DANGEROUS
Desires

DANGEROUS
Desires

A DANGEROUS BEAUTY NOVEL

J.T. GEISSINGER

Montlake
Romance

Published by Montlake Romance, Seattle

www.apub.com

Amazon, the Amazon logo, and Montlake Romance are trademarks of Amazon.com, Inc., or its affiliates.

ISBN-13: 9781542007979
ISBN-10: 1542007976

Cover design by Letitia Hasser

Printed in the United States of America

For Jay, because you never forget to put the toilet seat down.

A woman is like a tea bag. You can't tell how strong she is until you put her in hot water.

—*Eleanor Roosevelt*

ONE

Eva

The Chinese philosopher Lao Tzu once said that being deeply loved by someone gives you strength, while loving someone deeply gives you courage. But as I step aboard the sailing vessel *Silver Shadow* in the cool, misty darkness before dawn, I'm wondering if he missed the point.

Love's true power isn't in the strength or courage it gives, but in the selfishness it strips away.

I'm almost certainly going to my death, yet the only sadness I feel is for Naz. When he discovers what I've done, it will break his heart.

Better heartbroken and alive than dead.

Better me than him.

"Miss Evalina, I presume?"

The man who materializes from the dense shadows cast by the tall black sails is unfamiliar. Slight of build, wearing a tailored dark suit, he has silver hair and smiling blue eyes. He projects the air of a professional concierge, though I doubt he specializes in making dinner reservations.

"Yes, I'm Eva. Who are you?"

"My name is Raphael."

"Like the Renaissance painter."

He smiles pleasantly. "Quite so. He was my mother's favorite artist, hence my namesake. He was also killed by a fever after an excessive night of sex, if you can imagine. One wonders at the stamina death by copulation would require."

He has a precise, almost fastidious way of speaking that hints at too much formal education and a fondness for small, overbred dogs. Paired with a French accent, it lends him a sophisticated air. I'm inclined to like him, but I know only too well how deceiving appearances can be.

I slowly release the breath I've been holding. "Are you going to hurt me, Raphael?"

If he's startled by the bluntness of my question, he doesn't show it. He simply clasps his hands at his waist and says softly, "Oh no, my dear. Not I."

Emphasis on the word *I*.

His meaning becomes clear when a man steps out from behind him, appearing silently from the same dense shadows. But *this* man isn't a suave sophisticate with a polite demeanor. He's the exact opposite. Tall, tattooed, and heavily muscled, he has messy dark hair that brushes wide shoulders, a severe brow, and large hands that look made for crushing skulls.

Unsmiling, he gazes at me steadily with cold eyes and a ruthless slant to his mouth.

Hysteria threatens the edges of my forced outward calm. I steel my nerves, because I volunteered for this. I can't crack yet. Dimitri will give me ample opportunities to crack before he finally breaks me.

Or I break him.

I turn my attention back to Raphael. "Where's Dimitri?"

Raphael takes a moment to consider my question. "That I cannot tell you, but I am at liberty to disclose that I have been charged with taking you to him. And—please forgive the unfortunate intrusion on your privacy, but I'm sure you understand—I will advise Mr. Ivanov of your disposition throughout our journey."

Translation: I might be friendly, but we're not friends. Don't forget who's in charge.

"You should also know that Killian"—he gestures to the silent goon—"has been given instructions by Mr. Ivanov to punish any . . . unacceptable behavior."

Killian's hard mouth curves into a faint evil smile.

Oh God. This is new. Dimitri must be incredibly angry with me to sanction this. I pause to get my breathing under control before I answer. "I understand. Thank you, Raphael."

He beams at me. I know it's not my imagination that Killian looks disappointed that I'm being so accommodating, but I don't have time to dwell on that because he's moving toward me, reaching out with his big, meaty hands.

I flinch when he grabs me by my shoulders and hate myself for it. Then he's yanking my arms away from my body so he can search me for weapons.

He's thorough and rough. Hard fingers dig into my most tender parts—armpits, belly, thighs—making me wince with pain. When he slides a hand under the hem of my dress and moves it higher, toward my crotch, I twist away with a panicked yelp.

"That will do, Killian," says Raphael, sounding slightly nervous.

Killian rises. From under lowered brows, he stares intently at my face with the look of a predator stalking its prey. I look away, but from the corner of my eye, I see his evil smile appear again.

Raphael clears his throat. "Now that all the introductions have been made, we'll get underway. Welcome aboard, Miss Evalina."

He turns and disappears inside the main cabin, leaving me, Killian, and his hungry stare alone.

The lights of Hell's Kitchen glow against the dark night sky. The murky waters of the Hudson shimmer under a three-quarter moon. Though it's not yet Halloween, there's a sharp, foreboding chill in the evening air, a harbinger of the coming winter.

This is my final moment of freedom. Once I walk through the open cabin doors, I relinquish all that I was before. All power. All privilege. All hope.

I bite the inside of my cheek and blink against the water pooling in my eyes.

Goodbye, Naz. Maybe we'll meet again in another life.

To Killian, I say politely, "After you."

If he's amused or angered by my fake nonchalance, I can't tell. His smile has disappeared. His face is as unreadable as a block of wood. Apparently that's as much of an answer as I'll get.

I take a step forward, but he doesn't budge. When I step to the side, he moves in the same direction, blocking my way.

He's toying with me, like a cat with a mouse.

Annoyance gives me the boost I need to establish some boundaries and hopefully set him back on his arrogant heels. "Look. I've never seen you before, which means you're new to Dimitri's organization. Which also means you're nothing more than an errand boy. This position you've been given is a test. A test of your loyalty and usefulness, but also of your IQ."

Slowly, the tattooed thug lifts an eyebrow.

I take a breath and roll the dice. "If you think he won't kill you for touching me, you're overestimating your worth."

"And you're underestimating the situation. I'm not your babysitter, bitch. Short of death and penetration, I've been given permission to handle you however I like."

His voice is low and sandpaper rough, and lilting with an Irish accent.

I'm not surprised Dimitri would have a non-Russian working as one of his enforcers. Unlike the Italian Mafia, where only ethnic Italians can ever be "made," the Russian Bratva is much more inclusive. I am surprised, however, by the confidence in Killian's tone.

I might have been bluffing, but he's not.

Unthinkably, Dimitri has granted his rough enforcer power over me. The power to "handle" me however he likes.

A slick ripple of terror spreads through the pit of my stomach like a snake unfurling its coils.

As Killian notices the change in my expression, his awful smile makes a reappearance. His eyes glitter with malice. "What doesn't kill you makes you stronger, right?"

The comment resonates with me because of all the painful things I've endured. Not only the years with Dimitri, but also the earlier years spent training to become a ballerina, when many times my toes would bleed right through my pointe shoes.

I lift my chin. "What doesn't kill me better run."

"Tough words from such a little girl."

He's not intimidated. I don't blame him. I'm wearing a white cotton sundress and espadrilles. I have no weapons and no skill in self-defense. I'm trembling from cold and still shell-shocked from being in a car explosion, shooting two men at point-blank range, and making a bargain with the evil bastard who abused me for seven years that I'd return to him in exchange for his sparing Naz's life.

But that doesn't mean I'm completely defenseless.

If faith can lead Moses out of the wilderness after forty years, it can certainly help me.

"I might be small," I say evenly, holding Killian's gaze. "But I'm bigger than you'll ever be. There's nothing you can do to me that hasn't already been done, and I'm still standing. You can break as many of my bones as you like, but you'll never break *me*."

In the beat of silence that follows, several emotions flash across his expression. First there's surprise. It's followed by admiration. Then, most oddly of all, what looks like regret.

Regret?

It's the last coherent thought I form before he grabs me by the throat.

TWO

NAZ

I jolt upright in my hospital bed, my heart hammering with a sudden bone-deep certainty that something is terribly wrong.

"Eva?"

My call dies to echoes in the empty room. Across from the bed, the bathroom door is open. She's not in there, either.

Maybe she's in the waiting room talking to Tabby and Connor. Maybe she's getting something to eat. Maybe she had to stretch her legs. Took a walk. Yeah, that could be it.

My theories are all shot to hell when Connor barges through the door and announces, "Eva's gone."

"What do you mean, *gone?*"

"I mean Tabby pulled footage from the security cameras of Eva leavin' through an employee break room door."

The heartbeat monitor I'm hooked up to goes crazy, screeching as if it's the one having a heart attack and not me. Connor reaches over and bangs a fist against it. The room falls into silence.

Fighting a wave of dizziness and the rush of adrenaline crashing through my bloodstream, I try to focus. "I don't understand. Why would she leave? How did she get past our guys? Where the hell is she going?"

"All good questions, brother," says Connor grimly. "But I'm afraid we don't have answers to any of 'em."

Gone? Eva's gone? That can't be right. I have to find her. I have to protect her—

"Whoa!"

Connor grabs me by the arms when I stagger out of bed and almost fall to my knees. I'm weak. Too weak. Fucking anesthesia. Fucking car bomb.

Fucking Dimitri Ivanov.

The thought of him sends another rush of adrenaline through my veins. It gives me the strength to steady myself. I shake my head like a dog, trying to clear it.

"Start at the beginning."

Connor doesn't need more of a prompt than that. He knows I need all the facts, and I need them *now*.

"Just after two this morning, I drove Tabby to Metrix so she could get a few hours' sleep. I checked in with the boys at headquarters, put the word out to all my contacts in law enforcement and the military that we'd been hit, called an old buddy at Langley to see what strings he could pull. The feds are gonna take over the investigation from NYPD, and I wanna be kept in the loop. He'll give me whatever intel he can as the investigation moves forward."

I jerk my hand, impatient for him to get to the important part.

"Then I called Smith, one of our guys stationed outside your door. He gave me the all clear. Nobody'd been in or out of your room. Building perimeter was still locked down. No sign of trouble. I came back to the hospital, put my feet up in the waiting room, closed my eyes, caught a few *zs* 'cause I was fuckin' exhausted, and I'm no good to anybody if I can't think. When I woke up, I checked in with Smith again. No change, he said, but I came up to see for my own eyes that everything was good.

"Which is when I discovered Eva wasn't in the room with you. Smith says she never left. Only this is when I realized he came on shift before *I* left."

"Which means she was already gone by then," I say, my heart crashing.

Connor's nod is grim. "Searched the cafeteria, restrooms, chapel, everything. Then I called Tabby and had her do her thing."

I blink against the bright sunlight streaming in through the window blinds. "What time is it?"

"Seven fifteen."

"Jesus. If you left at two, that means she's been gone for more than five hours!"

Connor watches without comment as I lurch unsteadily toward the small closet on the other side of the room. A saline drip on a rolling metal stand clatters along behind me. I rip the bandage off the back of my hand and yank the needle out of the vein, throwing them both aside. Inside the closet in a clear plastic bag are what's left of my clothes. Shredded tactical pants. Combat boots. Filthy T-shirt encrusted with blood.

"Naz."

I look over my shoulder at Connor. He points at a black duffel bag on the chair next to my bed. "Clean threads and a cell phone."

I don't bother with a thank-you or ask who brought them. A sense of doom has settled over me, as heavy and dark as a thundercloud. I tear open the duffel's zipper, pull out pants, a shirt, and a pair of boots, and quickly start to dress. The stitched-up gash torn in my thigh from the piece of shrapnel from the car bomb screams in protest when I shove my leg into the pair of jeans. I grit my teeth against the pain and keep shoving.

"What else did Tabby find? Anything?"

"Yeah. Right after you got outta surgery, Eva made a collect call from a pay phone down the hall."

I whip my head around and stare at him. The thundercloud of doom spreads out to engulf the room. "Who'd she call?"

"International operator first. From there . . . we don't know. Number was spoofed. Routed through an anonymous web server to a burner, blah, blah. You know the drill." He pauses. "Sixty seconds after that call, she got a call back."

We stare at each other as blood pounds in my temples. "Lemme guess. No ID on that number, either."

"Bingo."

I know what he's thinking by the way he's looking at me. I briefly close my eyes, forcing myself to swallow the roar of frustration building in my throat. "It can't be."

"You got any other theories? 'Cause I doubt she called her grandma for a little untraceable chitchat."

My tenuous hold on my panic finally breaks. I shout, *"Why the fuck would she call Dimitri?"*

Connor doesn't bat an eyelash at my tone. "You know her better than I do, brother. You tell me."

I'm blank for a moment, then it hits me all at once: *to negotiate.*

I must've said that aloud, because Connor frowns. "Negotiate what?"

"The terms of her surrender," I whisper, cold with horror.

I stagger sideways a step and have to brace an arm against the wall for balance. It doesn't stop my body from shaking.

"I'm never going to forget a second, Naz, I swear."

I knew that sounded like a goodbye when she said it before I fell asleep. I *knew* it! Goddammit all to hell.

"Well, whatever Eva's motivations, Tabby's hacked into the city's traffic cams and any other security systems with video in the surrounding areas she can find, tryin' to get a bead on her last location. It's only a matter of time before we discover where she went."

"Check the airports," I say, breaking into a cold sweat. "Bus terminals. Taxis. Trains."

"She can't have gotten that far. She doesn't have money. Or ID."

My mouth is bone dry. I can't catch my breath. I rip off the hospital gown, yank on a clean black T-shirt, and button the fly of my jeans, battling every frantic emotion inside me for control. I shove my bare feet into the boots, not bothering to lace them.

I say, "She wouldn't need either if Dimitri's involved. Let's go."

⌾

Half an hour later, we're striding through the reinforced steel front door of Metrix's headquarters. There's something seriously wrong with my lungs, because the inside of my chest feels as if it's on fire, and I can't get enough air. Fire's scorching my gut, too, but I know that's not an effect of the explosion I was in a few days ago.

That's fear, plain and simple.

I know exactly what kind of sick, soulless criminal Dimitri Ivanov is. The thought of Eva going anywhere near him again makes my blood curdle.

Almost worse is the knowledge that when we made love, Eva already knew she was leaving.

Tabby greets us inside the door, wearing the same clothing she was wearing yesterday. She's pale and yawning, with dark circles under her eyes from lack of sleep. I suffer a twinge of guilt that everything has turned into such a shit show, but push it aside. I'll say my apologies later, after we get Eva back and my brain is working right again.

"Princess." Connor grabs her into a bear hug, burying his face into her neck.

She says softly, "Hey, sweetie." Then, with a laugh: "Don't break my spine, jarhead. I'm using it."

He releases her, and she turns her gaze to me. Her eyes are the color of fresh-cut grass and, as usual, miss nothing. "Damn. I hope you feel better than you look."

"I don't. Talk to me before I lose my fucking mind."

She assesses my body language for a moment. Whatever she finds makes her cut right to the chase. "Long story short: I've got nothing."

I didn't think it was possible, but the blazing heat in my chest gets worse. I've got a forest fire raging under my rib cage, searing my throat. I'm almost exhaling flames.

"What do you mean, *nothing?*" I manage to grit out.

"I mean she took the subway to Penn Station, then disappeared."

"So she's on a train!"

"It's possible. It'll take a lot more time for us to review all the footage to confirm, but . . ."

When she trails off, I prompt impatiently, "What?"

"Penn is one of the busiest passenger transportation hubs in the Western Hemisphere. More than 350,000 people pass through there a day."

"So you're saying we need to get more eyes to help you look?"

"I'm saying that it's the perfect place to accomplish two things: vanish into a crowd, and plant a red herring."

My brain is working better than my lungs, because I put two and two together quickly. "She wanted to make it *look* like she took a train?"

Tabby lifts a shoulder. "I can't be sure. But from what I know of Eva, she's smart, resourceful, and thinks on her feet. She'd have known you'd look for her as soon as you discovered she was gone."

She doesn't add the obvious—that if Eva went to the trouble of trying to make it look as if she went one way while actually going another, she didn't *want* to be found.

Guess we've got more acquainting to do, because if she thinks I'm not going to find her, she obviously doesn't know me very fucking well.

Anger gives me the edge I need to focus above the pain in my body and the fear in my heart. "Okay. Going with that theory, she's probably still in New York."

Connor cuts in, nodding. "We need to start looking outside Penn Station. Exits and the immediate surrounding area."

"She's on foot," I mutter, my mind going a million miles an hour. "Unless she stole a bike—"

"Or a car," Tabby supplies, a little too calmly, I think. When I glare at her, she says, "Just covering all the bases, Nasir."

"She doesn't know how to drive," I say. "She's not in a car."

"And nobody in this city's pickin' up a hitchhiker," says Connor.

"So she's on foot," I say more loudly, my pulse an uneven, throbbing rush in my ears as a new theory presents itself. "What's another big transportation hub close to Penn Station?"

"Port Authority Bus Terminal's the closest," says Tabby.

I try to picture Dimitri leaving a bus ticket for Eva at the counter, but decide it doesn't fit. A bus is so common. Public transportation is something a billionaire would find repugnant. At least trains have a certain style. Plus, buses are slow. If you're looking to make a quick escape, you don't take a goddamn Greyhound.

A memory hits me. The night I first read Eva's file months ago, the night before I left Los Angeles for New York to start my job with Metrix, I was alone in a room at my friends' house in the Hollywood Hills while my farewell party raged outside. I opened the computer file Connor had sent me, and had my first introduction to one beautiful and mysterious Evalina Ivanova . . .

Who'd disappeared into the sea after jumping off a yacht in the middle of the night.

"The docks," I say, knowing even as it's leaving my mouth that I'm right.

Connor looks doubtful. "That's a long walk from Penn."

"Not if you're motivated." I turn my attention to Tabby. "Can you find out what ships left the harbor between midnight and now?"

Tabby snorts. "Can I." Without another word, she turns and leaves, her chin in the air and her red pigtails swinging.

I look at Connor. "Is that a yes or a no?"

He sighs. "It's a 'Just fucking watch me,' brother. With a side order of 'Don't insult my intelligence' and 'Dumbass.'"

"Right. Shoulda guessed."

When I make a move to follow Tabby, Connor stops me with a hand on my shoulder. "Hold on a sec. I want to talk to you."

"We don't have time—"

"We need to consider an alternative scenario for Eva's disappearance, brother."

I stare at him, already knowing where he's going with this. "She wouldn't go back to him unless she thought it would keep me safe. You read the hospital reports yourself. You know what he did to her. She fucking hates him."

"No doubt," he says gently. "But what if she didn't go back at all?"

I blink, startled. "Come again?"

"She could have contingencies in place for something like this. Secret bank accounts, other identities, there's a hundred ways she could've set herself up to disappear again if Dimitri caught up with her. Like Tabby said, Eva's smart. I can't see her going to all that trouble to escape and disappear from her old life without having a plan B. Maybe even a plan C, D, and E."

"What exactly are you saying?"

"I'm saying maybe she isn't headed back to Dimitri. Maybe she's headed to Thailand. Australia. Fuckin' Iceland, who knows? My point is that you might want to consider the possibility that she's not going back to him . . . but she didn't want to stay with you, either."

Man, that feels like an ice pick plunged right into the center of my fucking chest. "She loves me," I say, hearing the growl at the back of my throat.

"She tell you that?"

When I thin my lips and don't respond, Connor drops his hand from my shoulder and folds his arms over his chest.

"Okay. I just want you to be prepared for the possibility that she might not be all that happy to see you if we find her."

"*When* we find her. And *you're* the one who suggested it was probably Dimitri she called."

"The odds are good, considering the situation. But she could've also called a handler. Someone who moves her money. Someone who helped her get away the first time. There's no way to know. We know virtually nothing about this woman except that she was with Dimitri for seven years—"

"Against her will!"

"—and then she was with you, briefly, and now she's gone."

I take a moment to check my anger before I speak. I know he's only trying to help, and I know what he's suggesting is reasonable.

Just as I know he's 100 percent wrong.

"I hear you. And I respect your opinion. And now I'm gonna ask you this: If the shoe was on the other foot, and it was you standing here listening to me call Tabby's motives into question, how would you feel about that?"

His face darkens. His eyes, black as the bottom of the ocean at midnight, begin to burn.

"Yeah, I thought so. And now if you don't mind, I'm gonna go find my woman."

I stalk down the hallway in the direction Tabby went. The sound of Connor's low chuckle follows behind me all the way.

THREE

Eva

When I'm finally able to sit up and open my eyes, I feel like a person returning from the dead.

Everything hurts. My head, my body, my ridiculous pride.

It takes only a few moments of tentatively stretching my limbs and testing the limits of my pain tolerance before I come to the conclusion that nothing is broken. I swing my legs over the edge of the bed I've been curled in since Killian threw me into it and take an inventory of my injuries.

A big ugly bruise darkens my left wrist. My bare knees are red and raw with rug burn. That metallic taste in my mouth is blood, and my throat aches. I'm sure it's mottled with ugly bruises, too.

Killian is nothing if not dedicated to his work.

Stupid. I should've known that a man with the word *kill* right there in his first name would take my little "you can't break me" speech as a challenge.

Wincing, I rise unsteadily to my feet and look around. I'm in a large, elegant stateroom decorated in soothing shades of cream and gray. Through three round portholes in the opposite wall I see blue ocean and clear sky, though the gentle rocking motion of the ship is all I need to determine we've left the docks behind us. The digital clock on the nightstand tells me it's still early in the morning, just after dawn.

I make my way, gingerly, to the door. It's locked. I do a quick inspection of the room, checking the closet, bathroom, and dresser drawers for anything I can use as a weapon. I already know I won't find anything, but it never hurts to be thorough.

I return to the bathroom, use the toilet, wash my hands, and gulp water from the faucet, then brace myself for a moment before I face my reflection in the mirror.

My stomach drops when I do.

My lower lip is split and swollen. My left cheek is swollen, too, and turning an interesting shade of purple. Also, I was right about my neck. I trace the perfect outline of Killian's thumb over my trachea. Then I touch the painful raised knot on the back of my head and curse the day that son of a bitch was born in four different languages.

At least my hair still looks good.

It's the old, familiar gallows humor that helped me survive a life of horrors, back again when I need it most. My mother used to say she could forgive anyone anything except not having a sense of humor. That was before she became acquainted with Dimitri and discovered firsthand there were far more terrible shortcomings a man could have than not being able to make her laugh.

A pang of sorrow grips my heart when I think of my mother, but I quickly smother it. Grief won't help me. The only thing that's useful to me now is clear, cold resolve.

I've already killed two men. Shoved a gun under the first one's jaw and blew his brains out without a hair of hesitation. Shot the second one in the chest. There was a time when I would've sworn I wasn't capable of such a thing, but necessity is a ruthless teacher. And although I know it's a sin to take a human life and the only way the stain can be removed from my soul is if I repent and pray for forgiveness . . .

I'm not sorry for what I did. Therefore, I can never be forgiven.

Bottom line? I'm damned.

On the bright side, however, that means a little more blood on my hands won't matter.

Ready or not, Dimitri, here I come.

A flash of brilliance catches my eye. On the dresser across from the bed, the facets of a crystal vase fracture a sunbeam into a prism. Slices of gold, red, blue, and green illuminate the room in blinding washes of color that vanish as quickly as they appeared when the ship rocks in a different direction.

I stride over to the vase, pick it up, and throw it as hard as I can against the opposite wall.

With a loud crash, it smashes into a million satisfying pieces. I instinctively raise my arm to protect my eyes, then find a big chunk on the floor and head back into the bathroom.

I grab a handful of my hair. Using the jagged edge of the broken vase, I saw off a hunk at the base of my neck.

Dimitri always loved my hair. He brushed it obsessively, stroked it as I lay weeping after he beat me, used it as a leash wrapped tightly around his wrist to hold me in place as he used my body in the most brutal of ways. Killian found it useful, too. Easy to grab hold of and yank so I lost my footing. So I couldn't get away.

"Won't be so easy for them now," I mutter to my reflection as I grab another handful and start cutting.

When I'm done, the sink is full of long golden-brown tresses. I stare at the pile of glinting locks, feeling strangely euphoric. *I should've done this years ago.*

A loud knock on the door. "Coming in."

My pulse jumps at the sound of Killian's voice. I thrust the shard of crystal into a pocket in my dress and walk out of the bathroom just as he's striding through the door.

He's carrying a tray. A glass of water clatters against a plate as he jolts to a stop when he sees me. After a long, hard look at my new haircut, he says, "I see you've been busy."

I say nothing, fighting the urge to run my finger against the sharp edge of the hidden shard.

He walks to the small desk beneath the portholes and drops the tray onto its surface. Then he pulls out the chair, swivels it around to face him, and lowers his bulk to the seat, folding his arms over the back and staring at me expectantly.

When I don't move, he jerks his head toward the tray of food. "Eat."

My mouth has already begun to water at the smell of bacon. I can't remember the last time I had food, but I'm in no mood for company. Especially *his* company.

I'm also in no mood to get knocked around again, so I do as I'm told.

I take the tray, sit on the edge of the bed, set the tray on my lap, and start to eat. With my fingers, because no cutlery has been provided.

Killian grunts in approval.

I could kill this bastard with my bare hands.

Swallowing proves difficult due to the swelling in my throat. I have to take several small sips of water in between bites. My discomfort is made worse by the intensity of Killian's gaze, which is unwavering. I want to tell him to get lost—and oh, by the way, go straight to hell, you pathetic excuse for a human being—but I'm well practiced in the art of biting my tongue and biding my time.

As I'm tearing into a piece of buttered toast, he says, "There's arnica ointment in that white tube next to your plate."

I freeze. Arnica?

"For the bruising." He looks at my neck. His Adam's apple bobs as he swallows. A muscle flexes in his jaw.

When his gaze flashes up to mine, I wipe the quizzical frown from my face and swallow my mouthful of toast. I take another careful sip of water and consider how to respond. Finally I go with a stiff "Thank you."

"You're welcome."

Color me extremely confused.

We sit in silence as I finish the rest of the food on my plate. Wheat toast, scrambled eggs, four pieces of bacon—it all goes down under Killian's fixed, hawklike stare. When I'm done, I wipe my hands and mouth with the linen napkin, then set it back on the plate.

Then I stare at my knees and wait.

If he tries to hit me again, I'll slice his neck open.

Just as the silence is becoming excruciating, Killian stands. I keep my gaze lowered as he takes the tray from my lap. He turns and steps away. I start to breathe easier, but when he turns back, my blood stops circulating.

With my chin between his fingers, he lifts my head. He inspects the bruising on my cheek, his eyes and face unreadable. Then he turns my head the other way and stares at my neck.

I hold perfectly still, not flinching or recoiling, not daring even to breathe. A fly caught in amber.

"That hurt?"

You know it does, bastard. My nod is almost imperceptible, but he understands.

"Learned your lesson, then?"

That low, raspy voice reveals nothing, but I know an offer when I hear one. I hate him, but I'll take it if it means no more repeat performances of my unprotected flesh vs. his fists.

"Yes."

The muscle in his jaw slides again. He exhales. It's probably my imagination, but that quiet release of breath sounds relieved.

"Good. Give me that piece of broken vase in your pocket."

When I don't comply quickly enough, he adds gently, "Don't make me tell you twice."

I withdraw the piece of crystal and set it on the tray in the middle of the plate where the eggs had been, trying my best not to look guilty.

"When I come back, that mess will be cleaned up." He glances at the shattered vase littering the floor, then back at me. "And you won't try to hide anything from me again. Understood?"

Why is he being so nice? "Yes."

He examines my face. Apparently finding my expression appropriately obedient, he drops his hand from under my chin and turns and leaves without another word, shutting the door quietly behind him.

The key turns in the lock and I'm left alone, wondering what I'm missing.

I've known my share of psychopaths, but I've never met one quite like this.

⚮

There's no television, phone, or computer in the stateroom, and nothing to read, either, so after I pick up all the shards of crystal from the floor and toss them into a wastebasket, I give in to the fatigue dogging me and sleep.

I dream of Naz. Of him holding me in his strong arms and softly asking, "You ever think about kids?"

When I wake up, my cheeks are wet.

I'm sorry. I'm so sorry. Please don't hate me for this.

The knock on the door comes just as I'm standing up. This time Killian doesn't bother announcing his entry. He simply walks in, holding a bundle of folded clothing.

When he catches sight of my face, he stops. His lips thin. His brows draw down over his eyes.

I suppose tears will get me a beating, so I quickly swipe my fingers over my cheeks to dry them and stand up straighter. My head feels so light without all the hair, but also naked in an uncomfortable way. I run my hand nervously over the back of my neck, waiting for him to say something. Waiting for the next move in our sick little game of chess.

Silent as a panther, he moves slowly to the unmade bed.

How can a man so big be so quiet?

"Get cleaned up and put these on." He sets the clothing on the mattress, then turns to look at me. "Then come up to the main deck."

I bite back my automatic *Why?* and simply nod instead. He exits as silently as he came, leaving the door wide open behind him.

I stare out into the empty corridor, hearing nothing but the sound of the wind and the waves and my own erratic heartbeat. *Is this some kind of test?* I don't know, but I'm unsettled.

Perhaps that's the point. Keep me rattled. Keep me guessing. Get my defenses down so he can get off when I slip up and he's "forced" to punish me again.

I close the bedroom door, then go into the bathroom and lock that door, though I know it's the most superficial kind of defense. Killian and his dumb bulging muscles could break it down with a flick of his wrist.

Under the spray of the shower, I soap my body and use the lemon-scented shampoo, then rinse off, turn off the water, and dry myself with a thick white cotton towel. There's no comb or brush in the drawers, so I finger comb my hair. The short cut suits me, even if it is shaggy and botched.

I look like someone else. Like a woman who doesn't have time for frivolities like a nice hairdo because she's too focused on more important things. More *deadly* things.

"Vengeance is mine, says the Lord," I tell my reflection, watching my eyes glitter. "But nobody ever said you weren't allowed to help him along."

It occurs to me that I might not be of completely sound mind at the moment—the combination of physical and mental trauma might have set me off my rocker—but I'm oddly unmoved by the thought.

Which is also probably more proof that my brain has taken a vacation and I'm in a mental no-man's-land, but I'm feeling one big *meh* about the whole thing.

There's no need for sanity where I'm going, anyway.

I get dressed, dab the arnica cream on the worst of my bruises, and head upstairs.

In daylight I can see how luxurious the yacht truly is. Polished wood, gleaming mirrors, and white leather furnishings are accented by tasteful oil paintings and objets d'art. I wind my way up a curved glass staircase and find myself in a large main salon, with a media room and sitting area on one side and a big open sundeck on the other.

Outside in a chaise longue, enjoying the sun with a glass of champagne in hand, sits Raphael. He's dressed head to toe in crisp white linen. His face is tipped up, his eyes are closed, and though in all other respects he looks utterly relaxed, there's a furrow between his brows, like he's thinking of something unpleasant.

He must sense me standing there, because he turns his head and opens his eyes. When he sees me, he stiffens and his face goes white, as if he's been slapped.

"Good morning," I say, unmoving from my place at the top of the stairs. "I'm glad one of us is enjoying himself."

He rises, unable to hide his expression of horror. In his hand, the champagne glass trembles. He walks slowly inside the main cabin, so clearly shocked by my appearance I can't help but wonder what he thought all that screaming was about last night.

And what he expected any "punishment" Killian saw fit to dole out would look like.

Whatever it was, it surely wasn't this. The man looks as if he's going to pass out.

"My dear," he says faintly. Pale and shaken, he stops a few feet away from me and puts a hand to his throat. "Oh my dear. Whatever has he done to you?"

"His job, I presume."

He opens his mouth, closes it, swallows. In what looks like a gargantuan effort of will, he produces a pinched smile. "Yes. Of course." He smooths a shaky hand down the front of his shirt. When he notices the ice bucket with the champagne bottle on a mirrored console to our left, he brightens.

"Would you like some champagne?"

I narrow my eyes. *What's going on here? Why is he acting so weird?* "No."

He doesn't let my answer deter him from topping off his glass. He guzzles it in one go, like he's hoping it will help steady his nerves.

Speaking of nerves, mine are singing with intuition. I sense Killian before I see or hear him. He's a dark presence approaching from behind, all pressure and powerful intensity, as electric as an advancing storm.

His arm brushes mine as he passes, raising all the little hairs on the back of my neck.

He flicks a cool gaze in Raphael's direction, then stops a few feet away, crosses his arms over his chest, and looks at me.

It feels like being crucified.

I glance down, my heart banging around in my chest like a kicked can.

"That color's good on you."

His voice is a throaty grumble. I hesitate to answer, feeling again like this might be some kind of test. I'm wearing the clothing he left me, a dress of soft jersey knit in butter yellow, tied around the waist with a sash. It's a simple thing, the kind of dress you'd pack for a casual weekend getaway to the beach. It's also a perfect fit, a fact I found interesting.

This isn't the style of clothing Dimitri would choose for me. Nor is it his preferred color. He favored me in jewel tones—sapphire, emerald, ruby—and couture. Elaborate, expensive confections he very much enjoyed ripping to shreds with his hands.

23

He'd consider what I'm wearing a rag. In fact, it's more like the clothing I chose to wear on Cozumel. Light, airy, and ultra low-maintenance, made for hot climates and stuffing into a travel bag.

I wonder who bought it, because I already know who didn't.

"Thank you," I say, still looking down. Then, carefully: "I like it, too."

Silence. When I glance up, Killian's eyes are smoldering. His expression makes my mouth go dry.

"Did you use the arnica?"

When I nod, he licks his lips. "Good girl."

After a sharp look in Killian's direction, Raphael clears his throat. "My dear, won't you have a seat on the sundeck while lunch is brought up?"

I want to snap something about how this isn't a pleasure cruise, but decide against it with Killian's weird intense energy throbbing all around. I'll go with prim and proper instead and keep my ears open to see if I can find any clue as to what strangeness is afoot.

Last night, I thought Raphael was in charge. Now, I think he's window dressing.

I think Killian is really the boss here, only I'm not supposed to know it.

Which makes me wonder what else I'm not supposed to know.

And what else these two are hiding.

FOUR

Naz

I find Tabby in the war room, the central command of Metrix's operations. A huge black conference table dominates the center of the space. Two walls are covered with big screens depicting various satellite and video images from around the world. On the floor below the screens, operatives wearing headphones and the standard Metrix work uniform of black cargo pants, black T-shirt, and black combat boots man consoles bristling with colored buttons and switches.

All of them have Glock semiauto handguns strapped to their waists.

Looking distinctly out of place in her pigtails, tiny leather miniskirt, and hot-pink tee, Tabby sits in front of another console, this one operating a larger screen that takes up almost the entire third wall of the room. She doesn't turn when I approach, but says over her shoulder, "Give me a sec. I just got started."

Standing behind her chair, I watch as her fingers move lightning fast over a keyboard. Several windows open on the large screen, atop a background image of what I assume is the root directory of some external computer system she's already hacked into, judging by the directory tree of dozens of files and subfiles on screen. Her fingers keep moving.

In a few seconds, another window opens, this one with a wide-angle picture of a harbor at night.

"Is that what I think it is?"

"If you think it's the New York Port Authority's recorded video footage from their security cameras at the harbor from this morning, then yes. It's what you think it is."

I watch in fascination as she accesses footage from various angles, obviously taken from different cameras stationed throughout the harbor. The time stamp on all the screens reads today's date and 00:01. A minute after midnight. Then each image starts to speed up.

"Wait—you're going too fast to see the hull identifiers of the ships."

"Don't worry about that. Just keep your eyes peeled for a woman in a white dress. If Eva was here—assuming she didn't change clothes from the last time I saw her—she'll stand out like a beacon. Once we see her, we can follow her to the right ship."

"Oh. Right." I feel silly that I didn't think of that.

We watch the sped-up video feeds in silence for what feels like a long time, until I'm convinced this is a useless effort and I was wrong about Eva being headed to the docks. But then I spot a flash of white in the corner of one dark screen, and my heart leaps. "There!" I shout, pointing.

Tabby hits a button. The video stops. She slowly rewinds the feed using a dial until we see a woman walking backward, her head lowered and her arms wrapped around her body in an attempt to ward off the chill she was surely feeling due to her lack of proper clothing for such a cold, misty night.

Short-sleeved white cotton dresses aren't good for keeping warm.

It's Eva.

The rush of emotion that hits me is overpowering. I can't do anything but stand still and breathe heavily for a moment as a powerful blast of adrenaline rockets through my body, setting every nerve on fire.

Connor walks up beside me and folds his arms over his chest. "That didn't take long."

Supple as a cat, Tabby stretches her arms overhead. "Girl power puts everything in turbo mode."

"Play it," I say, gravel in my voice. "Let's see where she went."

Tabby taps a finger on another button, and the video comes to life. The three of us watch in silence as Eva hurries down the wide main path along the harbor's edge, then turns down one of the piers. She seems unsure of her destination, stopping every so often to squint at a docked vessel before moving on.

"What's she doing?" asks Connor. "Trying to find a contact?"

"Doesn't seem like she knows where she's going," offers Tabby.

When Eva stops again, I figure it out. "She's looking at the ships' names."

"If that's the case, she isn't familiar with the vessel by sight." Connor glances sideways at me. "It's not one of Dimitri's."

This again. "So he sent someone else to pick her up."

Tabby says, "Whoever it belongs to, Eva found it."

Connor and I turn our attention back to the screen and watch as Eva ascends the gangway of a large black sailboat. Sailing yacht, more correctly. The picture is grainy, but the size of the ship is evident by how it dwarfs the ships moored around it.

I try not to be freaked out by the billowing black sails, which strike me as all kinds of wrong. "Can you get a better angle? Anything closer so we can see the name?"

"Hang on."

She tries to zoom in, but the picture quality isn't good enough. The hull becomes one big blur of pixels. Then the screens change images as Tabby tries to find the next closest camera, switching from one to another as her fingers move swiftly over the keyboard.

The next camera must be mounted on a light pole or other high object, because now we're looking down onto the foredeck of the black ship. Three people stand together. There's no audio, so there's no way to hear what's being said, but suddenly one of the people—a man with silver hair wearing a dark suit—turns and disappears into the main cabin. The two left facing each other are Eva and another man, much larger than the first. I don't need to see anything other than his size, his posture, and the amount of tattoos covering his arms to get a bad feeling about him.

Then he reaches out and grabs Eva by the throat, and my bad feeling morphs to incendiary rage.

My roar of anger is so loud everyone in the room stops what they're doing and stares at me.

"I'll fucking kill him!" I slam both fists on the console next to Tabby's keyboard. Then, when the man knocks Eva to her knees and drags her into the cabin by her hair as she writhes and kicks helplessly against his grip, I let loose a bellow of such fury I'm sure all the major arteries in my body will explode under the pressure of it.

The room is perfectly silent, except for my labored breath. Then Tabby swivels around in her chair and looks at me.

"Good," she says calmly. "You got that out. Now batten down the hatches, soldier. Eva needs you at the top of your game, and so do we."

I whirl away and drag my hands through my hair. Then I start to pace, just for something to do.

If I don't keep moving, I might kill something.

"I can't see the name of that ship from any of these angles, so I'm going to check the port registry and the marine traffic satellite and see what we've got. It'll be a few more minutes."

That loud, angry rumble of noise echoing off the walls is coming from me.

Connor watches me with a steady gaze as I pace the length of the room, then back again.

How could she have left? Didn't she trust that I'd keep her safe? Or that I'd handle Dimitri myself? Didn't she know this would kill me?

Oh shit—what did that fucker do to her after he dragged her inside?

I'm furious, panicked, and in shock. I'm also in a fair amount of physical pain from my busted-up leg and whatever the hell is going on with my lungs. Pretty sure I've got a concussion, too, because my head is throbbing like some asshole's working it with a jackhammer.

Eva. Eva, *why?*

Connor says thoughtfully, "That didn't make sense."

Another growl tears from my chest. I'm so enraged the power of speech has momentarily left me.

"If those guys are Dimitri's, they wouldn't treat her like that. He's the boss. She's his property"—he shoots an apologetic glance in my direction—"or at least they *think* she is. You don't damage the boss's property."

I reply through gritted teeth. "They're *thugs*, Connor. Criminals. They don't have a code of honor like ours."

"No, not like ours, but every criminal organization has a hierarchy, and Dimitri Ivanov is at the top of the ladder in his. The men who work for him would know he'd kill them without hesitation for stepping out of line. And that"—he gestures to the video screen—"was definitely out of line."

I stop pacing and look at him.

He says, "But if they weren't Dimitri's guys—like I was saying before, if they were friendlies, her plan B or C—they wouldn't treat her like that, either." He pauses for a moment, his black eyes drilling into mine. "So if they're not Dimitri's men, and they're not hers, who are they?"

"That's a big leap you're making based on ten seconds of video."

"He's got scary good instincts," Tabby throws over her shoulder. "Like spooky scary. And I totally agree with him. Nobody on Dimitri's payroll would dare pull a stunt like that. He's got a reputation as a psycho for good reason."

My heart is beating so hard I think everyone in the room must be able to hear it. I swear, this shit is gonna kill me. "Tell me what you're thinking."

Connor turns his speculative gaze back toward the screen. "I'm thinking that we've got another player in the game."

Cold flashes over me, then heat. "Tabby, *find that fucking ship*."

"Funny thing about that." She swivels around in her chair and looks first at Connor, then at me. "The marine satellite's got an unresolved DNS. And the port registry's displaying a 404 error."

"Tabby. For the love of God. Speak English."

"She's saying both systems are down," says Connor.

"And not by accident. They were *taken* down, both by the same elegant little piece of malware."

This shit just keeps getting better. "Somebody wanted to make sure they weren't followed."

Tabby nods. "Somebody smart."

"Not smart enough, if they forgot to wipe the Port Authority security feed." I exhale and try to gather my scattered thoughts. "Okay, so we just have to go through all the video from the harbor cameras and hope we get a clear-enough image of the name of the ship Eva boarded—"

I'm cut off by Tabby's laugh. "What's funny?" I ask, confused.

"You are, soldier. If you want to spend hours going through the security feed to find the name of that ship, knock yourself out. Or you could just give me five minutes and I'll tell you."

"What? How? You just said both systems were down!"

Her sigh is small and disappointed. "Honestly, I have no idea how people with penises are in charge of anything." She swivels around to face the console and starts tapping on the keyboard.

When a satellite image of the harbor comes up on-screen after a few moments, I shake my head in disbelief. "I don't get it."

Connor chuckles. "Join the club, brother."

Tabby scoffs. "What, you think there's only *one* satellite orbiting the friggin' earth at any moment in time? Dude. There's so much hardware in space it's like a metal asteroid field circling the planet." *Tap, tap, tap.* "Only about two thousand are operational, though. Let's just see what NASA's got for us . . ."

I look at Connor. "Are you ever afraid for your life, living with this one?"

He replies seriously, "Only every day."

"Here we go, kids. Big black sailboat leaving port at zero dark thirty."

"How are we gonna see the name of the fucking thing from above?"

Tabby sighs again, mutters something under her breath, then does her tapping thing. Then she sits back in her chair, smiling. "Like taking candy from a baby."

The image angles, zooms in, and clarifies, revealing script lettering along the transom, backlit in white.

"She's a beaut, that *Silver Shadow*," says Tabby.

My pulse is a roar in my ears, and my mind is already leaping ahead as I turn on my heel. "Find out who she belongs to and where she's going and send me everything."

Tabby grumbles, "Oh, *now* he has faith in me."

"Naz, where're you going?" shouts Connor at my back.

I answer him on my way out the door. "I've got a shadow to catch."

FIVE

Eva

Raphael, Killian, and I sit together at a table under a sunshade on the aft deck of the ship as a silent uniformed crew serves us lunch.

If my bruised appearance alarms them, they don't mention it. The two men and one woman never raise their gaze to mine as they efficiently lay out platters of meats, cheeses, and fruits, pour sparkling water into crystal goblets, and drape linen napkins on our laps.

The entire time all that's going on, Killian's watching me.

And Raphael is watching him.

From the corner of his eye, trying not to make it obvious, but still, he's watching. It's evident from his pinched lips and the furrow dug between his brows that he doesn't like what he sees.

The female of the crew—a slender African American girl in her early twenties with gorgeous long-lashed brown eyes—quietly asks me if I'd enjoy a glass of wine with my meal.

"No, thank you."

Killian orders, "She'll take a chardonnay."

Raphael glares daggers at him. Interesting. I decide to press my luck to see what will happen. There's a power struggle going on here, and friction between the two of them might prove advantageous to me.

Using my most docile voice, I murmur, "I'd prefer red." I lift my lashes and hold Killian's gaze longer than is comfortable. "If you don't mind, of course."

A faint smile curves his mouth, but it isn't the evil one I've seen before. This one is far more intimate, softer and darker, hinting at dangerous desires. "Careful. Keep looking at me like that and I'll think you're sweet on me."

In a wave that starts at his neck and moves swiftly upward, Raphael's face turns red. "That's enough," he snaps.

Still gazing steadily at me, Killian says, "I say when it's enough. What do you think, Eva? Have I had enough yet?"

I don't understand exactly what's happening, but I do know with absolute certainty that Killian is used to giving orders, not taking them. I'm not dealing with an errand boy, like I originally thought.

I'm dealing with an alpha.

I sit back in my chair and consider him with new interest. The pretty African American girl stands perfectly still beside me, her eyes lowered, waiting silently for instructions. She's been trained well.

Just as I once was.

"Permission to speak honestly?"

Killian's smile deepens. I've amused him. He grants me a kingly nod.

"No, I don't think you've had enough. I don't think you've even really gotten started yet. In fact, I think that when you *have* had enough, you'll be standing alone on top of a pile of bodies so high it blocks out the sun."

I lean over and select a piece of Havarti cheese from a silver platter. Then I tell the girl, "I'd actually like a glass of rum, please. Mount Gay if you have it. With a slice of lime and no ice."

She flicks a glance at Killian. His smile is still in place. He doesn't spare her a glance when he nods, giving his permission for my choice of drink and granting her leave.

Raphael appears to be on the verge of a stroke. He takes a long drink of sparkling water to manage his dismay at the turn in conversation.

I wait for the crew to leave before I say calmly, "I have no idea who you two really are, but when he finds out you've kidnapped me, Dimitri will kill you both."

Water bursts from Raphael's mouth, spraying a fine mist through the air and over the assorted meats and cheeses. He falls into a fit of hacking coughs while Killian and I stare at each other across the table.

It was an absolute shot in the dark, but damn did it hit its mark. Dimitri didn't send them for me. The only relevant questions remaining are who did . . . and why. And—I'll worry about this one later—exactly what they've got planned for me.

"It wasn't my idea!" gasps Raphael, sputtering. "You have to believe—"

"Another word," says Killian mildly, "and I'll cut out your tongue."

With a comical gulp, Raphael shuts up.

I gaze at Killian with my heart up in my throat and all my nerve endings screaming. He inspects me for a long time in thoughtful silence, drumming his fingers on the table in a slow, steady beat. On each knuckle is a tattoo. Initials. Flowers. A knife plunged through a skull.

Finally he says, "You think your darling love cares enough about you to start a war?"

"I never said he was my darling love," I snap, repulsed by the idea anyone could think I cared for the man who abused me so badly and for so long.

Killian leans forward and rests his arms on the table. His eyes—rich hazel in the sunlight—focus with the intensity of lasers on mine. "Are you saying you don't love him?"

Anger makes my mouth form words it otherwise wouldn't. "What difference should that make to you?"

His jaw hardens. "Don't test me."

"Why, because you'll beat me again? Personally, I think that was just to establish dominance, get me nice and scared so I'd be easier to handle."

His voice drops so low it's almost lost in the sound of the sails snapping in the sea breeze. "Is that what you think?"

I refuse to break eye contact, though I'm 90 percent sure my eyes are about to roll back into my head from terror. "I think you felt bad about it."

"My dear," whispers Raphael, stiff and white beside me. "Please don't."

I realize then that he's my best chance at getting to the truth. Killian is too poised, too smart, too controlled. He'll never reveal anything.

Unfortunately, however, things are going to have to get ugly before Raphael breaks.

Killian sees my calculation. With deadly softness and a glint of violence in his eyes, he says, "Choose your next words carefully. Because I lied when we met."

My pulse is a fast, faint thrum under my skin. I nervously moisten my lips. "Lied about what?"

He gazes deep into my eyes. "About the rules regarding no death or penetration. In fact, there aren't any rules at all."

I feel the wild, painful beat of my heart.

I've made a fatal miscalculation. Whatever Killian's plan, my part in it is disposable.

I'm disposable.

The girl returns with my rum. The moment she sets it down beside my plate, Raphael falls on it as if he's spent a decade in the desert. He swallows the entire thing in one gulp.

"I'm so sorry, sir," the girl says. "I didn't realize you wanted one, too."

Killian tells her, "Bring us the bottle. I have a feeling he's going to need it." He rises abruptly, his gaze murderous and zeroed in on me.

35

Heart racing, I jump to my feet so quickly I knock my chair over. It falls to the deck with a clatter.

Killian lunges.

He's fast, but I'm faster. In half a dozen long, running strides, I've reached the side of the deck. It's hardly an effort at all to jump up on the rail and hurl myself over.

I fall like a stone, the skirt of my dress flipped up over my face so the world is all yellow.

The ocean greets me as an icy, brutal slap against my skin, forcing the breath from my lungs as I plunge into it and go under. I surface after a moment, gasping and coughing, then kick my legs and start to swim.

But there's nowhere to go. We're somewhere out in the Atlantic with no land visible in any direction. Despite the sunshine, the sea is dark and freezing, and most likely infested with sharks.

But I'd rather drown or be ripped to shreds and eaten alive than let Killian get his hands on me again, so I plow ahead, cresting white-capped waves and squinting into the desolate blue horizon.

After a while, the roar of an engine drones over the sound of my labored breathing. A small boat pulls up about ten meters away and slows. It's the tender from the *Silver Shadow*, driven by one of the uniformed crew.

Gazing down at me over the edge, Killian stands with his arms folded, watching me with hooded eyes.

I keep swimming and ignore him.

For a long time, he does nothing but watch me. The tender puts along slowly, keeping pace as I swim, never surging ahead or lagging behind, just staying even. When I stop to catch my breath and tread water, they cut the engine and float silently. When I begin to swim again, the engine starts anew.

And still Killian watches me, patient as a predator lying in wait for a meal.

Soon enough, I'm close to exhaustion. The initial surge of adrenaline has burned out, and all my muscles are shaking and sore. The sea is choppy, and the water is frigid. I know I've only got moments left before hypothermia sets in and I lose consciousness.

Naz.

I accidentally inhale a mouthful of brackish water and cough so hard I can't catch my breath. My eyes sting, my legs are badly cramping, and I suppose this is as good a way to go out as any.

To be sure, I've faced far worse deaths than this.

I tilt my head up to the sky and let the sun blind me. The next inhalation I take is all water, and God, how it burns.

Naz. Thank you. You made it all worth it in the end.

I'm yanked out of the sea by a pair of brutally strong hands that pull me over the edge of the tender and throw me, violently hacking and wheezing, onto the floor.

"Stubborn," mutters Killian as he looms over me, a giant casting shadows.

I can't stop coughing, and I can't see. Water streams from my nostrils and mouth. My entire body heaves again and again, instinctively trying to expel the rest of the water from my lungs.

Killian pounds me on the back. Punishingly hard, because that's his default setting.

I spit out a mouthful of water. He thumps me on the back over and over until I can finally breathe, sucking in great gasping breaths. Then he shoves me onto my stomach and says something else in a language so beautiful it sounds like music. Even though the tone is angry and it's probably a curse, the words sound as smooth and lovely as water flowing over stones.

"A chonách san ort!"

Huddled against the unforgiving metal floor, I curl into a ball and close my eyes. I'm shivering uncontrollably. My teeth chatter. The smell of diesel fuel burns my nose.

I must fall into a daze or lose consciousness, because the next thing I know, I'm being hauled out of the boat by my wrists. We're on a platform inside an opening in the side of the yacht where the tender is kept. As soon as my feet touch the deck, I crash to my hands and knees. My legs are too rubbery to hold me up.

Killian sweeps me up into his arms.

When I stiffen, he says, "Stay still or I'll strangle you."

Far too exhausted to put up a fight, I close my eyes and let my head fall against his shoulder. "Not if I strangle you first."

His response is a wordless sound. I can't tell if it's a grunt of anger or a chuckle.

We move through the ship's corridors quickly and silently until we arrive at my room. Killian stops at the edge of the bed and sets me on my feet, steadying me with his hands gripped around my shoulders.

"Take off the dress."

I recoil in horror, my weak limbs finding just enough strength to pull against his grip before he gives me a swift, forceful shake that snaps my head around like a leaf on the end of a twig.

He puts his face close to mine and says slowly, "Take it off. Don't make me say it again."

I hiss, "You'll have to kill me before I'll volunteer to make it easier for you to rape me."

Enunciating each word but not raising his voice or losing any of his perfect control, he says, "Rape is beneath me. But murder isn't."

The room tilts. I can't think. I'm too weak to run, and all the fight has drained out of me.

Suddenly, all I want is for it all to be done.

"Funny, I never thought Death would speak Gaelic."

His eyes turn icy. "You don't believe me?"

"Oh, I believe you. I just don't care. The only thing I had worth living for is behind me."

Frowning, Killian cocks his head. "Behind you? What are you talking about? Dimitri—"

"Is a monster who stole seven years of my life," I say, my voice raw with pure hatred. *Wait—why is the room getting dark?* My legs give out. I go slack in his grip. My head falls back and my lids slide shut.

The last thing I remember is Killian's eyes, hard and speculative, narrowed and dark, and shadowed with obvious confusion.

SIX

NAZ

I'm headed for the front door, but Connor catches up with me before I'm even halfway down the hallway.

"Hold on!" He reaches out and grasps my shoulder. "Nasir, wait a minute. We need to make a plan!"

I shrug off his hand, but stop long enough to look at him when I answer. "The plan is I'm gonna get Eva. Boom. There's the fucking plan."

He holds up both hands in a surrendering gesture. "We're on the same side here."

He's right. We are on the same side. And I'm being all sorts of twitchy and unreasonable, but I can't get rid of the image of that big tattooed motherfucker putting his hands around Eva's slender throat.

I'm gonna tear his heart out of his chest and eat it while it's still beating.

I drag my hands through my hair, then lace my fingers behind my neck and stand there breathing hard through my nostrils and trying to ignore the shooting pains in my leg. And the band of steel swiftly tightening around my chest. And the horrible feeling that I might already be too late.

My sweet, soft, beautiful girl could be badly hurt.

Or worse.

"Listen. If we go in all shock and awe, balls to the wall, whoever's got her might panic. Panic isn't gonna be good for her, if you know what I'm saying."

Good for her health, he means. Good for her future in the land of the living.

"Copy that," I say gruffly. *"Fuck!"*

He steps closer and drops his voice. "I know, brother. Believe me, I know. I've been exactly where you are. When Tabby was in harm's way, I thought I'd lose my ever-lovin' mind. Just breathe for a minute, and let's think. Haste equals mistakes."

I blow out a hard breath, nodding. "Okay. This is me thinking." I pause. "I'm gonna go get Eva."

Connor props his hands on his hips. I can tell he's trying not to roll his eyes. "Yeah, we've already established that. The question is *how?*"

"Submarine. Parachute. Helicopter. Teleportation. Pick one, I'll make it happen."

He waves me off like I'm being ridiculous. "We could get the feds involved, have them waiting at wherever Tabby discovers the *Silver Shadow*'s final destination is."

"The *feds?*" I repeat, incredulous. "You wanna *guarantee* this thing gets fucked six ways to Sunday?"

He thinks for a moment. "You have a point."

"I know I do! Here's another one: *we're* the specialists in extraction!"

"Yep," he says, his voice even. "But you're operating at about fifty percent capacity right now, and I'm responsible for the lives of everyone in this building. Dimitri could have another strike team waiting for us as soon as we roll out the front gate."

"He could've already hit us if he wanted to. He could've gotten to us in the hospital, if it was really us he was after. But it wasn't us he was after, it was Eva. And she knew it, so that's why she left. *To save all our*

41

asses. And if you're right and it *isn't* one of his guys *or* her guys who has her on that ship, it can only be bad news for her. So the longer we wait the worse it gets. So . . ." I make an impatient motion with my hand. "Let's get this goddamn ball rolling."

Tabby pops her head out of the war room door and shouts down the hall. "Boys!"

Connor turns around. We both look at her, waiting.

"Before anybody goes anywhere, you might want to check this out." She disappears, leaving us no choice but to hustle back the way we came.

We find her in the same spot she was in when we left, sitting at the console. Only now she isn't tapping on the keyboard, she's simply staring up at the big screen.

The big screen showing nothing but ocean—vast, blue, and alarmingly empty.

"What happened? Where'd the *Silver Shadow* go?" says Connor.

"Oh, it's still there," replies Tabby. "We just can't see it."

The way she says it gives me a very bad feeling. "Meaning what?"

She swivels around in her chair. "Meaning the CYGNSS-6 satellite we had eyes on went out of range. We're going to be looking at the North Atlantic until the sat hits the west coast of Africa."

"Shit!"

"Indeed."

"Is there another satellite you can hack into?"

"Sure, the Landsat 8."

I examine her expression, knowing whatever she's about to say won't be good. "You might as well just tell me and get it over with."

"Well . . . unfortunately the Landsat 8 won't be in range for a little while."

Saliva pools in the back of my mouth. I might be about to vomit. "When you say a little while . . ."

"I mean six hours."

My mind makes some swift calculations about approximate horse-power of the average luxury yacht and how many knots it might travel per hour. I repeat slowly, "Six *hours*."

Sounding apologetic, Tabby says, "It makes sense, really. The Northern Atlantic's enormous and there's basically nothing out there, so there aren't nearly as many satellites on that rotation as there are over the continents."

"Ship that size under full power could eat up a lotta ocean in six hours," says Connor.

Tabby nods. "And if they change headings—"

"It'll be like looking for a needle in a haystack," I finish, my voice faint.

"That's not the worst part."

I groan and scrub my hands over my face.

"Sorry, but you did say to tell you."

"What is it?" prompts Connor.

Tabby says, "The Landsat 8 has a higher orbit than the CYGNSS-6, so we won't have the same clarity."

"So it'll basically be useless." The earth is crumbling beneath my feet.

"Correct. Unless you know *exactly* where to look, the resolution is too low to spot a ship."

"What about marine radar satellites?" asks Connor. "They comb the sea in big chunks. Every vessel captured would be a blip on the radar screen."

Tabby swivels around to her console and hits a few buttons. "Good thinking, honey, except for one thing."

A big two-dimensional map of the East Coast of the US appears on-screen. Thousands of small multicolored dots forest the blue area of the Atlantic off the Eastern Seaboard.

"None of this is real time. The automatic identification satel-lites functioning as part of the international maritime systems weren't cutting edge to begin with, but budget cuts from the last administration made things worse. So this tanker here, for instance"—she clicks on a green dot and a small screen pops up—"isn't actually *here*. This was its position three hours ago."

"For fuck's sake!" I can't stand still anymore, so back to pacing I go. "We have their last known coordinates. It won't take us that long to reach them. Let's just get in a bird and head out!"

Connor keeps an eye on me as I stalk back and forth, my limp getting more pronounced by the second. "They'd see us coming a mile away."

"That was an interesting sound, Nasir," says Tabby after a moment. "Very bear-with-a-thorn-in-his-paw-ish."

"Oh, I've got a thorn all right," I mutter, clenching and unclenching my hands. "I've got a thermonuclear thorn I'm gonna shove right up that bastard's—"

"Soldier!" says Connor loudly. "Focus!"

"Would this be a cool time to tell you the good news?" Tabby says calmly, examining her nails.

Connor and I stare at her. "*What* good news?"

She looks up at me and smiles. "The owner of the *Silver Shadow* is a wealthy French businessman by the name of Raphael Bergé."

I don't even bother to ask how she knows that. The woman puts the Oracle at Delphi to shame. "*And?*"

"And he has *really* good GPS on his LEO phone."

A LEO phone is the only kind of cellular phone that provides worldwide coverage with no gaps. The system works through low earth orbit satellites, hence the acronym.

More importantly, the LEO system can track a unit's precise location anywhere on the planet.

My relief is indescribable. "He's on the ship, isn't he?"

"Yes."

With quiet wonder, Connor says, "You discovered all that in the time it took me and Naz to walk down the hall and back?"

She bats her eyelashes at him, the picture of innocence. Then she spins around in her chair, grinning. "Shazam, bitches!"

I could kiss her, but I'd be dead within seconds. Connor's standing less than an arm's length away. "So let's call this motherfucker!"

Tabby stops spinning and looks at me like I'm nuts. "*Call* him?"

In a tone like you'd tell your kid to knock off the crying or you'll give him something to really cry about, Connor says flatly, "We're not calling him."

I growl, "Fine. Send Frenchy a text. Tell him if Eva's in anything other than perfect health when I get there, I'll cut off his arms and legs and hang him on the wall and name him Art. And then I'll kill his entire family, all his friends, his pets, and everyone he's ever worked with. And then I'll burn down his house and take a rocket launcher to that fucking ship and send it to the bottom of the ocean with him lashed to the mast, and his bloody stumps will attract all kinds of hungry sea creatures who will eat his goddamn guts out and lay their eggs inside his skull and gnaw on his bones. And then I'll drag up his picked-over carcass and cremate it and make urinal cakes from his ashes and piss on his remains every day for the rest of my life."

Without missing a beat, Tabby says, "Do you want that all in *one* text, or . . ."

Connor looks at the ceiling, shakes his head, and sighs. "It's like feeding hour at the zoo around here."

I've had enough of this. "Let's look at what we know so far. First, we know that Eva made an untraceable international collect call while I was in surgery. Right?"

Tabby nods. Connor says, "Right."

"Second, we know that Eva was on board the *Silver Shadow* when it left New York."

Connor agrees again.

"Third, we know at least two men were on board—one of whom got physical with Eva. Fourth, we know someone disabled both the marine satellite and the port registry, but failed to wipe the surveillance footage from the Port Authority security cameras covering the harbor."

"Ookaay," says Tabby, looking unsure of the direction I'm headed.

"Fifth, and most importantly, we've wasted precious minutes talking about this while Tabby could've hacked into Frenchy's sat phone account and figured out who this guy's been talking to and, from there, hopefully, found out who we're really dealing with. And from there— *possibly*—where the *Silver Shadow* might be headed."

Tabby makes a face at me, apparently insulted I felt the need to point out the obvious.

"I've already started a bot to crawl his records. We'll have a list of all his calls shortly."

When a cheerful electronic *ding* sounds from the console behind her, she points over her shoulder. "And there's the report now." She spins around in her chair, but then spins right back, holding up a finger. "One other thing I forgot to mention."

"Yeah?"

She looks me dead in the eye, her chin lifted and her voice low. "I don't like to be patronized, second-guessed, or told how to do my job. Do you?"

I release a heavy breath, close my eyes briefly, and shake my head. "No. I apologize."

When I open my eyes again, Tabby's smiling at me. "Apology accepted. We all handle stress differently. You should see Connor when he's really stressed out."

I look at him, curiosity momentarily overriding my panic. "I can't imagine what that might look like."

Connor sniffs and looks at me down his nose. "I'm way too cool to stress out."

"Ha!" When Connor's look turns sour, Tabby laughs again, then blows him a kiss. "You're right, honey. There's *never* any stress eating at our house. No gallons of mint chocolate chip ice cream wolfed down in four bites, no bags of chocolate chip cookies inhaled as fast as rails of cocaine, no jumbo-sized Reese's Peanut Butter Cups wrappers littering the coffee table."

He twists his lips. "So I enjoy an occasional sweet. That proves nothing."

"You're right, babe," she says softly, her eyes warm. "You're Teflon. My bad."

Watching them gaze tenderly at each other unravels the last bit of patience I have. "Okay, I'm apologizing in advance for this, but I'm about to rip out my hair by the roots here. So if we could please get a move on, I'd really appreciate it." I look at Tabby, lay a hand over my heart, and bow. "With deepest respect."

Tabby turns her warm green gaze to me. "Now that was a proper request."

She spins around in her chair and engages in a truly impressive display of furious keyboard typing, quickly launching several pop-up windows on the main screen. More dazzling typing. More screens appear. Then she executes some kind of command that makes all the screens begin to cross-reference one another. Numbers are highlighted, moved to one side, and bunched in order of most frequent appearances.

She opens yet another screen, copies and pastes the frequent number list, and hits "Enter." Then she says, "Hmm."

I don't realize I'm gnawing on my thumbnail until I try to talk and discover my thumb jammed in my mouth. "What does that mean?"

"It means our friend Raphael Bergé is definitely acquainted with Dimitri Ivanov."

A jolt of electricity runs down my spine, making me stiffen. I scan the screen but don't see whatever the connection is that she's seeing. "How can you tell?"

She double-clicks one of the phone numbers. A map appears on-screen with latitude and longitude coordinates of a pinned red spot.

Connor recognizes the location immediately. "That's Dimitri's home in Russia."

"So they *are* Dimitri's men." I start to pace again. I'm so upside down, I can't decide if this is good news or bad.

"Or at least Bergé is," says Connor.

"The big one must be, too, or he wouldn't be on the ship."

"Could be an associate. An employee. A friend, maybe, not necessarily even acquainted with Dimitri. What else we got, Tabby?"

She takes a while to answer, clicking down the list from number to number. Finally she shakes her head. "These others in the top ten are all spoofed numbers, rerouted through anonymous servers, mapped to nowhere. Could be Dimitri, too. Or Raphael knows a lot of other bad dudes." More clicking, then Tabby stops short. "Oh. Well, there you go."

I squint at the screen. Displayed is an unidentifiable mass of numbers, letters, and characters that don't look to be in any particular order. It might as well be hieroglyphics. "What are we looking at?"

She turns around, crosses her long legs, folds her hands in her lap, and looks back and forth between me and Connor. "We're looking at a SWIFT message."

She says that like I have a fucking clue at all what she's talking about. I bite my tongue, inhale a calming breath, release it, then ask politely, "What is that, and what does it mean?"

Her smile comes on slow and smug. "It's the format banks use to send messages to each other. And it means that nobody ever told our friend Raphael that you shouldn't transfer payment orders through a porous international financial network when you've got a bona fide computer genius crawling up your booty hole."

Electricity crackles through my veins. "We've got his bank account."

"Yep. Which means we've got access to his entire financial history and all his personal information, including address and national identification number. Which means we have him by the balls." Tabby looks at me with lifted brows and an innocent expression that's as fake as they come. "Think you might be able to use his balls for anything?"

My heart starts to beat so hard it leaves me breathless. "I can think of a thing or two. Let's get started."

SEVEN

Eva

"Are you *insane*? Do you have any idea what he'll do when he sees what you've done to her?"

"Aye. He'll give me what I want."

"He'll slit both our throats is what he'll do! All those bruises! And the hair! *Mon dieu*, how *could* you?"

"She cut the hair herself."

"Did she split her own lip, too? Did she strike herself in the face?"

"No. I did that."

"*Why?* You said all you'd do is scare her!"

"She's not intimidated by threats. I had to show her I meant business so she'd be easier to handle."

"Like she said!"

"Aye. She's smarter than I thought she'd be." A short pause. "And much more beautiful."

The voices are indistinct. Both male, one is high-pitched, borderline hysterical, the other low and controlled. Coming from somewhere nearby, they're muffled by the drone of the ship's engines. I try to lift my head, but find I can't. My eyelids are so heavy I can barely crack them open.

My body is so hot. I'm on fire. I'm roasting alive.

I do *not* want to roast alive.

The hysterical voice says, "What was that sound?"

"I don't know. Stay here. And you've had enough champagne."

A whisper of footsteps on floorboards. A creak of a door hinge and a breath of fresh air on my face, then the steps fall silent.

When I feel a hand on my forehead, I groan in relief. It's so cool. If only I could be that cool everywhere. My skin is engulfed in flames. I'm being turned on a spit over hot coals, like a suckling pig.

"Shit," murmurs a voice. The low, controlled one. The one that belongs to the cool, soothing hand.

I move my legs restlessly under the covers—*bed, I'm in bed*—trying to get some relief from the flames. I try to speak, to ask for water, but my tongue is thick and I can't seem to form coherent words. It's only the feeble groan that passes my lips again.

The hand withdraws. The footsteps start up again, moving quickly, headed off to my right. The sound of running water is torture. More footsteps, then the mattress on my left dips with a heavy weight. A big hand slides under my head and cradles it. Something is pressed to my lips.

"Open your mouth."

I obey on pure instinct and am rewarded by deliciously cold fluid sliding over my parched tongue. I sip and swallow, sip and swallow, until I can't drink any more and turn my head away.

The big hand supporting my head rests it gently back against the pillow.

"Hot," I whisper, hearing how weak my voice is. How cracked and weak.

Nothing happens for a moment. Then, all at once, the suffocating weight on top of me is stripped away. Cold air washes over my flushed skin. I sigh in relief. A shiver like pleasure passes through my body.

"Christ," mutters the voice.

It no longer sounds quite so in control.

51

Then I'm dreaming or hallucinating. I don't know which, but it feels very real. I'm running through a dense forest at twilight, dry leaves crunching underfoot, my heart pounding fast and terror chasing me. No—some*one* is chasing me. Someone who wants to hurt me is chasing me. They're reaching out with clawed hands. They've almost got me—almost—

Naz! Help me! Where are you?

"Shh. Hush, *bhrèagha*. You're okay. You have a fever."

The voice is almost tender now. The hand comes back, cool and comforting, resting lightly on my forehead.

I want that coolness all over my skin. I need that soothing coolness everywhere.

The faintest tremor runs through the hand. "Stop writhing or I'll pull the covers up."

All the softness in the voice is replaced by strain. The words are spoken through a clenched jaw.

I make an incoherent pleading noise. I have to escape from this bonfire engulfing me. I need to get away or I'll die.

The hand disappears again, but it's back quickly, and this time it's brought me a gift.

Something cold and wet presses against my fevered neck. A towel? A washcloth? I don't care. Whatever it is, it's pure heaven.

The cold cloth slides down my left arm. Heat evaporates behind it. I make soft sounds that mean *yes please more* and shiver again when the cloth slides down my ribs. It follows the dip of my waist, traces the rise of my hip bone, slips down the length of my thigh.

I lie still, feeling goose bumps rise all over my skin, the dull, constant drone of the ship's engines not quite drowning out the erratic breathing close to my side.

Then everything goes black and I sleep.

The next time I open my eyes, the light has changed. It's twilight, and everything is washed in shades of purple and gray. I lie still for a moment, heavy lidded and heavy limbed, just breathing into the gathering gloom. The gentle rocking motion of the ship lulls me. The room is quiet and still. My mind is sluggish, lazily sliding from one thought to the next, unable to hold on to anything long enough to disturb me.

At least I'm not burning up anymore. I'm warm, but not uncomfortably so. I must've been sweating, because the pillow beneath my head is damp, and so are the sheets under my naked body.

My heart skips a beat. I'm naked. *Why am I naked?*

I sit up so fast the room spins. I have to close my eyes and breathe slowly for a moment to get it to stop. When it does, I look down at myself. Thighs, belly, and breasts all bare. A baby-blue washcloth wadded up in a ball on the floor by my feet.

My stomach lurches. I desperately search my memory for a clue as to what happened, but the last thing I remember is Killian holding me by the shoulders and demanding I take off my wet dress.

Horrified, I clap a hand over my mouth.

Oh God.

No.

I stumble into the bathroom and flick on the light, recoiling at the sight of myself in the mirror. I look like death. Pale and blotchy, bruised and puffy, dark circles nestling in the hollows under my eyes. My pulse is fast but faint, and I feel light-headed. I recognize the signs of dehydration and stick my head under the faucet and drink until I'm full.

Then I take a scalding-hot shower and scrub my body until my skin is raw.

I won't think about it. Whatever he did, I won't think about it— until I have a weapon in my hand.

When I come out of the bathroom with a towel wrapped around me, Killian is sitting in a chair by the desk.

I freeze, my stomach clenching into a fist. He does nothing but sit and gaze at me with an inscrutable look in his eyes. After a long span of silence, I'm finally able to speak. "You said rape was beneath you."

"I did."

"And yet . . ."

He quirks a dark eyebrow. "And yet what?"

Though I barely have the strength to stand, my voice shakes with rage. "Don't make me say it."

He tilts his head, lets his gaze roam up and down my figure, unabashedly intimate, then meets my eyes. "If I'd had you," he says quietly, "you'd know."

Heat burns my cheeks. My legs are trembling, so I cross to the bed and sit on the edge, trying to manage my breathing while Killian watches me with those dark, impenetrable eyes.

"Who's Naz?"

I jerk my head around and stare at him in shock. "What?"

"Naz. Who is he?"

Despite all the water I drank, my mouth turns desert dry. I swallow, my palms going clammy, and look away. "I don't know what you're talking about."

He drums his long fingers slowly on the arm of the chair. "Really? How interesting. Because you cried out his name. Several times."

I fight a strong urge to make the sign of the cross over my chest. "I don't know anyone named Naz."

The drumming stops. "Look at me."

When I glance over at him, he leans forward, rests his elbows on his knees, and pins me with his cold stare. "If you lie to me again, I'll punish you. This time I won't go easy."

Astonished, I choke out a broken laugh. "Easy?"

"Aye," he says, holding my gaze. "It's your choice. Now tell me."

I want to be brave. God, how I want to be bold and so scary he backs off and leaves me alone, but the hot prick of tears is stinging my eyes and I'm so damn tired and spent and frankly depressed that I'm fresh out of courage.

So I tell him the truth. I don't even bother trying to hide the emotion in my voice when I do it. "Naz is . . ." I inhale a hitching breath. "The kindest and most honorable man I've ever met."

"Honorable."

Killian repeats the word with a curl of his lip, as if it tastes bad in his mouth. The sneer sends a needed burst of strength through me. I sit up straighter, lifting my chin. This piece of trash will *not* talk shit about Naz in my presence, no matter what it costs me.

"Yes, *honorable*," I say with heat. "You're probably not familiar with the word, but it basically means the opposite of what you are."

He contemplates me for a moment with a faint air of disapproval, as if I'm a foolish girl with silly ideas in her head. "Honor is nothing but narcissism dressed up for dinner. It's code for men who care too much about what other people think."

There's a lifetime of weariness behind that statement. Oceans of darkness and suffering color his words, but I refuse to be curious about anything to do with him. "That's quite eloquent for a cold-blooded, woman-beating bastard. Even if it is wrong."

"Calling me names isn't in your best interest, Evalina."

The proprietary way he says my name gives me chills, but I sit there and pretend it doesn't, aching for the moment he leaves and I can be alone again. *Might as well get this over with as quickly as possible.*

"Naz," I say flatly, bringing us back on topic. "You want to know who he is? He's the man who gave me back my faith in humanity. He gave me something to live for. He gave me something to die for, too, the most precious thing one person can give another."

Killian's gaze turns piercing. "What's so precious that you'd die for it?"

I answer simply, without so much as a breath of hesitation. "Love."

55

He stares at me in eerie stillness, his eyes glinting in the dim, all the lines of his big body simmering with tension. "And here I thought you were bright."

"It doesn't matter to me what a monster thinks of my intelligence."

He laughs as if I'm highly amusing. "You haven't even glimpsed the monster I really am. If you had, all that pride and stubbornness of yours would be a distant memory. Instead of sitting there with your nose in the air, you'd be cowering like a dog."

There doesn't seem to be a proper response to that, so I keep my mouth shut. Anything I'd say might be taken as an invitation.

"So you've been unfaithful to your husband?"

Husband. That startles me. He thinks Dimitri and I are married. I open my mouth to answer, but close it again, unsure if my position becomes more or less precarious if I tell him the truth.

With infinite gentleness, Killian murmurs, "Eva. Don't make me do it. You know I will."

I turn my head to avoid his gaze. I feel too naked when he looks at me. Vulnerable and weak, like a child. "Can a slave be unfaithful to his master? Can a dog be unfaithful to the one who holds his leash?"

A moment passes. Then I suck in a breath and jerk back because Killian is crossing the room. He shoves me back onto the mattress, straddles my body, and grabs my wrists. He pins them above my head and leans so close to my face our noses almost touch.

"I asked you a simple question. I expect a simple answer."

I'm breathing so hard I'm almost hyperventilating. His grip is far too strong for me to escape, and I know if I run he'll catch me anyway. I'm too weak from exhaustion, hunger, and fever to do anything but lie here.

Then I notice the knot I tied in the front of the towel has come undone.

I'm lying naked beneath him.

When I cry out in distress, he says, "I've already seen all of you there is to see. How do you think you got out of your wet clothes after your pointless little swim?"

"Get off me!"

"If I stand without an answer, you'll pay the price."

My entire body shakes with anger. He's big and heavy and utterly in control, and I despise him so much it's a physical thing. It's a vat of boiling lava in my stomach.

Through clenched teeth, I say, "Dimitri and I aren't married. We never were. And to answer your earlier question, no. I don't love him. I hate him with my whole heart."

His response comes fast and hard. "And yet you've been together for years. If you hate him so much, why didn't you leave?"

My laugh sounds semi-hysterical, even to my own ears. "You've never met him, have you?"

Killian's jaw hardens. He says nothing. He only watches me, waiting, his dark hair draped around our faces like a curtain cutting off the world.

"I didn't think so. If you had, you'd know that no one leaves Dimitri. I've tried and failed many times. The only way to escape him is death."

"You stepped on this ship of your own free will to go back to him."

"Yes, I did. To save someone else's life. Not that a man like *you* could ever understand that."

Killian's breathing is unsteady. His hands around my wrists are iron bands. Unblinking, we stare at each other in hostile silence while the clock ticks on the wall and I brace myself for the moment those hands move from my wrists to my throat.

But then, as quick as two fingers snapping, he releases me and rises from the bed.

The moment he stands, I sit up and cover myself. My hands shake so badly I almost can't manage to tie a knot in the towel over my breasts.

He walks a circle around the room, pacing the length of it and back, his hands on his hips, as restless as a caged tiger.

It's the first time I've seen a crack in his iron control.

"You're not married."

"No."

"You hate him."

"Yes."

"And the only reason you're going back to him is to save this Naz person."

"Yes."

He turns and paces the other direction, muttering something in Gaelic under his breath. Abruptly he stops and sends me a lethal, burning glare. "If I find out you're lying—"

"I know," I say, exhausted by all this. "You'll beat me."

His smile is small, yet profoundly cruel. "No. Since you enjoy swimming so much, I'll throw you overboard."

You'd think the sound of your mind cracking would be more of a roar, a chaos of noise that rises to a deafening crescendo, but really it's the smallest little *snap*, like a twig crushed underfoot.

I meet his burning glare with a level one of my own. "The hell you will."

His brows lower, temper settling over him like a fog, but I'm not backing down.

"Whatever it is you need me for, you haven't gotten it yet. And by the way, in case you hadn't noticed, *I can take whatever you dish out.* That isn't bravado, it's a fact. Dimitri is far more inventive and dedicated to savagery than you. I survived seven years of his particular brand of brutality, so you'll excuse me if I'm underwhelmed by your threats. So stop them. Beat me or don't, either way it doesn't matter. I'm done playing this cat-and-mouse game."

I stand, pushing back a wave of dizziness through sheer force of will. "Oh, and speaking of intelligence? If you had even half a brain, you'd tell me what you want from Dimitri and let me help you get it. Because I'm the only weakness that man has."

There's a beat wherein he simply stares at me with his nostrils flared and his lips thinned, as if he's debating whether choking me or setting me on fire will kill me the quickest.

I'm so over it.

"Here's what's going to happen. I'm not speaking another word to you unless you come back with food, clean clothes, and antibiotics. Whatever gave me that fever probably isn't done with me yet, and I need medicine, nourishment, and rest. In the meantime, you're going to figure out how you want to handle our situation. If I end up overboard again, I'll consider that my answer."

He just keeps staring at me as if picturing me swinging from a tree branch with a noose around my neck.

Fine. Let him be angry. I've leaped off higher bridges than this and survived.

I tiredly wave a hand toward the door. "That's it. Piss off."

Then I hobble back into the bathroom, lock the door behind me, curl up in the tub, and promptly fall asleep.

EIGHT

Eva

Sometime later, a thunderous banging noise wakes me.

"Come out," orders Killian through the door after he's finished punishing it with his fist.

He sounds calm. That either means he's brought what I've asked for and we're going to talk, or he's standing there holding a machete and my head will soon be separated from my body.

"Give me a minute."

I lift my head, wincing at the crick in my neck and the soreness in my limbs. Slowly, I climb out of the tub, rolling my head when I stand, stretching my arms toward the ceiling and hearing my spine crack. All my muscles groan in protest. I don't look at myself in the mirror—I'm not that much of a masochist—but spend several moments mentally gathering myself and making sure the knot in the towel over my breasts is snug. I have no idea where the yellow dress or the white one I wore when I came aboard went, but this is the only thing I have to wear, so it will have to do.

I open the door to find Killian standing right beside it. Startled he's standing so close, I jerk back a step.

"Hullo."

His pleasant expression and cordial tone immediately make me suspicious. "Hi."

He takes a moment to examine me. I can only imagine the unholy mess I look like, but except for a slight narrowing of his eyes, he doesn't react. "You slept on the floor?"

"The tub."

He repeats slowly, "The tub."

I lift a shoulder. "It seemed like the thing to do. Are you going to throw me overboard?"

The faintest hint of a smile lifts his lips, there and then swiftly gone. "You don't have a talent for small talk. That's unusual for a woman."

His words make my chest ache with a sudden, violent longing for Naz. He'd told me the same thing several times, lovingly teasing me about how hopeless I was with making light conversation and how abruptly I changed subjects, two random aspects of my personality he found charming.

Naz. God how I miss you. I look at my feet and moisten my lips. "My life hasn't been one where small talk was necessary. Or encouraged."

After a moment that feels charged, Killian says, "Mine either."

I glance up. He's looking at me with a new expression, one of piercing curiosity and focus, his hazel eyes almost glowing they're so intense. It rattles my nerves.

"What do you want from Dimitri that you kidnapped me to get?"

Now his smile really comes on, widening across his face to reveal a dimple in one cheek and a slew of straight white teeth. Whatever circle of hell he emerged from, they obviously had a good dental plan.

But that dimple is damn disturbing. On a ruthless face like his, with all its hard angles and straight edges, it adds a touch of softness that seems completely out of place yet all the more compelling because of it.

"There are fresh clothes on the bed for you. Come up to the main deck after you've dressed and we'll eat."

"So I'm not going overboard. Good to know."

"Not yet."

When I scowl, the dimple flashes as if it's winking at me. I find it so irritating my next words are laced with acid. "What about the antibiotics?"

He says drily, "Did you think there was a pharmacy on board?"

"I thought there might be a medical kit, or maybe one of the crew . . . never mind."

His expression turns sly, which makes me even more suspicious than when it was tranquil. Oh, who am I kidding? Every one of his expressions makes me suspicious as hell. The shady bastard!

Then, from the back pocket of his jeans, he pulls out a small white bottle and holds it up. He shakes it, rattling the contents. There's a yellow prescription label on the side that tells me those pills aren't aspirin.

When I meet his gaze, his is the smug look of a man who enjoys surprising people.

"Wow. If you were any more pleased with yourself, we'd have to get a priest so you and your ego could get married. Where did those come from?"

"The captain."

"Oh. I'll have to thank him."

"Nice thought, but you can't."

I sharpen my look at the edge in his voice. "Why's that?"

"I broke his neck."

I go cold with horror and stare at Killian with wide eyes. He smiles blandly, turns away, and says over his shoulder, "See you above deck."

❧

Another casual dress awaits me on the bed, this one a lovely shell pink under a pattern of white palm fronds. It has cap sleeves and a scoop neckline and fits as perfectly as the yellow one did. There's a lightweight jacket to go with, crisp white linen with a ragged-edged hem that hits me right at the hip and looks trendy and cute. The panties are simple white cotton. There is no bra. The tan leather moccasins are a size too big.

Did someone die for this outfit?

I shudder to think of how many female crew members there might have been before the *Silver Shadow* set sail from New York. If Killian would murder the captain for a few pills, the man is capable of absolutely anything.

Or did the captain meet his fate before today? Or even, perhaps, was Killian simply lying? I don't know, but I do know I need to be extraordinarily careful with him. The man is too unpredictable.

I slowly make my way upstairs, fatigue weighting every cell in my body. I suspect I've caught an infection, possibly picked up something from the hospital and made it worse with my swim in the sea. I'm achy, feverish, and have a headache that throbs with every beat of my heart.

When I reach the top of the stairs, I stop and listen. I see no one, but I hear muffled conversation from somewhere nearby, behind a closed door or through an open porthole perhaps. I catch only snippets of sentences, the occasional word here or there, but it seems as if someone is having some kind of money problems. Something to do with his accounts being emptied, the money mysteriously transferred out to untraceable destinations.

I can tell by the French accent that someone is Raphael.

"Tabby," I whisper, feeling a thrill in my blood.

It has to be. She did the same thing to Dimitri. Hacked into his bank accounts and drained them to zero using whatever magical knowledge she possesses in that genius brain of hers.

It hits me like a thunderbolt: *they know where I am.*

If Tabby is messing with Raphael's money, it means she knows I'm on this ship. *Naz* knows I'm on this ship.

And he'll be coming to get me.

Like buckshot from a shotgun, my mind blasts into a dozen different directions at once. My heartbeat accelerates until it's so fast I'm breathless. Emotion lashes through my body. Hope and euphoria and terror and desperation all fight for dominance, leaving me frozen with ambivalence, my thoughts tearing this way and that.

Maybe I'm wrong. Maybe this gut feeling is only whatever illness I'm coming down with. Maybe I'm jumping to conclusions and this is merely a coincidence . . . but holy hell does it feel like I'm right.

One flashing warning light underscores all the chaos, something that in my exhausted haze escaped me earlier. If I don't make it back to Dimitri, if Naz rescues me from this ship before Killian and Dimitri can make a deal about whatever it is Killian wants, it will be a disaster.

No matter the reason, no matter even if I'm dead, if I don't return to Dimitri, he'll kill Naz.

Maybe not this week. Maybe not next week, or even next month. But eventually he'll find a way to eliminate him, to bring down the hammer on Naz's head and end his life, inevitably in the most gruesome way possible.

No matter what, Dimitri always holds up his end of a bargain. It's how I knew he'd keep my mother alive if I complied with his sick wishes. It's how he's earned such respect from everyone in his employ. Even his enemies know that Dimitri Ivanov—vicious psychopath though he might be—does whatever he says he's going to do.

Always.

I can't let Naz find me or he's a dead man.

A door down the hallway past the media room opens, and I turn toward it as Raphael and Killian step out. Killian's gaze sharpens as soon as it lands on me, as if he can read my mind. I look away, desperately trying to compose myself and think of a plan.

"Ah, there she is! How lovely you look in that dress, my dear."

Raphael sounds strangely happy to see me. He probably thought Killian had dismembered me and thrown me piece by piece into the sea. "Hello, Raphael."

Wringing his hands, he advances toward me with an expression of barely contained hysteria. "How are you feeling? Still feverish?"

I shoot Killian a glance, but look away quickly when I meet his eyes. It's always difficult to look directly into them, but there's something new in his gaze, beyond all the calculation and hardness. Something even more strange than Raphael's relief to see me still alive.

Whatever it is, it's profoundly disturbing. Worse even than that incongruous dimple of his.

"I'm fine, Raphael. Thank you."

He stops in front of me and stares at me with his brow crinkled, then takes my hands. "Hair is fine, my dear," he says, gently cradling my hands in his. "People are either well or they aren't."

"Oh. In that case, I'm not only well, I'm great. I'm excellent. I'm positively *splendiferous.*"

His face falls at my tone, which is as dry as bone. He produces a small sigh. "Yes, I see your point," he says sadly. "And I want you to know I'm very, very sorry about all this—"

Killian's hand closes so quickly around Raphael's throat I barely register it when his arm lashes out. It's a literal blur, then Raphael is clutching at his neck and making awful gagging sounds as Killian begins to crush his windpipe.

Instinctively, I launch into action. "Stop! Killian, stop it!" I shove him as hard as I can in the chest, which manages to do nothing but make him whip his head around and stare at me while Raphael struggles and gasps, his face turning beet red and his knees beginning to buckle.

"Move away."

Killian doesn't even sound as if he's exerting himself. His voice is level, his expression is calm, but his eyes on me are burning.

Raphael's face is turning purple. He drops to his knees, but Killian doesn't let go. Spittle flecks his lips, which work soundlessly as he struggles for air, clawing with both hands at Killian's arm.

I think I might be about to watch him die, right here in front of me.

My heart beating like mad, I step closer and look up into Killian's eyes. "Let him go *right now!*"

There's something wild in Killian's gaze. Something unleashed, animal, as if he's no longer human. It's deeply frightening, mainly because I've seen this before.

Unfortunately, when you're dealing with an animal, you have to appeal to an animal's instincts.

I set my open palm in the middle of Killian's chest and lower my voice. "Please. If you let him go, I'll—"

Killian releases Raphael so abruptly I gasp. He topples sideways to the floor, where he's racked by a fit of coughing, curling up into a fetal position and holding his neck.

Then I'm no longer paying attention to Raphael because Killian takes me by my shoulders, drags me roughly against his body, and bends his head down so his face is close to mine. "You'll *what?*"

His voice is that sandpaper snarl again. He stares at me, unblinking, his jaw as hard as granite.

Careful, Eva. Careful. I say, "Behave. I promise I'll behave."

When his gaze drops to my mouth, I stop breathing. The moment stretches out until it becomes unbearable, but then Killian drags his blistering gaze back up to mine.

His fingers digging into my skin, he dips his head and puts his mouth next to my ear. "You'll have to do better than 'behave.'"

I hear the innuendo in his voice, and everything inside me rebels against it. I have to take a moment to steady myself so I don't scream bloody murder in his face. "This is me reminding you again that you said rape was beneath you."

His breath washes warm and soft against my neck when he replies. "It's not rape if you're offering."

"I'm not offering!"

I try to pull away, but he's got me in too tight a grip. So tight my breasts are smashed against his chest and the heat of his body burns me right through my clothing.

On the floor, Raphael wheezes. "Stop it, you barbarian! Leave her be!"

Killian and I are locked in a silent push-pull embrace, my head turned to the side and his cheek against my neck, his stubble rough against my skin, scratching it. My palms are flattened over iron pecs. He smells like soap and smoke and leather, a hint of masculine musk.

He says deliberately into my ear, "If you disobey me again, or interfere in any way with my orders or decisions, or pull another stupid trick like jumping off the ship, I'll put a knife through Raphael's thorax. In fact, if you do *anything* that displeases me *at all*, I'll put a knife through Raphael's thorax."

He pulls away slightly so we're eye to eye, letting me see how serious he is. And I do. This isn't just a threat to see if I'll listen. He means it.

Then he smiles. "Since you enjoy playing the hero so much."

That dimple flashes again, mocking me like a middle finger in the side of his face.

This time when I try to yank away, he allows it. He releases me, adopts a bored expression, and turns a sour eye to Raphael, still wheezing pathetically on the floor. "Get up."

I help Raphael to his feet. It's no easy task, because he's as weak kneed as a newborn giraffe, stumbling over his own feet and clinging to me. I think he's about to start weeping.

"You're okay, Raphael," I say firmly, trying to shore him up. "If you can still breathe, your windpipe wasn't damaged. You'll be sore and bruised, but you're going to be okay. Understand?"

He looks at me with big, watery blue eyes. "I don't know what's worse," he whispers hoarsely, sniffling. "My poor bruised windpipe or the fact that you must know from experience that if I can still breathe, it wasn't damaged."

My laugh is grim. "I'm a walking encyclopedia when it comes to all the ways a human body can be hurt. Here, put your arm around my shoulder. Let me help you to that chair." Then, in French, I tell him not to worry because I won't let Killian lay a finger on him again.

His shock at hearing me speak his language is so profound he almost falls to the floor again.

Still in French, I tell him, "I speak Russian, English, French, and German. I understand a smattering of Korean, too, but not enough to hold a conversation. Only enough to know when arms negotiations are being held."

Killian says loudly, "Congratulations on your linguistic talents, but you're not the only person around here who speaks French."

Under his breath, Raphael whispers, *"Schwanz."*

It's the German word for dick. And it's spoken with such ferocious hatred it gives me an idea.

As quietly and quickly as I can, I ask Raphael in German if he can get me a phone.

Before his loyalty or the extent of his fear of Killian can be tested, however, I'm grabbed by the scruff of my neck and hoisted away, leaving Raphael gasping, collapsing into the chair I was leading him to.

"What did you say to him?"

Killian has one hand gripped around the back of my neck. He closes the other around my throat. He looms over me, glaring, six-plus feet of danger, the look in his eyes purely lethal.

I'm not a good liar. My emotions are always clearly written on my face, and my voice betrays the truth in elevated pitch and guilty wavers. And considering I believe Killian's threat about sticking a knife in Raphael's thorax, my choices are limited. So I simply tell him the truth.

"I asked him if he could get me a phone."

Killian seems surprised by my honesty. He hesitates for a moment, as if unsure how to proceed. "So you could call this Naz of yours?"

"No. So I could call Dimitri."

My answer angers him. He drags me closer, his hand clamping tighter around my throat. I don't bother struggling, because I think it might make the situation worse, but I have to steady myself by gripping his wrists. They're as thick as tree branches, corded with muscle, and iron hard.

"You said you hated Dimitri."

My voice comes out choked from the pressure on my larynx. "I do. But if I don't get back to him soon, he'll kill Naz. I have to let him know it's not Naz's fault if I don't return."

His look is one of total astonishment. He stares at me, examining my expression, his gaze darting all over my face. His grip on my throat loosens, but he doesn't release me. If anything, he draws me closer, until we're practically breathing each other's breath. Finally, a look of understanding dawns in his eyes.

"You'll do anything to protect him, won't you?"

"Yes."

"Including risking my anger and returning to a man you claim to hate."

"Including anything, even sacrificing my life."

"That's pathological."

"That's love."

Killian has completely forgotten Raphael exists. He's focused on me with extraordinary intensity, his brows drawn together, his eyes unblinking. In a hushed, unguarded tone I haven't heard him use before, he says, "You keep saying that word. *Love.* Like it's a real thing."

I can breathe easier because his grip around my throat has loosened to the point where he's simply resting his hands around the front and back of my neck. His touch is gentle now, as soft as a lover's caress.

69

"It's the *only* thing," I reply vehemently, looking into his eyes. "It's the only real thing there is."

A faint tremor runs through his hands, a current like electricity. Something shimmers in the depths of his hazel eyes, an ancient, urgent pathos welling to the surface. "Show me."

I blink. "Um. What?"

His gaze drops to my lips. His expression changes. It softens somehow, but also warms with an emotion that's not quite desire. It's more like . . .

Longing.

"I said show me. I want you to kiss me the way you'd kiss him."

My heartbeat goes arrhythmic. Suddenly I can't draw a breath.

"Or Raphael suffers," Killian adds, still intently looking at my mouth.

My stomach knots. My armpits go damp. My pulse takes off like a rocket and my knees start to shake. *I can't do this. There's no way on God's green earth I can kiss this man. This* brute. *I'd rather kiss a shark. But Raphael—he'll hurt Raphael. I can't let that happen, I have to—*

"Decide," Killian orders in a gruff whisper.

God, if you're listening, I know I'm damned, but I could really use a miracle right now. Please strike Killian dead. A massive brain hemorrhage would be perfect.

More loudly, Killian says, "Decide." He shoots a dark glance toward Raphael.

I go up on my toes and press a swift, closed-mouth kiss to Killian's lips.

When I withdraw, he stares at me. Then he shrugs, drops his hands from my neck, walks over to Raphael, grabs him by the throat, and raises his other arm overhead, the hand closed to a fist. Raphael lets out a shriek and cowers.

"No!"

I leap between them, managing to shove Killian back so he releases Raphael.

He's undisturbed by my interference. He merely gazes at me with cool composure. Then he withdraws a folded knife from his back pocket. He opens it with a practiced flick of his wrist, causing Raphael to produce another shriek of terror, this one even higher pitched.

I throw up my hands. "Wait!"

Killian's look is bland, almost bored. "This isn't a negotiation."

This man is getting on my last nerve. I set my shoulders, close the few steps between us, take his unshaven face in my hands, and kiss him.

Really kiss him, with tongue and heart and total abandon, pressing the length of my body against his, forcing myself to recall every kiss I ever shared with Naz. I imagine it's *his* strong arms closing around my back and crushing me to his chest, *his* heartbeat hammering against my breasts, *his* hot mouth and surprisingly soft lips and low, anguished noise rising in the back of his throat.

I give myself over completely, knowing in the recesses of my mind that this is only for Raphael, and also that it's a terrible, terrible mistake.

Because Killian kisses me back with the desperation of a man trying to save himself from drowning.

There's uncharted passion in his mouth and his embrace, a kind of ravenous darkness that has no end. His kiss contains a black, bottomless hunger that could consume everything in its path or burn it to cinders, like an uncontrolled wildfire. He drinks deep, so deep I'm bent back at the waist, clinging to his shoulders, drawing short breaths through my nose as he ferociously ravages my mouth.

Finally, after what seems a lifetime, he breaks away from my mouth with a ragged intake of breath, his chest heaving. We stand frozen for uncounted moments, locked together, silently staring into each other's eyes.

He blinks slowly, his lids drifting open and shut, his pupils dilated as if he's been drugged. His voice shaking, he breathes, "Thank you."

Then he shoves me aside, picks up his knife from where he dropped it on the floor, strides over to Raphael in the chair, and plunges the blade deep into the center of his chest.

NINE

Naz

Halifax, Nova Scotia. An Atlantic Ocean port in eastern Canada, it's known for its maritime history, charming waterfront boardwalk, iconic lighthouses, and the Citadel, a star-shaped fort first established in 1749 to defend from various enemies approaching by sea.

It's also so cold it can freeze your goddamn balls off.

Especially in the water.

In October.

At night.

"So here's how this is gonna go, Catherine," I tell the well-dressed middle-aged woman Connor's got gagged and handcuffed on her knees in two feet of icy black water on a deserted part of the rocky beach south of town. "I'm gonna ask you a question, and you're gonna give me an answer. If I don't like your answer or I think you're lying, my colleague here will dunk your head underwater and let you reconsider for a while. Then we'll start over.

"I should warn you, though, that he's got a pretty crappy sense of time. Thirty seconds, ninety seconds . . . it's all the same to him." I adopt a concerned expression. "How long can you hold your breath?"

She stares at me with hatred, not fear, blazing in her eyes.

Interesting.

Connor is wearing a sour face, which I know is because I called him my "colleague" and not my "superior officer" or simply "boss." He doesn't like these kinds of breaches in protocol. The military has a definitive hierarchy it enjoys drilling into the brains of its recruits, and though we both left the corps behind years and years ago, there are some things you just can't shake.

"Oh, hang on a sec." I pull my cell from my pocket and snap a few pictures of her wet and bound. "In case we need it for your obituary," I say cheerfully, and put the phone away.

That didn't intimidate her, either. She looks like she's mentally putting a voodoo hex on me. This broad's a tough nut to crack.

"So. Question one. Are you ready? Here we go: You and your husband own a yacht by the name of *Silver Shadow*, correct?"

Her fury is momentarily waylaid by confusion, evidenced by the way she stops glaring and squints at me.

"Nod or you're going under. Salt water stings like a bitch when you inhale it through your nose."

She nods.

"Okay. Good job! Question two: Your husband is currently aboard the *Silver Shadow*, correct?"

More nodding.

"Beautiful! You see, you're a pro at this!"

Connor shakes his head and rolls his eyes, but I ignore him. We all have our ways of interrogating hostiles. Mine might be a little unorthodox, but I find having to frighten a woman extremely distasteful—sheerly on principle, though I've known a few women who were *way* more evil than any man, and it's not fair to discriminate based on gender, but c'mon, you just shouldn't be mean to girls—so I go with a few easy questions and a lot of support and encouragement so hopefully they won't be too traumatized or have too many lasting mental and emotional scars for their therapists and romantic partners to deal with later on.

Although this particular hostile doesn't seem to require kid gloves. I suspect I could strap her with explosives and a dead-man trigger and she'd spit in my eye.

"Question three, and this one is very important, so think hard before you answer." I drop my friendly smile and my voice and stare right into her eyes. "Where. The *fuck*. Is he going?"

She makes a sound like a growling animal. I let her stew in her juices for a while as I continue to stare at her, then motion for Connor to remove her gag.

As soon as the cloth is free of her mouth, she takes a deep breath, then launches into a long and passionate speech about how we better kill her or she's going to slice off our balls and choke us to death with them. Disembowelment will also occur, as will severing of limbs, etc. etc., before she dissolves our corpses in vats of acid and dumps them at sea.

Damn. I've met less-hardened prison wardens.

"We're not going to kill you."

When she looks surprised, I add, "I mean, *probably* not. We don't want to. Well, *I* don't want to, but . . ." I point at Connor while hiding my finger behind my other hand. Then, in a stage whisper: "That one's nuts. He loves knocking broads around." Then I spread my hands, like *What are you gonna do?*

She looks at Connor and makes that animal growl again. Connor stifles a sigh.

I'd feel sorry for her if I didn't know what she and her husband have been up to for the last few decades, namely money laundering, facilitating transfers of illegal weapons from bad guys to even *worse* guys, and drug trafficking. A few hundred kilos of coke and fentanyl here and there to pad their bank accounts and bankroll their lavish lifestyle.

Oh, and let's not forget the girls.

All the underage kidnapped girls the seemingly ideal citizens Mr. and Mrs. Bergé shuttle from one port to another aboard their luxury sailing yacht, the *Silver Shadow*, headed toward short, brutal new lives of degradation, humiliation, and unimaginable abuse from men who pay top dollar for virgins.

It is truly mind-boggling what you can discover if you know how to scour the dark web the way Tabby does.

So no, I don't feel sorry for this fat little worm in a soaked Chanel pantsuit, but she's still a person of the female persuasion, so she won't get the worst of my temper.

Her husband, on the other hand, is a different subject. I cannot *wait* to get my hands on that son of a bitch.

Catherine takes a few moments to get the growling under control, then snaps, "He's headed here."

Connor and I look at each other with raised brows. *"Here?"* I repeat, my head cocked. That certainly isn't what the last position of his LEO phone indicated. At last look, the *Silver Shadow* was headed due east from New York, out into the open ocean toward Europe, not north up the Atlantic coast.

"Yes. He'd sailed from Barbados and stopped in New York to drop off a . . ." She trails off, looking slightly guilty.

"We know what your typical cargo is, lady," I say sourly. "Get on with it."

"After New York, he was coming back here. To Halifax. At least, that was the plan the last I heard. He hasn't checked in with me since last night."

Connor sends me a questioning look I interpret as *Should I dunk her?* I shake my head, because I think she's telling the truth.

Apparently Raphael got new marching orders. The question of the hour is: From whom?

"Who's on the ship with your husband?"

"The captain. And crew. And go fuck yourself, pig."

"Charming. How many crew?"

"There's four of them. Three men and a young woman."

"What about the big guy with the tattoos? He part of the crew?"

I get the confused squint again. "Big guy?"

Resisting the urge to kick water in her face, I say, "Yes. Shoulder-length dark hair. Lots of tattoos."

She shakes her head. "There's no one like that on staff."

Just to confirm, I make her tell me what everyone looks like. She describes two African Americans, a Filipino, and two Caucasians, none of whom fit the description of the man who grabbed Eva on the deck of the ship.

"You ever deal with a guy who looks like what I'm describing? Any of your business contacts look like that? Friends? Acquaintances?"

Catherine shakes her head. "No. Are we done here? Because I've got my fucking book club meeting to get to and I'm responsible for the booze. If those bitches don't get their wine, they lose it. I'll hear about it for months."

Connor and I share a look of disbelief.

We'd nabbed her just as she was leaving her house, which happens to be conveniently close to the shore—which is conveniently close to the landing zone where the bird dropped us off—and so we decided to bring her down to this wide deserted beach for a little evening dip to see if we could determine where her husband was en route to.

We could've just interrogated her inside the house, but getting handcuffed and gagged, thrown into the trunk of your car, and driven to a remote location is always more terrifying and truth-inducing than sitting in your recliner at home, so here we are.

Except for her not being terrified—at all—it's worked out.

I ask a few more questions, but get nothing that can help us discover where her husband is headed with Eva. Short of removing her fingernails with pliers, which I'm not about to do, we've reached a dead end. So we take her back up to her Mercedes and toss her back into the trunk.

Then Connor and I climb inside and sit in the darkness, watching the waves roll onto the shore and listening to the human filth in Chanel in the trunk call us every name in the book while we drip salt water all over her Corinthian leather seats.

"Looks like it's time to send the Mr. a pic of his Mrs."

Drumming his fingers on the steering wheel, Connor says, "It's dangerous. He could overreact."

I drag a hand over my face, ignoring the burn in my chest that is progressively getting worse. I won't think about what's happening inside my lungs. They can collapse later, after I've gotten Eva back.

"We're out of options. My guess is whoever this tattooed bastard is, he wasn't expected. From what Tabby discovered, the Bergés operate as a team. The wife would know this guy if he'd been around before. If hubby was supposed to be coming home but made an unexpected detour, it was probably under duress. Doubly so since he didn't call her to let her know his change of plans. So maybe he finds out his wife is in danger and agrees to give us some intel if it saves her ass."

"Or maybe he asks us to do him a solid and put a bullet in her head. Imagine what living with her must be like. Jesus. I'd already be swinging from the rafters. He probably won't give a rat's ass what we do to her."

"You got any other suggestions? I'm all ears."

"Only what I've suggested before. We wait until they land somewhere, then go get her. Once they're out of the water, it'll be much easier to track them."

My temper flares. I had my shit under control on the two-hour bird ride up here from New York that we arranged as soon as Tabby had Raphael's home address, but now I'm starting to lose it again. "I'm not waiting. We've been over this. Time is of the essence, you know that."

"Only other viable option is to guess at where they're heading based on their trip so far and get out in front of 'em and wait."

I don't like that option, either, as it involves guessing. I fucking hate guessing. I need to *know*. It also involves sailing all over the goddamn North Atlantic, which at any time of year is treacherous. Between the currents, the wind, and the sheer amount of luck it will take to get close enough to the *Silver Shadow* to get on board, there's also the obvious problem of being spotted. I could take a dive from a plane, but it'd be like trying to thread a needle from outer space.

Tick tock.

Eva. Fuck, sweetheart, please be okay.

I blow out a hard breath and decide on a course of action. "Let's see if Frenchy wants to make a trade."

Fingers crossed he loves his nightmare of a wife.

TEN

Eva

The scream that rips from my chest is one of absolute horror, disbelief, and rage.

He stabbed him. *Killian stabbed Raphael in the chest!*

Blood pulses from the wound in surges that quickly saturate Raphael's shirt and spread down to the velvet seat of the chair. Lurid crimson blooms over white linen like a flower as he stares in shock at the knife protruding from his breastbone. He slumps lower in the seat, weakly grabbing at the handle, his mouth working but no sound coming out.

"You bastard!" I shove past Killian and fall to my knees in front of Raphael. His blue eyes are wide and disbelieving. A thin line of blood dribbles from the left corner of his mouth.

I'm going to be sick. There's so much blood. It's everywhere. On Raphael's clothing and hands, sprayed in fine droplets on his neck and chin, on my own hands as I helplessly try to put pressure on the wound, which makes ghastly sucking noises every time Raphael draws a breath.

I know enough not to remove the knife. It will only make things worse.

He'll bleed out faster.

"Get a doctor! Help! Someone help us, *please*!"

My desperate plea dies to echoes in the empty rooms. A new surge of horror washes over me when I realize no one is coming to help us. There's no one aboard this ship who can help either one of us.

Killian knocks me aside, yanks Raphael to his feet, and drags him moaning from the room.

"What are you doing? Where are you taking him?" I leap to my feet, my hands slick with blood and balled into fists, my face hot and my legs weak.

I shout my questions again, but Killian ignores me. Blood splatters over the polished wood floor, smearing into wavy lines as the toes of Raphael's shoes drag through the drops. Killian lugs him along like a sack of potatoes by his side.

Then we're outside on deck. Cold wind whips my hair around my eyes. The sky is leaden gray above, the cloud cover low and threatening. The wind sounds like the howling of wolves. I cling to a railing for support because my legs are so unsteady, worse even than my stomach, which is roiling. The hot sting of bile burns the back of my throat.

He stabbed him. He stabbed him. I can't wrap my mind around what I just witnessed, but I don't have time to recover from that before the next horror begins.

Killian drags Raphael to the edge of the deck, picks him up as if he weighs nothing, and tosses him over the railing.

He seems suspended in midair for an impossibly long moment, a tangle of arms and legs against a background of white-capped waves in the vast blackness of the ocean. Then he falls, twisting and spinning, the knife still protruding from his bloodied chest. I catch a final glimpse of his white, gaping face before he tumbles out of sight.

My entire body is jolted with adrenaline. It floods my cells, enabling me to push past my horror and spring into action.

I hurtle toward the railing, screaming into the wind, my arms out-stretched and my hands flexed wide open, grasping. *I have to help him I have to help I need to help him—*

I'm caught. Snatched away from the handrail by a pair of iron arms that bind me tight even as I kick and thrash against their hold.

"Let me go!" I scream. "What are you doing? *What the hell did you do?*"

Killian pulls me indoors, backing up step by step, his grip on me as relentless as his retreat. I fight him desperately, instinctively, but it's no use. He's too strong.

When we're inside, he sinks to a crouch, taking me with him to the floor. His arms around me are a cage; there's no escaping. When I lift my head and scream my frustration at the ceiling, Killian turns his face to my neck.

"It's done, Eva. It's done."

"Why? I promised I'd behave! I promised and I kissed you! *I gave you what you wanted!*"

"It's not your fault. He was never going to make it off this ship alive."

All of me starts to tremble. My legs are folded beneath me, but they tremble, too. I think I'm going into shock. "I don't understand."

"You don't need to. But don't bother shedding any tears for Raphael. That man caused more human suffering than almost anyone I've ever known. And I've known the worst humanity has to offer."

"I don't believe you! He was kind to me! He was angry when you hurt me!"

"Only because he was afraid of the consequences. He was afraid of Dimitri. He valued your life as much as he valued all the hundreds of girls he's delivered into Dimitri's hands over the years—only for what it would gain him."

Girls. A chill like death raises all the tiny hairs on my body.

He feels my sudden stillness and says softly, "Did you think Dimitri ordered them from Amazon?"

Several things come together at once in a sudden flare of illumination. "You thought I *helped* him with that?"

There's a loaded pause before he answers. "I thought you were someone you're not."

I sag against his arms, all the fight drained out of me. When my stomach clenches and I taste bile again, I'm helpless to stop it. I retch, my stomach heaving, but nothing comes out.

Killian murmurs something in Gaelic. His arms turn from binding to supportive as I heave, my eyes watering and my nose stinging. I flatten my bloody hands on the floor and stare at them as my empty stomach tries over and over to rid itself of sickness, not understanding that the kind of sickness plaguing me can never be eliminated.

It's the kind of sick that goes all the way down to the marrow of my bones.

❧

He carries me to my room. This killer. This mercenary with zero regard for human life carries me in his arms as gently as you would a child. He sets me on the bed and brings me a cup of water. I take it from him with shaking hands and drink it all in one go, focusing on a spot on the wall beyond his shoulder so I don't fall over.

"You need food."

He drags a chair to the bedside and sits, gazing at me with an unreadable expression, which I'm grateful for. I don't want to know what's going through his mind. I don't want to know anything except how I'm going to stop Dimitri from harming Naz.

"You should send him pictures of me." I gesture to my bruised face, distantly surprised by how shaky my voice sounds and by how hot the room feels. Hot and suffocating. "Dimitri, I mean. You should send him close-ups of my face and neck."

Killian leans back in his chair. His tone is faintly amused. "Is that what I should do?"

I nod. *How is he so calm? He must murder people a lot.* "Or a video. I'll scream and beg very convincingly."

Now his voice is thoughtful. "I bet you would."

The door swings on its hinges as the ship makes a slow roll over a wave. My stomach rolls with it. "Oh." Hit with a new thought, I look up at Killian. "Or were you going to kill me first?"

Our gazes hold for an uncomfortably long time before he speaks again. "You know I'm not going to kill you."

I sit with that for a moment before answering. Then I nod again. "Yes."

"What else do you know?" He leans forward, sets his elbows on his knees, and threads his fingers together as he stares at me.

I look down at my hands holding the empty cup. My trembling, bloodstained hands. *How did I get here? What happened to me? How is this my life?*

"I know that you didn't want to beat me, but you did. You felt you had to." I hear only silence in response, so I continue. "I know that Raphael tried to pretend he was in charge." My laugh is soft and hollow. "But clearly he wasn't. I know Dimitri has something you want." I look up at Killian again. "And I know you think bartering me is the way you're going to get it."

"And am I right?"

"Yes."

"Good. I hate to think I went to all this trouble for nothing."

"But there are many things I don't know."

He tilts his head, considering me, which I take as permission to continue. I think for a moment, then decide to go with the most pressing question.

"Who are you?"

He smiles, but it's the cruel one again. The one that makes him look homicidal. "A better question is not who, but what."

"Oh, I already know what you are."

The smile turns mocking. "Do tell."

"You're a man who'll do anything he thinks he needs to do to get what he wants. Anything at all, including things he *doesn't* want to do. Including violence. Including murder."

"Ah. A monster with a conscience, then?"

"No, just a monster. If you had a conscience, you wouldn't do the things you know are wrong. But you do them anyway."

He gazes at me for a beat. "The world has enough heroes already. Idealists with pretty morals but weak stomachs, loud mouths but no grit. Even the noblest of wars are paid for in blood. What the world really needs are more monsters willing to get the ugly stuff done so everybody else can sleep safe at night."

"Is that what you tell yourself so *you* can sleep at night?"

"Let me ask you this: If you had to kill one person, but it would save countless lives, would you do it?"

"It's not for me to decide."

Impatient, he shakes his head. "Hypothetically."

"Hypothetically or not, it's God's job to decide who lives or dies, not mine."

He scoffs. "If there is a God, he got bored with us a long time ago. He moved on to other projects. He's not paying attention to us anymore."

I've heard this argument before, and as always, I'm not buying it.

Just because we don't understand how something works doesn't mean it isn't working.

"I know it's easier to be cynical," I say, holding his gaze. "I know the world is filled with misery, and people hurt each other terribly, and it can feel like we're alone. But we're not alone. He's always there, waiting for us to turn to him."

I sense his growing impatience with this topic. He says, "Why should we *want* to turn to him? This God of yours is a petty little dictator who doesn't deserve our worship. Have you actually *read* the Bible? It's a horror story. God is a genocidal maniac. Your faith is wasted on him."

I stare at him, surprised he has such strong feelings on the subject and that someone like him would have even a passing familiarity with the good book.

He presses, "Why would your God allow someone like Hitler to exist? Why would he let the rape and enslavement of children occur? Why would he allow so much suffering?"

"Because we were given free will. We weren't created to be slaves. How we live our lives is our choice, and if we choose to be evil . . . he allows it."

He says flatly, "That makes no sense."

"Neither does love. Yet it exists. It's real, even if you don't believe in it. Just like God." I blow out a hard breath and set the empty glass on the bedside table. "I'm a hypocrite, though."

I feel his attention sharpen. He asks, "How?"

"I said it was God's job to decide who lives or dies, but . . ."

"But what?"

I glance up at him. "But I've killed two men."

He's shocked, I can tell, though he tries not to show it. I can also tell he's intrigued, but he waits for me to continue without prompting.

"They were Dimitri's men. They blew up the car I was riding in and tried to kidnap me." I pause for a moment. "You're lucky I don't have a gun."

"You wouldn't shoot me," he says instantly.

"That's the thing, though," I say faintly. "The thing I discovered about myself. The thing I never would have believed. If it comes right down to it, I'm capable of taking a life."

"Only to protect yourself. Self-defense isn't the same as what I did to Raphael. You're not a murderer."

"I realize you probably have a lot of experience on the subject, so I hate to contradict you, but technically anyone who has committed murder is a murderer."

His expression is a combination of amusement at my sarcastic tone and intense curiosity about what I'm saying. "Let's go back to what you said a second ago. About Dimitri's men trying to kidnap you."

"What about it?"

"Why would they do that? Were they going to barter you to get something from him, too?"

"No. Dimitri ordered them to."

He furrows his brow.

Exhausted, I exhale a heavy breath. "This would be much easier to explain if you'd tell me your side of the story first. What you want from Dimitri, how you came to be aboard this ship, what the deal between you and Raphael is . . ." That sick feeling returns. "Was."

He answers without hesitation. "The less you know the better."

I consider that and have to concede he has a good point. Dimitri will no doubt want to know everything that was said on this ship, and he'll surely have terrible ways of extracting that information. If I know nothing, I might get away with only a few broken bones before he's convinced.

So I start talking.

I tell Killian the story of how I met Dimitri when I was twenty, how he saw me dance in a production of *The Firebird* and introduced himself backstage after the show. How polite and generous he seemed at first, how flatteringly smitten, how he courted me and even brought my mother flowers. Ashamed, I tell Killian how awed I was by Dimitri's wealth—having come from a poor family myself—and how easy it was to be seduced by his charm and sweet, boyish face.

I tell him how, after a few dates, I refused to sleep with him because I was a virgin and wanted to save myself for marriage. I also tell him how enraged that made Dimitri. How he beat me.

How I lost consciousness. How I woke to him violating my body. How from then on I was a kept thing with no will of my own, no voice, no options. How he moved my mother and me into his mansion and held me hostage on threat of her life. How I was always under lock and key, under surveillance, under his cruel, demanding thumb.

How I hated myself more and more with each passing day.

I tell him how, after seven years of suffering for us both, my mother finally died of a protracted illness. I tell him how I escaped.

How I met Naz.

How, for the first time in my life, I fell in love.

How completely I was loved in return.

I tell Killian every good and horrible thing that led me to this moment, sitting across from him on the edge of this bed in this room. When I stop talking, it isn't until I feel something hot and wet drip onto my wrist that I realize I'm crying.

After a time, his voice thick, Killian says, "And for all that, you're *willingly* going back to Dimitri."

My exhalation is a great gust of a thing and takes the last of my energy with it. "I told you. If I don't go back, Naz dies. Also"—I manage a sick laugh—"back to me being a hypocrite. Because I'm going to find a way to kill Dimitri."

The room has begun a gentle, slow spin, all the world tilting and topsy-turvy. I'm queasy, hopeless, and bone-tired. "So I guess that makes us the same."

"What do you mean?"

"I know it's wrong to take a life, but I'm going to do it anyway."

I lose the ability to hold myself upright. Killian catches me as I topple sideways. He lowers me gently to the mattress, brushes a lock of hair off my forehead, and pulls the too-big moccasins from my feet.

Just as I'm tumbling into unconsciousness, he murmurs, "We're not the same, *bhreagha*. You've still got a soul."

ELEVEN

Naz

I compose the text to Raphael, attach the picture of his wife, and hit "Send."

"Might take a while," says Connor, settling back into the driver's seat. "He'll have to think how he wants to—"

The phone rings. Connor and I share a surprised glance.

"That was fast."

I hit the "Answer" button and hold the phone to my ear. I don't say anything, I just listen, gauging the quality of the silence and waiting for him to speak.

After a moment, a deep, rough male voice says, "This must be Naz."

I'm so shocked I almost drop the phone. The anonymous, untraceable burner phone. I didn't include my name in the text message, so how the hell does he know it's me?

"Raphael?"

"Raphael's dead. I stuck a knife in his chest and threw him overboard."

His voice has an Irish accent, not French as I was expecting. Judging by that and his words—which sound honest—this isn't Raphael playing some kind of game.

"Who is this?"

"This is Killian."

Killian? Who the fuck is Killian? All my senses have sharpened until it seems I can hear the atoms vibrating in the air around me. Then it hits me.

This is probably the big motherfucker who put his hands on Eva. Unless it's one of the crew, but I don't think so. Especially considering what he said. Yacht crews don't generally find it in their best interests to kill their employers and throw them into the sea.

The words leave my throat in a gravelly scrape of pure hatred. "You have something of mine."

After a pause, he says disapprovingly, "I doubt Eva would be keen on hearing you call her a 'thing.'"

My eyes flare as wide as my nostrils do. The way he said her name is bad enough, but the implication that he knows how she'd feel is like a sword of fire shoved down my throat.

I demand, "What have you done with her?"

"She's in good hands," comes the calm response to my heated question. "You don't have to worry."

Is he fucking kidding me?

Beside me, Connor is frowning and tense, but I can't pay attention to him because of all the murder and mayhem wreaking havoc in my nervous system. "What do you want? What is this about? Where are you going with her? If she's hurt, I swear on my mother's grave—"

"It's beautiful, you know."

His tone has changed. Now it's soft, thoughtful, and I have no clue what he's talking about. "What? What's beautiful?"

"The way she loves you."

It feels as if King Kong just punched me in the chest. Eva told this man she loves me? This man who grabbed her by the throat and dragged her across the deck of a yacht? She hasn't even told me herself.

My God, has he tortured her for information?

Before I can respond, he says, "I hope you deserve it. To be honest, you sound a wee bit unstable. Are you sure you're good enough for her? You might have to convince me. After everything she's been through, she deserves the best." His voice drops. "And Christ, she's exquisite. Those eyes. That body. That *fire*. No wonder you and Dimitri are so desperate to get her back."

Breathing hard, my heart feeling as if it's about to explode, I say, "Put her on the phone."

"She's sleeping."

I growl, "Listen to me, you son of a bitch—"

"Naz. What kind of a name is that? Is it short for something?"

Connor is motioning for me to give him the phone. I think he can sense things have gone completely off the rails. I wave him away, frustrated and needing to hit something.

"Yeah. It's short for, 'If you hurt her, I'm gonna kill you in every way there is to be killed.' It's short for, 'I will track you down to the ends of the earth and make you and everyone you've ever met pay a thousand times over for any pain you cause the woman I love.' It's short for, 'I WILL NEVER STOP UNTIL I GET HER BACK.'"

There's a pause, then what sounds like a satisfied grunt. "All right. You're a little too hotheaded, but you sound sincere. So I'll answer your questions. What I want is something Eva's going to help me get. What this is about is the future of nations. Where I'm going with her is . . . well, I can't tell you that yet because if I do you'll probably be here before I can get what I want from Dimitri and then all my careful plans will be ruined."

I let loose a frustrated holler and Killian laughs.

"I get that a lot. Eva made almost the exact same noise a short while ago. She didn't like what I did to Raphael." His voice turns wistful. "She's sensitive that way, isn't she? Concerned for the well-being of other people. Even to the point of sacrificing herself. Honestly, Naz, she's remarkable. I've never met anyone like her. She's . . ."

In his pause, I hear how loudly I'm breathing.

"*Compelling*, I think is the right word. Or maybe fascinating. Once you start looking at her, it's impossible to look away." He chuckles. "But you know that already. You sound obsessed."

"Killian—"

"I'm going to destroy this phone after we're done talking, because I'm sure you're tracking it. But I want you to know I was truthful when I told you she's safe with me. And I'll try to get my business with Dimitri concluded as quickly as possible."

He hesitates. When he speaks again there's a new tone in his voice that raises all the hair on my arms.

"Because the more time I spend with your woman, the less I want to give her back."

The connection drops, and he's gone.

I sit frozen for a moment, listening to dead air, my nervous system rapidly shutting down until my body feels as cold and immobile as an iceberg. I can't think clearly. I can't form words. The only thing I'm conscious of is the primal, almost violent need to see Eva's face.

I have to get to her.

I have to get to her *now*.

"Nasir. What happened?"

I turn and look at Connor. His black eyes glint in the dim interior of the Mercedes, reflecting moonlight spilling through the windshield. My voice comes eerily calm and hollow.

"You have any pull with the Canadian Armed Forces?"

"Yeah. Got plenty of contacts who can arrange whatever I need for an op on Canadian soil. Why?"

"Because we need a long-range cargo plane and a parachute rig. By the time I get to the nearest air base and get geared up, there should be another satellite within range of the *Silver Shadow* so we can pinpoint their exact location. I'm gonna jump in."

"Who's Killian? What'd he say?"

"Enough for me to know that if we don't get Eva back soon, we're not getting her back at all."

I face forward and stare out the windshield, seeing nothing, everything inside me the darkest shade of black. Then I throw open the passenger door.

"Move over. I'm driving."

TWELVE

Eva

I'm dreaming. Fevered, delirious dreams of running through streets that are deserted and on fire, the soles of my feet blistering from the heat. Firestorms rage all around me, the flames so hot they create their own winds.

I run as fast as I can, my clothes smoking, my lungs burning, hot ashes landing like scalding rain on my skin. But there's nowhere I can escape to. There's no safe quarter for me and there never will be, because this is hell.

I hear the low drone of conversation somewhere behind me, but I don't turn to look. I just keep on running as my skin starts to turn black and peel off my body.

"How long has she been like this?"

"Since I called you. She's getting worse."

A cool touch on my wrist. A thumb pressing down, seeking my pulse, finding it. An electronic beep near my ear.

"Well?"

"She has a weak, rapid pulse and a dangerously elevated temperature. Any vomiting or diarrhea?"

"Yes to the first, no to the second."

"Dizziness? Fainting?"

"I don't know."

"Allergies?"

"I don't know."

"Well, something nasty's causing that rash."

"What is it?"

"Could be anything from an allergic reaction to an infection to a bad flu. Or a hundred other things. There's no way to tell without running tests. I'll leave you with a broad-spectrum antibiotic and general care instructions."

"No. She needs proper medical attention."

"You're not suggesting . . ."

"I'm suggesting we get her on a helicopter and head to a hospital."

"Hospital! You could compromise the entire operation!"

"If you don't shut up and get out of my way, I'll compromise the shape of your skull."

I'm being moved. Lifted by a pair of massive arms that cradle me close and shush me when I whimper. I must not be dreaming anymore because the fire is extinguished, doused by the sudden freezing slap of salty wind on my skin.

"Easy, *bhrèagha*. I've got you."

I'm laid on something cold and hard. My limbs are gently rearranged. A heavy blanket is placed over me. I don't have the strength to open my eyes, and I barely have the strength to care what's happening to me.

Except . . .

"Naz," I whisper through cracked lips.

A warm, rough hand wraps around my ankle and squeezes. "I took care of it. Dimitri knows you're with me." Then the voice commands to someone else, "Let's move!"

A stomach-lurching weightlessness and a deafening roar of engines make me wince and curl, shuddering. Everything hurts, especially my heart, which feels as if it's breaking. Every beat is accompanied by stabbing pain. Then the world fades to black.

The last thing I remember is the feel of that warm, comforting hand on my skin.

∽

An hour or a day or a hundred years later, I hear murmuring voices.

"It's endocarditis."

"I don't know what that means."

"It's an infection of the inner lining of the heart chambers and valves that's spread through the bloodstream. We typically only see this with patients who have underlying heart problems or previous damage to the heart muscles."

"Is it bad?"

"It's not good. If not treated quickly, it can destroy the valves and lead to life-threatening complications."

"What's the treatment?"

"For now, IV antibiotics. Once we see how she responds and what the extent of the damage is, we'll decide if further intervention is required."

"Such as?"

"Surgery. We're also looking at possible complications including stroke, seizure, embolism—"

"How soon can she be moved?"

"Moved? She can't be moved. She'll need to be hospitalized for several weeks, at least!"

"You've got twelve hours. If she's not stabilized and on her way to perfect health by then, I'll put a bullet in your brain."

"Don't threaten me. And it would take a miracle for this woman to be well enough to leave in twelve hours."

The voice I recognize as Killian's says darkly, "Better start praying, then, Doc. Because even a miracle won't save you if she isn't."

95

THIRTEEN

Naz

We're waiting inside a frigid hangar at the Canadian Forces Base Halifax for the C-130 to fuel up when Connor gets a phone call from Tabby.

"Princess," he says, picking up. He listens for a moment. Whatever she says in response makes him say, "Hold on. I'm putting you on speaker." He taps a button. "Say that again so Nasir can hear."

Tinny but clear, her voice comes through the phone's speaker. "Hi, Nasir."

"Tabby. What's happening?"

"What's happening is that the *Silver Shadow* sent out a call to the coast guard over channel sixteen."

Channel sixteen is a marine VHF radio frequency designated as an international distress frequency. Ships use it in Mayday situations when serious threats to life and safety occur.

Like, for instance, when the ship is sinking and everyone on board is about to die.

"Oh fuck."

"Well said. The good news is that now we've got their exact coordinates."

"What's the bad news?"

There's a short pause. "Their coordinates don't matter anymore, because according to the person who placed the call, the pirate who commandeered the ship—"

"Pirate!"

"—is no longer aboard."

"The mysterious Killian," muses Connor.

I demand, "Where did he go?"

"You're not going to believe this, but apparently he was picked up by a US Navy frigate."

"*What?* The navy? How is the navy involved in this?"

"I don't know yet, but I'm afraid there's more, Naz." Tabby takes a breath. "He killed Bergé and all the crew except the girl who made the call. When he left the ship, he didn't leave alone. And the woman he took with him was unconscious."

Eva. It becomes impossible to breathe.

"But I do have something we can work with."

"Tell me."

"The caller said she overheard the pirate on a phone call mentioning Angra do Heroísmo. She believes that's his final destination."

Connor says, "Where the hell is that?"

"The Azores." I recall a trip to Portugal I took long ago. "If memory serves, Angra do Heroísmo is the capital of Terceira Island, one of the ancient volcanic islands that compose the archipelago."

Connor and I look at each other.

Into the silence, Tabby says, "I'll hack into everything I can to see if a navy frigate shows up anywhere near there. But it will take days for them to cross the Atlantic from the last position we had for the *Silver Shadow.*"

"Good," I say, energy thrumming through my body. "By that time we'll already be there waiting."

FOURTEEN

EVA

I'm in his arms again. I have no sense of how much time has passed, if any. I'm thirsty, groggy, and as weak as a foal, but the nausea is gone and the fever that once was a forest fire has burned down to a few glowing embers.

"Hmm. Back from the dead, I see. Maybe your God has some use after all."

I force my lids open, though it feels as if they're weighed down with lead. I see a hard jawline covered in scruff and a thick masculine throat with tattoos peeking above the collar of a white T-shirt.

"Killian," I whisper, disoriented.

"At your service."

Beyond his face is blue, blue sky edged in palm trees. Below is a hill forested with white houses with red-tiled roofs and a small, charming marina dotted with boats. We're moving along a tree-lined path in the golden glow of a humid afternoon, and I have no idea what's happening or where I am.

"Naz—"

"Christ, woman, is he all you can think about? I told you, I took care of it. Now be quiet before you piss me off and I throw you over the cliff."

I close my eyes and let my head rest against the broad expanse of his chest. "You're not going to throw me over the cliff."

A grunt is my only answer.

In short order we arrive at a white stucco bungalow sitting alone at the end of a lane. Killian punches in a series of numbers on a keypad hidden behind a giant *Monstera* bush, then we go inside.

"Is this a safe house?"

He slants me a look, his brow cocked. "What do you know about safe houses?"

"More than you'd think. I'm full of surprises."

He mutters, "I know." It doesn't sound like a compliment.

He kicks the door shut behind him and carries me over to a sofa that's as soft as a cloud. He arranges my head on a pillow and tucks the blanket in under my feet. Then he points at me and orders, "Stay here."

I gaze up at him. It's like looking up at a skyscraper. "Shoot, and I was just thinking of going on a nice jog."

His look is disapproving. He props his hands on his hips. "Careful with that smart mouth, *bhrèagha*."

I smile drowsily. "Or what, you'll put a knife in Raphael's thorax? Oops. Too late."

He mutters something, dragging a hand through his hair. "You're still loopy from the pain meds."

"What's that thing you keep calling me? That Gaelic word."

His expression sours. "Witch. It means mouthy, troublesome, pain-in-the-ass witch."

"Okay. May I please have some water?"

He stares at me for a beat. Then he shakes his head, mutters something under his breath, and stalks off across the living room toward the kitchenette. He returns with a glass and kneels beside the sofa, sliding his hand beneath my head to support it.

Annoyed at being treated like a baby, I grouse, "I can do it myself."

"Oh, sure, go ahead, then."

He pulls his hand away, and my head drops back to the pillow. I try several times to lift it to a high-enough angle to be able to drink, but for some reason the damn thing weighs five thousand pounds.

"I guess I can't do it myself," I admit sheepishly.

"No kidding."

"But if you leave the glass on that coffee table, I'll try again in a little bit."

His exhalation is slow and sounds murder-y. "This Naz of yours must have the patience of a damn saint."

From whatever bizarre combination of illness and trauma and drugs I may have been administered, hearing Killian say Naz's name makes me teary.

Watching my expression, Killian asks sharply, "What is it?"

"I miss him so much. God, I feel like death. This safe house is cute. Did you save my life?"

He closes his eyes just longer than a blink, shakes his head, and presses his lips together. I think he's trying not to laugh. Then he rises and goes into the kitchen. He rummages around in the cupboards, pulls something out of the fridge, then comes back with a baby bottle–shaped plastic container filled with pale yellow liquid, a roll of tape, and something in a bulky green wrapper. When he tears open the package with his teeth, that something turns out to be syringes and a catheter.

I've been in the hospital often enough to know this is an IV infusion set.

I watch with interest as Killian unwinds a length of slim tubing from the container with the liquid and readies the catheter. Then he uncaps the part with the needle and takes my hand.

"You have to swab it first."

When he pauses to look at me with his brows lifted, I nod. "With rubbing alcohol. So bacteria from the skin doesn't get into the needle."

With the beleaguered air of someone of great intelligence dealing with a certified idiot, he says, "Extensive studies have shown that disinfecting the skin prior to injection has no measurable benefit."

I frown at him. "That makes no sense."

He deadpans, "Neither does your belief in love or God, but here we are."

He slips the needle into the vein on the back of my hand on the first try, without causing the slightest sting. Then he tapes it to my skin, uncaps the short length of tubing attached to the catheter, and injects one of the syringes into the tube.

"Saline to clear the line of air bubbles?"

"Cyanide to stop your heart. Be quiet."

He removes the protective cap on the infuser tubing and screws it into the extension tubing on the catheter. Then he opens the clamp on the infuser so the yellow liquid begins to flow.

When I sigh, he says, "What?"

"You didn't wash your hands first."

"For the love of God, woman."

"You know, for someone who doesn't believe in God, you sure mention him a lot."

"If you don't shut up, I'll duct-tape your mouth."

"I'm only saying that you've gone to all this trouble to kidnap me and save my life and everything, but you didn't wash your hands—*or* disinfect my skin—before you started treatment. I could die from some random secondary bacterial infection."

He glowers at me. "I should be so lucky."

When I shudder and gasp, he demands loudly, "What now?"

"It feels like you injected ice water into my veins! You didn't bring the meds to room temperature!"

He leans down over me, props a hand on the cushion under my head, and says into my face, "*You're* going to be room temperature soon if you. Don't. Shut. Up."

I purse my lips. "Can I say thank you, though? For saving my life, I mean."

He groans, rises, and turns away, heading back into the kitchen.

"I know it was only because you haven't gotten whatever it is you want from Dimitri yet, but still. He'd be none the wiser. You could've pulled it off."

With his back turned, he starts rummaging through cupboards again, muttering to himself the whole time about mouthy women and stupid infections and how he should call Naz again and tell him to hurry up and come get me before he loses his goddamn mind.

"Wait—what did you just say?"

Killian stops and looks at me over his shoulder.

My heart beating madly, I struggle to sit up. "About Naz. You *talked* to Naz?"

"Oh, *now* you find the strength to lift your head. I bet if I said his name three times in a row, you'd start levitating."

"When did you talk to him? What did he say? Does he know I'm okay? How did he sound—is he worried? Is *he* okay? Oh God, Killian, *please start talking before my heart explodes and I drop dead!*"

He considers me with a look of mild disgust. "So this is what love does? Turns you into a blathering moron with a flair for melodrama and zero sense of self-preservation? I'd rather keep my dignity, thanks. This love nonsense is pathetic."

"Killian! *Please!*"

He leans against the counter and folds his arms over his chest. "Aye. I talked to him."

No longer able to hold myself up, I flop back against the pillow and struggle to breathe through the onslaught of emotion. Trembling and almost panting, I whisper, "Tell me what he said. Tell me everything."

"May I remind you that you're not the one in charge here?"

I look at him beseechingly. "Please just tell me if he's all right. Please . . . how did he sound?"

Killian makes a face. "He sounded like a bloody maniac, to be honest. Threatened to kill me with every other breath."

My body is flooded with relief, then guilt, as hot as my earlier fever. Imagining how Naz must be feeling, I squeeze my eyes shut and whimper. How angry he must be. How frantic and lost.

In a gentler tone, Killian says, "He's all right, Eva."

"He must be so fucking worried."

After a pause, Killian says, "That's the first time I've heard you curse. I've kidnapped you, beaten you, threatened your life over and over again, stabbed a man three feet away from you and then threw him to his watery death, and *this* is when you decide you're upset enough to curse. When you think Naz is *worried*. Unbelievable."

I open my eyes and look at Killian. "Did he sound mad? At me, I mean. Is he angry with me for leaving?"

"You're completely mental."

"Please tell me. I have to know."

When he cocks his head and narrows his eyes, I start to get concerned. Then, when he asks lightly, "Are we negotiating?" and a crafty smile curves his lips, I get downright nervous.

"I . . . don't know. Negotiating for what?"

"Well, generally in a negotiation, two parties ask for what they want, then discuss terms. Hence the word '*negotiate*.'"

"I have a bad feeling about this."

He pushes off the counter and saunters over to me, then sits on the edge of the coffee table and props his elbows on his knees. "Do you want to know what Naz said or not?"

"Quit playing games. You know I do. What do *you* want?"

Very deliberately, he looks at my mouth.

Alarmed, I shrink back into the sofa.

Utterly nonchalant, he shrugs. "Have it your way. I couldn't care less."

But he doesn't move, and he doesn't stop looking at my mouth.

Desperation sets in. "I'm in no shape to be kissing anyone right now."

"I didn't say it had to be now."

I pull the blanket up to cover the lower half of my face and stare at him.

"What, did you like it too much the first time? Afraid you'll start wanting more?"

I look at the ceiling, silently ask God to grant me patience, then flip the blanket down. "Don't flatter yourself."

He temples his fingers under his chin and gazes at me as if he's my psychiatrist, all ears and full of concern. "You did, though."

"No, I definitely didn't."

"Your nipples got hard."

Heat floods my face. I open my mouth, close it again, and look away, mortified by this turn in conversation.

"I know because you weren't wearing a bra."

I say through gritted teeth, "Because you didn't give me one."

"Because I wanted to see if your nipples would get hard when I kissed you."

Shocked, I look at him. "You . . . *planned* that?"

His smile manages to be sweet, smug, and condescending all at once. In a husky voice, he says, "I've got all *sorts* of things planned, pet."

Anger lights me up like a Christmas tree. I glare at him, wishing I had the strength to claw his eyes out. "I'm not your pet. And if my nipples did get hard—*which they didn't*—it was only because the entire time I was kissing you, I was thinking of Naz."

"Oh, she's mad at me now," he says mockingly. "Must've touched a nerve."

When I turn my head to the side with my lips clamped shut, he chuckles.

"So that's a no, you *don't* want to hear what he said, then?"

I refuse to look at him. I stare up at the wall instead, following a hairline crack in the plaster up to the ceiling and wishing the entire thing would fall down and smash his head.

His tone turns thoughtful. "Because he had a lot to say."

I glance back at him, desperation beating a drumbeat through my bloodstream. I have to bite my lip not to ask *Like what?*

Then the bastard starts to calmly examine his fingernails. He's waiting, as patiently as if he has all the time in the world, because he knows—he *knows*—that I'll crack. He understands my weakness and exactly how to exploit it.

I clear my throat. "What if I . . ."

Eyes blazing, he turns his full attention to me. It's like standing on a dark stage and being hit with a blinding white spotlight, full bore.

"What if you *what*?"

I swallow. "Um. How about . . . a hug?"

As if I've just suggested I'd like to slather his body in dog poo, he grimaces.

"A long hug?"

Slowly, holding my gaze, he shakes his head. "Quid pro quo, Clarice. I give you what you want, you give me what I want. Or no deal."

"A *Silence of the Lambs* reference. Coming from you, Hannibal Lecter Jr., that's very apropos."

"So we have a deal?"

"I can't make that deal. It's like cheating."

His brows shoot up. "No, it's blackmail, which isn't *at all* like cheating. Especially because—as you claim—you don't like kissing me. And let's not forget, you've already done it once."

"Only because I thought it would save a man's life."

I see the moment when a new idea crosses his mind. His smile turns dangerous, and a glint of violence lights up his gaze.

"Killian," I say hotly, "don't you dare threaten Naz's life to get me to kiss you. *Don't you dare.*"

"Or you'll do what?"

"I don't know yet, but you won't like it!"

He stares at me for a long time in silence, simply examining my expression, his own expression thoughtful. Then he exhales, and all the light in his eyes dies with that breath.

"There's a price to pay for everything in life, Eva. We both know that. The greater the prize, the higher the price. I already know you're willing to sacrifice anything to keep him alive. And you know I'm a man for whom the end justifies any means. We'll both do whatever is necessary . . . and that makes us dangerous. No limits means no rules, and without rules we're basically animals."

His voice drops an octave. "And this animal wants to kiss you again enough to kill a man I've never met and have no quarrel with. So like it or not, I'm threatening his life."

So angry I could scream, but too weak to do anything but lie here, I stare at Killian, willing his head to explode. When it doesn't, I say, "You're a despicable human being."

"Is that a yes?"

I close my eyes and blow out a frustrated breath. "If I agree, you'll only up the ante. This time it's a kiss. Next time it will be something worse. I can't trust you to keep your word."

When I feel a gentle touch on my cheek, my eyes fly open. Killian traces his fingertip over my cheekbone and down to my lips. Very softly, looking at my mouth, he says, "You can trust me with anything."

"Please. Enough with the BS. I'm not the idiot you think I am."

His thumb brushes my lower lip. "You're only an idiot when it comes to Naz, but what I said is true. You can trust me." He drags his gaze from my mouth to my eyes. "You have no idea what I'm risking for you."

My heartbeat ticks up a notch. "I would if you told me."

After a moment, he says quietly, "Millions of other people's lives."

I'm horrified to discover I believe him. We stare at each other in silence until I gather the courage to say, "Tell me what that means."

He sits back and scrubs a hand over his face. "Can't. Wouldn't even if I could. And now it's time for me to go." He glances back at me. "But I'm not going to forget our bargain, *bhrèagha*. You owe me a kiss."

He stands and walks toward the front door. I call out after him, "I never said I'd kiss you again!"

He opens the door, pauses, then looks back at me over his shoulder. "You didn't say you wouldn't, either."

Smiling, he walks through the door and closes it behind him.

❧

A short while later, as I'm drifting off to sleep, Naz kicks it open with a booted foot and bursts inside.

FIFTEEN

Naz

The door crashes open with a thundering *boom* that rattles the windows. With Connor two feet behind me, I rush inside, my M16 raised. I sweep the rifle left and right as I search for any movement, adrenaline burning white hot through my veins.

I spot a small figure lying still on the sofa, covered in a blanket, and freeze.

Moving swiftly and silently past me, Connor goes down a short hallway to my left, sweeps the room, and says, "Clear."

I'm still not moving. I can't. I'm frozen in horror and disbelief.

Eva's face is pale and blotchy, her normally glowing skin like wax. Her hair is shorn off at jaw length with what must've been a very dull knife. Her eyes are open but unfocused, and there's an IV inserted into the back of one hand.

Worst of all is the bruising.

A large purple spot on her left cheek is yellowing around the edges. Her lower lip is split on one side. On her chin, an ugly black-and-blue mark is livid, and the delicate skin of her throat is mottled with fading discolorations in the shape of fingers.

Big. Strong. Fingers.

"Jesus Christ," I breathe. A jolt of pure rage flares through me. It powers through my shock and gives me the boost to run to her.

"Clear," Connor says from one of the back rooms, but I'm not listening. I'm on my knees beside the sofa, taking Eva's face into my shaking hands.

"Sweetheart," I rasp, desperate to hear her voice. "Talk to me. Eva—Eva, say something, please!"

As if trying to see if I'm real, she reaches out and touches my face with the tips of her fingers. Moisture wells in her eyes. She whispers, "Beastie. You're here."

"All clear," Connor says, returning to the living room with his rifle lowered just as I gather Eva into my arms and hug her tight.

"What did he do to you? What did that son of a bitch do to you, sweetheart?" I pull away and start to frantically check her for injuries, yanking back the blanket to reveal a pale-blue hospital gown. More bruises encircle her wrist and upper arms. Her knees are red and scabbed, as if she was dragged over carpeting.

"I'm okay," she says, her voice weak. "I have . . . I think I have a heart infection."

Connor kneels beside me and checks Eva's distal pulse. She turns her gaze to him. "Connor. You're here, too."

He grins at her. "Course I am. Wouldn't miss this for the world. How you feelin', slick? You had us a little worried."

She pulls her lower lip between her teeth and swallows. "I'm sorry," she whispers, looking back at me with a furrow between her brows. "I'm so sorry, Naz. I hated to leave like that, but it was the only way—"

"Shh, sweetheart, stop. I know why you did it, but that's over now. We need to get you somewhere safe."

Connor stands and pulls his cell from a pocket of his black tactical vest. "I'm calling for exfil now."

He makes the call as I pepper frantic kisses all over Eva's face, trying not to cause her any pain but unable to stop myself from kissing her. *She's alive.*

"You found me." Her voice breaks. "You came for me and you found me."

"Sweetheart." I press my lips to the corner of her mouth that doesn't have bruises. Then I gather her into my arms and squeeze her, pressing my cheek to hers and trying to catch my breath. "I'll always come for you. You know that. You should know that by now."

She nods wordlessly, clinging to me.

Then I can't help myself anymore. I kiss her because I think I might die if I don't.

She kisses me back, matching my passion, not seeming to care about her injuries, making small, desperate noises in the back of her throat and curling her fingers into my arms.

We're interrupted by Connor's voice, coming from the kitchen. "Got a note here for you, brother."

Eva and I break apart. When I look at him, Connor's holding up a piece of paper, a wry expression on his face.

"It's from Killian."

Judging from his tone, he's already read it. I hold out my hand, unwilling to let go of Eva even for a moment. Connor crosses to me and hands me the note, and I start to read.

> *The house is yours for as long as you need it. Eva's meds are in the fridge. I was told she shouldn't be moved, but I didn't heed that advice. I doubt you will, either, but if you take her to a hospital, check her in under an assumed name and keep a close eye.*
>
> *Dimitri's looking for her. He'll leave no stone unturned.*
>
> *My apologies to you both for the bruises. I was given some incorrect intel about her relationship with Dimitri,*

but rest assured the source will be terminated for the trouble.

Maybe we can meet in person when all this is done. I'm curious what kind of man could make a woman like her so hopelessly devoted. She told me she was going back to the hell she came from to save your life—can you imagine? I can't decide if that's heroic or insane.

I'm still not convinced you deserve her, but she's got her heart set on you, so . . .

Don't fuck it up.

Best regards,
Killian
PS—That heart-shaped mole under her left breast could be the most beautiful thing I've ever seen.

I crush the note in my fist and exhale slowly, fighting back the insane-o caveman yell clawing its way up my throat. *That fucker sure has some balls.*

I won't think about how he knows about the mole until later, when I'm alone and can break things in private.

"They're ready for us whenever we are, brother," says Connor, slipping the phone back into his pocket.

I brush a lock of hair off Eva's pale forehead. "I'm gonna pick you up now, sweetheart, okay?"

Her smile is tremulous. "You're here," she whispers, her eyes filling again. "You don't have to carry me, I could probably float."

Emotion swells inside my chest, but I need to concentrate on getting her to safety before I break down and let everything I'm feeling wash over me. I shove Killian's crumpled note into a pocket, then carefully gather Eva in my arms. She winds her arms around my shoulders and curls into me as I pick her up and stand.

Inhaling deeply against my neck, she shivers and burrows closer.

"I'll get the meds," says Connor. "Right behind you."

He picks up my rifle from the floor and slings it over his shoulder as I hold Eva against my chest and hurry toward the front door.

∽

We take a bird to the nearest safe house Metrix operates, in Cascais, Portugal, a wealthy coastal town not far from Lisbon. The flight is under two hours, but it's the longest of my life. Eva sleeps cradled against me, her breathing shallow, twitching and softly whining every once in a while as if she's having a nightmare.

I'm having trouble compartmentalizing the rage I feel toward Killian, the worry I feel about Eva, and the anger I feel at myself.

I should've gotten to her sooner.

I should've never let her go in the first place.

If only I hadn't failed to protect her, none of this would've happened.

When we touch down in a field in an industrial part of town, a car is waiting for us in a nearby parking lot, the keys in the glove box. Courtesy of Tabby, a woman for whom the word *impossible* doesn't exist. Connor drives while I sit in the back seat and hold Eva's head in my lap, stroking her damp forehead and tormented by thoughts of what she went through on that ship.

What she *put herself through* because she thought it would save me. Not to mention all the other horrors awaiting her if she'd made it back to Dimitri.

I hate to admit it, but Killian isn't the only one unconvinced I deserve her.

The safe house is in a modern condominium complex, one of those swanky high-rise security buildings that caters to rich childless couples and businessmen who travel internationally so no one knows or cares who their neighbors are. We drive into an underground parking garage and take a private elevator to the eighteenth floor. The view of the ocean from the floor-to-ceiling windows is stunning.

"Nice place," I tell Connor as I carry Eva inside.

He chuckles. "Can't take the Saudi princess you just extracted from six weeks in a kidnapper's basement to a Motel 6."

I find the master bedroom and, as carefully as I can manage, settle Eva onto the bed. She rolls to her back with a drowsy sigh as I pull up the blankets around her.

"Where are we?"

I lean over and kiss her forehead. "Somewhere safe. The doctor will be here soon. How do you feel? What can I get you?"

She turns her head and blinks up at me, her eyes hazy. "Killian told Dimitri I was with him."

My heart skips a beat. "What?"

She moistens her lips, appearing to have to concentrate on her words when she speaks. "Dimitri knows Killian took me, so he won't be coming after you." Her eyes drift closed. "Killian took care of it."

Killian took care of it. Those words sounded . . . grateful.

I'm motionless, except for my heart, which pounds wildly.

"I'll be back in a minute," I murmur, ignoring the tremor in my hands as I tuck the blanket in around her shoulders and smooth her hair off her face. I close the door quietly behind me as I leave the master bedroom and return to the great room to look for Connor.

I find him rummaging through the big stainless steel refrigerator for food.

"I gotta get on my supplier about stocking better snacks," he says sourly, holding up a plastic container. "Why's there always so much fuckin' fruit? Who wants to eat sliced apples after a job, for fuck's sake? Not a goddamn cookie or scoop of ice cream in sight."

I fold my arms over my chest, lean against the kitchen counter, and blow out a hard breath.

Connor glances at me. "Here." He holds out a bottle of beer. "You look like you need it."

I take it from him but just stand there without opening it, staring out the windows. The setting sun is turning the sky over the sea to fire.

Connor swings the fridge door closed, twists the cap off his own bottle of beer, and takes a long swig. Then he wipes his mouth with the back of his hand. "I can spot a mindfuck in progress from a mile away, brother. Talk to me."

After a long moment of mulling, I say, "Killian."

Connor takes another drink of his beer, letting me work it over in my head.

"He commandeers a ship. Takes a hostage. Kills the captain and crew, except for one. That he left one of the crew alive is important, but I don't know how. He beats the hostage and sets sail across the North Atlantic, but halfway through the journey gets picked up by the US Navy. He and his hostage are dropped off on an island near Portugal days later by the same frigate. He has a safe house. In his note, he mentions 'intel' and a 'source.'"

I meet Connor's eyes. "He's a spook."

Connor nods. "Probably a NOC, because Tabby can't find anything in the CIA or NSA databases on any assets fitting his name or description."

Operatives working under nonofficial cover, or NOCs, are off-the-books consultants to government agencies, working outside the prescribed channels on covert missions. They're highly trained in espionage and intelligence gathering and are tasked with everything from political assassinations to throwing foreign elections, and anything in between.

They're also extraordinarily dangerous.

They have a case manager who assigns ops, but they answer to no one. They have only one goal: complete the mission. No matter how, no matter the cost. If they're caught, they have no safety net, because the government that hired them will deny all knowledge of their existence, so they go to extremes to avoid detection because capture by hostile foreign governments inevitably equals imprisonment or execution.

Sophisticated in the ways of clandestine operations and unconventional warfare, they're the lone wolves of the spy world.

They're the guys who get the really bad shit done.

I know all this because my own father was one.

I say, "So he has a job. Something he thinks kidnapping Eva will help him with."

"Something to do with Dimitri," says Connor, nodding.

"But he decides for some reason to drop her off at his safe house instead."

"Maybe he got what he wanted from Dimitri. Gave him proof of life, cut a deal, cut her loose."

I shake my head. "I don't think so. Eva just told me Killian told Dimitri she was with him. I bet Dimitri assumes she still is."

"So what's the advantage to Killian in this scenario?"

"I don't think there is one." I meet Connor's confused gaze. "Which is what scares me."

After a moment, Connor's expression turns from confused to understanding. "You think he likes her."

I recall what Killian told me on the phone, the rough, needy tone in his voice when he said, *"Because the more time I spend with your woman, the less I want to give her back."*

"I think her superpower is bringing a man to his knees before he knows what hit him."

Connor tugs on his chin for a minute. "It might explain why he left the one crew member alive."

"Why?"

"So there was someone to call the coast guard and tell them what happened . . . and where she thought he was headed."

I say slowly, "So I'd know where to look for her."

"I mean, he left a note. He definitely knew we were on our way. I wonder if letting the crew member overhear where he was going was a setup." Connor's tone turns admiring. "Hmm. That's kinda genius."

I'm really starting to hate this fucking guy. "Genius or not, he put his hands on my girl, so he's at the top of my shit list."

Carefully, Connor says, "So . . . who do you think got her the meds?"

When I glare at him, he puts his hands up. "I'm just sayin'. Shape she's in, she didn't go out and get 'em herself. Label says it's vancomycin for infective endocarditis. That's not something you get by bein' roughed up."

I decide it's time to open my beer and do so by tearing off the bottle cap with my molars. I spit it out and take a giant swig.

"And he did apologize. Blamed it on bad intel. The way I figure it, he thought Eva was a team with Dimitri the way Bergé was with that troll of a wife of his." He pauses. "Wonder if she ever made it out of her trunk."

"We parked the damn car in her driveway. The way she screams, I'm sure her neighbors called the cops as soon as we left."

He shrugs. "Anyway. So Killian kidnaps Eva, roughs her up on principle, then finds out she's actually a nice person. Then she gets sick and he feels bad, so he takes her to a doctor for treatment. Which would explain why the navy showed up."

I nod slowly, thinking it over. "Right. If he's a high enough level asset, with a high enough level op, he's gonna have all kinds of interesting connections all over the place. If you're a valued back-channel intelligence source to the Pentagon, you can pretty much make anything happen. Including a military escort."

All this is giving me a headache. I down the rest of the beer and slam the empty bottle on the counter, feeling like I could breathe fire. "So whatever Killian is trying to get from Dimitri is extremely important. What does Dimitri have that he might want?"

"I don't know, brother," says Connor softly. "But whatever it is, it's not good."

SIXTEEN

Eva

A gray-haired man with kind eyes and gentle hands comes to see me. With Naz hovering silently in the background while I lie quietly on the bed, the man takes my vitals and draws blood, then asks me a series of questions about how I feel and the injuries I sustained on the ship.

When he asks if I have any injuries that might not be visible, Naz stiffens, knowing what the real meaning behind that question is.

I answer with a firm, clear voice, though it's all I can do to muster it. I'm so exhausted even speaking is difficult. "No. He didn't touch me that way. He didn't do anything inappropriate."

Naz mutters, "Those bruises are *definitely* goddamn inappropriate."

Then he starts to pace, cracking his knuckles and grinding his jaw.

After a few more questions, the doctor withdraws to converse in low tones with Naz in a corner of the room. I hear the words *bed rest* and *fragile* and get the distinct impression that I won't be running a marathon anytime soon.

When the doctor leaves, Connor comes in. He draws a chair up to my bedside while Naz sits on the edge of the mattress and takes my hand.

"You feelin' up to talking for a bit?" asks Connor gently, casting a worried eye at Naz, who's staring at me in unblinking intensity, as if not quite believing I won't disappear in a puff of smoke.

With my free hand, I make the thumbs-up sign.

"Attagirl. This won't take long. I gotta head back stateside, but you and Naz are gonna camp out here for a while, until you're up for traveling again."

I say, "He didn't tell me anything solid."

When Naz and Connor share a startled glance, I clarify. "Killian, I mean. He was careful not to give me any information I could pass along. But he did say that he was risking millions of people's lives for me. That was after he took me to the safe house. I don't think he was supposed to do that. He also asked—hypothetically—if I'd kill one person if it would save countless others."

It's quiet for a while, the only sound the grinding of Naz's back teeth. Then Connor says, "Uh-huh."

"My point is that I don't think either of those comments were random. I think whatever he wants from Dimitri has repercussions that could potentially affect a lot of people."

"If you had to guess, any idea what that would be?"

I look at Naz, then back at Connor. "Most likely . . . weapons."

Naz tightens his fingers on my hand. Connor sits back in his chair and folds his arms over his chest. They both stare at me, waiting.

I close my eyes, recalling several different meetings I was present for that Dimitri had with a variety of evil-looking men. They'd come to the mansion dressed in expensive suits or military uniforms, accompanied by an entourage of bodyguards and assistants, and drink whiskey and smoke fine cigars while young girls naked except for gags and leashed collars were exhibited for selection.

The men came for business. The girls were merely treats offered by their host. But discussions were held as the girls were paraded over the priceless handwoven Turkish rugs, discussions about trade and strategies and transfer routes, about shipments of various kinds, including drugs, people, and weapons.

They all wanted weapons. The bigger, the better. Despots need guns to crush rebellions, and so do opposing political parties plotting coups, and everyone needs a reliable supplier who can deliver expensive contraband undetected by authorities.

Dimitri has no political aspirations of his own, but he's very much interested in power. He discovered that a man who could provide things that bad men needed as they clawed their way to the top of the dog pile had the kind of power that wasn't affected by election results, regime changes, massive cultural and political turmoil, or even decades of passing time.

Violence is a timeless human endeavor. It will never go out of style.

"Or *a* weapon," I say, opening my eyes. "Something that could cause mass destruction. All Dimitri's clients were after that. Dimitri was the one who provided the sarin gas to the Syrian president who killed all those people in Khan Shaykhun in 2017. Dimitri had Soviet-made aerial bombs retrofitted to deliver the gas in an airstrike. He thought that was so clever."

Connor and Naz stare at me, their eyes wide with shock.

Their expressions fill me with shame. Had I any real courage at all, I'd have found a way to kill Dimitri years ago. That I didn't makes me complicit in all the suffering he's caused.

Hence my self-loathing.

Hence my decision to make it right.

Maybe Lao Tzu was correct about love giving you strength, after all. If it weren't for me falling in love with Naz and agreeing to go back to Dimitri to spare his life, I probably never would've had the nerve to decide I wanted to put a bullet between Dimitri's eyes.

The understanding of what remains to be done dawns over me clear and cold like a winter sunrise.

To the ceiling, I say, "Neither of you will want to hear this, but Killian was right. I'm the best way to get to Dimitri." I turn my head and look at Naz. "There's only one way to get to him, and that's me."

His voice deadly soft and his eyes blazing fire, Naz says, "No."

I love this man. I love him so much it's a physical thing, a bright hot spot in the center of my chest. But as I stare into his eyes, I realize that many, many things about me have changed since I met him. Loving him has changed me for the better . . . although at the moment he'd probably disagree.

Because I'm no longer the girl who complies with commands.

"I know you're only thinking of protecting me, and I hope to God you won't take this the wrong way, but . . . sweetie . . . it's not up to you to decide. I wasn't asking permission."

Naz stares at me in livid silence, while Connor starts to look nervous. "Uh, okay, let's back it up a step here, kids. We're gettin' waaay ahead of ourselves. First things first, which is you gettin' back on your feet, Eva. After that, we can discuss—"

"There's no discussion," Naz interrupts, still in that dangerously soft tone. "There will never be a discussion that includes Eva going anywhere near Dimitri again. That conversation isn't even on the table. That conversation will *never* take place."

I exhale an exasperated sigh, because good Lord, men can be trying.

Sensing things are about to get hairy, Connor stands. "I'm gonna let you get some rest now, Eva. Soon as you're feelin' up to it, we'll send a pickup and get you back home, okay?"

He leans down and gives me a peck on the cheek. I look up at him and smile. "Thank you, Connor. For everything. So much."

He leans closer and murmurs in my ear, "Go easy on him. He's practically fallin' apart with worry." Then he straightens and jerks his head at Naz. "Let's talk outside for a sec, brother."

With a wink at me, he walks out the door.

Naz is still holding my hand and glaring.

"Superior Man to the rescue," I say, smiling.

He says loudly, "Don't try to flirt with me right now. I'm very angry with you."

"I can tell." I pause. "Have I told you how grateful I am that you're here?"

"No." More glaring.

"Well I am. I'm so grateful, and happy, and relieved. It's so good to see you. I thought . . ." I inhale a hitching breath. "I thought I'd never see you again."

He squeezes his eyes shut, then mutters, "Fuck."

"Please don't be angry with me."

Without opening his eyes, he says, "You're doing that on purpose, aren't you?"

"What?"

"Using that small voice. The sweet one that comes with the big Bambi eyes."

"No." Pause. "Why, is it working?"

His eyes fly open. He pronounces, "No!"

When I chew on my lower lip, he curses again, then squeezes his forehead.

"I'm sorry," I whisper. "I know you were worried. It was killing me to think how worried you must've been. All I could think about was you the entire time."

I squeeze his hand and try to pull him closer. He leans forward a few inches, reluctantly, his hand still covering his eyes.

"Please. Naz." I run my hand up his arm and squeeze his strong shoulder, then touch his face. He needs a shave. He has circles under his eyes. He looks tired, haggard, and I know it's because of me. I beg, "Look at me."

He drops his hand and lifts his head, letting me see all the emotion in his beautiful dark eyes. All the anguish, all the worry, all the love.

That look goes through me like a burning sword.

"I love you, Naz," I blurt, my voice strangled because my throat is closing. "I love you more than I've ever loved anything in my life. More than I thought was even possible. I would kill for you. I would die for you. And I swear there's nothing in this world or out of it that will ever separate me from you again."

He hesitates for a moment, his eyes welling, until he breaks, exhaling what sounds like a lifetime of worry. He says roughly, "Now that's just downright unfair."

Then he takes my face in his hand and kisses me until I'm breathless.

"Your lip," he says, pulling back slightly to stare at my mouth. "I don't want to hurt you—"

"Please stop talking." I curl my fingers into his shirt and tug. With a husky laugh, he lowers his head again and gives me what I need until both of us are breathing hard and his hands on my face are shaking.

He stares deep into my eyes with a look of desperation. "Tell me again."

"I love you," I whisper, knowing what he needs. "I love you. *I love you.*"

His eyelids flutter shut. He exhales, then presses the gentlest of kisses to my mouth. Then he wraps his arms around me and buries his face in my neck.

I hold him like that for what seems like a long time, stroking his back, running my fingers through his hair, feeling his heartbeat crashing against my breasts and his breath warm against my neck. Every so often his arms tighten and he squeezes me harder for a moment, as if he's reminding himself I'm really here.

When he finally speaks, it's in the barest of whispers, his voice achingly raw.

"Don't. *Ever.* Do that again."

He raises his head and gazes into my eyes. His own are filled with water.

"Promise me you'll never do anything like that again. Promise me you'll never run away, or put yourself in danger for me, or do anything so . . . fucking . . . *reckless* again." He pauses to get his breathing under control. "I thought I'd go crazy. I thought I might lose you for good."

I frame his rough cheeks in my hands and nod. "I promise, sweetie."

He kisses my cheek, my temple, my neck. His fingers twist in my hair. "Okay. Fuck. Okay."

His exhalation is so relieved I feel guilty all over again.

"I'm sorry."

"No, no more sorries. And no more heroics. I'm a grown man, for God's sake. The last thing I want is for you to think I need saving. It's *my* job to protect *you*, not the other way around."

I can see this is a point of pride for him, so instead of arguing that I'll *still* do anything to protect him, I just nod and keep my mouth shut.

He kisses me on both cheeks, as if giving me a blessing. Then, surprisingly, he starts to softly laugh.

"What's funny?"

He sits up, drags his hands through his hair, and props his elbows on his knees. Looking at his feet, he says, "I'm in probably the worst shape of my life, you're lying there all bruised and sick, I can't remember the last time I ate, I haven't slept for a solid two hours in a week, and yet my dick is so hard it hurts. Every time I see you, it's like I chugged an entire bottle of Viagra."

I slant a look at his crotch. "I can see that. If I had the strength, I'd do something about it."

He glances at me, his look warm and his lips curved into a smile. "We'll have plenty of time when you're feeling better. Right now you need to rest. I'm gonna let you sleep and then feed you. Sound good?"

"Sounds good."

He leans over and kisses me on the forehead, then stands and walks awkwardly to the door, shaking his head and chuckling. He blows me another kiss before he walks out.

I sleep. I don't know for how long, because there's no clock in the room. But when I open my eyes, it's dark beyond the drapes pulled across the windows. Everything is quiet and still.

I desperately have to use the bathroom, so I carefully pull back the covers and sit up, swinging my legs over the edge of the bed. I feel light-headed but otherwise steady, so I stand and cross barefoot to the en suite bathroom, flicking the light switch on when I go inside.

The light is so bright it makes me wince. I stand for a moment inside the doorway, letting my eyes adjust and looking around. The bathroom, like the bedroom, is done in a contemporary design, all glass and white marble with dark wood cabinets and recessed lighting. I use the toilet, then groan when I look into the mirror over the sink.

"You look like you fell off the back of a garbage truck," I tell my reflection as I wash and dry my hands. "And what the hell are you wearing?"

I look at the pale-blue short-sleeved cotton gown, trying to remember anything about how I got into it. But my memory of recent events is a dark blur. I don't even know how many days it's been since Killian took me off the *Silver Shadow*.

Killian. Who are you?

I touch the fading bruise on my cheek, thinking of all his contradictions. How the same man who could so ruthlessly beat me could also go out of his way to save my life. How he could kill Raphael in cold blood without batting an eye but so carefully administer my medication.

How he could mock love but kiss like he's starving.

The man is a puzzle I'll never solve, because I'll never see him again. I'm grateful he diverted Dimitri's attention away from Naz by telling him I was with him, but for so much else he did, I'm still angry and probably always will be.

"Blackmailed me for a kiss," I mutter, frowning.

"I did no such thing."

I jump, startled, only to find Naz leaning against the doorframe. It's so good to see him that for a moment I just stand there and stare at him, until his smile falters.

He straightens, his eyes flashing with worry. "Are you all right?"

"I'm . . ." I close my eyes and inhale, then look at him again. "I'm just so glad to see you."

He closes the distance between us without another word, wrapping his arms around my body and pulling me close. I hug his waist, tuck my head under his chin, and close my eyes, breathing him in and holding him tight, my heart banging so hard it's painful.

"I need to shower." My words are muffled because they're spoken into his chest.

Naz kisses me just below my earlobe, in that spot that makes me shiver. "Okay. I'll get the water started for you."

"No," I say when he starts to move away. He looks down at me with his brows pulled together. "I need to shower *with you.*"

His eyes darken with desire. "Don't tempt me. You know I have a certain part of my anatomy that likes to make his presence known during all kinds of situations. The two of us naked in the shower is definitely at the top of that list."

I slide my arms around his shoulders and go up on my toes to give him a kiss. "I know. That's why I suggested it."

He says sternly, "You're sick."

"Not that sick." I kiss him again, nibbling his lower lip. "And I missed you," I breathe, feeling my blood start to sing. "I need you. I need *us.*"

He groans when I rub my chest against his. "You're killing me."

"I could be doing something else you like better."

He sets me away from him firmly, his hands on my shoulders and his jaw tight. "I can't believe I'm saying this, but no."

Dejected, I stare at him. "No?"

He gazes at me in silence for a moment, examining my expression, then mutters, "Fuck."

"Is that a yes?" I ask, brightening.

"It's a sort of."

I lift my brows. "Sort of? You're 'sort of' going to make love to me? What would that involve, pantomime? Drawing dirty pictures?"

His expression sours. "You must be feeling better. All your signature sass is back."

"Yes, sir. I am one hundred percent cured."

He rolls his eyes at my cheeky grin. "You're supposed to be on bed rest, sweetheart. And before you say it, *no*, not everything you can do in a bed is restful. Especially where we're concerned."

I stare at him for a beat, then reach around to the back of my neck and pull open the tie holding the hospital gown together. It slithers off my body and lands on the floor in a pile of rumpled cotton, leaking air.

Burning bright with desire, Naz's eyes drink me in. A muscle flexes in his jaw. His voice comes low and gruff. "How are you always so goddamn beautiful?"

But he doesn't move, and he doesn't touch me.

Is there something else in his eyes? Something like . . . doubt?

"Hey."

He lifts his gaze to mine. I wonder if he can see my sudden terror. "Are we okay?"

He tilts his head in a quizzical way.

"Are you . . . you know what I said about Killian was true, right? That he didn't—"

"Stop," he says gruffly, and pulls me into his arms. He gazes down at me with those burning dark eyes, his expression both tender and severe. "I can't stand to talk about him right now. I can't stand to look at you and know that he did this to you." He touches my bruised cheek, then lowers his hand and rests it on my neck, which is still tender. His voice grows hoarse. "Most of all, I can't stand to know I wasn't there to stop it from happening."

"Naz—"

"Sweetheart, stop." He presses his finger gently over my lips. "Please. I'm still decompressing, and you're not well. I want you—I *always* want you—but honestly right now it's all I can do to keep my shit together because I want to kill that bastard so bad I can taste it. I'm . . ."

He stops abruptly, then laughs, but it sounds dark and scary. "Honestly, I think I'm a little fucked up."

My throat tightens and my chest starts to ache. "Okay."

He groans. "Oh God. Don't sound like that."

Hiding my face in his chest, I whisper, "This is my fault."

His big exhalation stirs the hair on top of my head. "Jesus. We're gonna need a shit-ton of therapy."

At the same time, we both start to laugh. It's grim and humorless, but still laughter, and so it's a start.

"All right, Annie Oakley," he says, using the nickname he gave me when we first met. "It's shower time. Except I think we'll take a bath instead. I need to sit. My leg is killing me."

"Oh my God." I pull back to stare in horror at his thigh. "Your operation. Your *leg*."

He says drily, "Yeah. And you don't wanna know what's going on with my lungs. We're two busted-up peas in a pod, sweetheart. C'mon, I'll start the water."

SEVENTEEN

NAZ

The bathtub is big enough for both of us to recline comfortably with Eva on top of me. Our legs are entangled. She's snug in my arms in the warm, bubbly water, her head resting against my chest, her body fitted to mine, back to front, in perfect alignment.

Well, not *perfect* alignment. There's a big—if I do say so myself—item lodged in between us.

"Scientists should sample your testicles to see what kind of super sperm you've got running the show," says Eva with a soft laugh as she adjusts her butt over my erection. "Your testosterone levels must be stratospheric."

"I wasn't nicknamed Superior Man for no reason."

"As I recall, you gave that name to yourself."

"Well, if the shoe fits . . ."

She tilts her head and smiles up at me. "They must be big shoes."

I whisper, "Humongous," and waggle my eyebrows.

She tsks. "Humility definitely isn't one of your superpowers, my love."

Her lips are so irresistible, I have to lean down to steal a kiss. She arches into me, responding instantly as she always does, tightening her fingers around my biceps as my tongue touches hers. I try my best to keep the kiss soft and slow, but we're so hungry for each other it quickly turns passionate.

I break away first, breathing hard. After a rough throat clearing, I say, "God, you're so unattractive. How much weight have you gained since I saw you last? I think you're crushing me. I can't feel my legs."

She tilts her head back farther and kisses me on the throat. Then—the minx—she slowly begins to rub her bottom against my crotch, tiny little movements that otherwise might not be so devastating, but the head of my stiff cock is sliding between the soft, slippery globes of her ass, and dammit all to hell because she knows exactly what she's doing.

"Can you feel that?" she asks in a throaty whisper.

"I'm dead from the waist down, I'm afraid."

"Um, not exactly."

She reaches into the bubbly water and takes my cock in her fist. I suck in a breath because it feels so good. Then she starts a casual conversation, all the while lazily stroking my dick.

"Where are we?"

"Oh, time for a geography lesson, is it?"

Her shoulders shake with silent laughter. Her slim fingers slide up my shaft.

"We're in a town called Cascais, on the Portuguese Riviera."

"Sounds romantic." She swirls her thumb around the crown, then gently presses down on the slit.

We both pretend to ignore the involuntary shudder that runs through me. "It's one of the wealthiest towns in the Iberian Peninsula—" I cut off with a sharp intake of breath when my balls are gently cupped and fondled, then continue, less evenly than before. "Edward the eighth and his wife, Wallis Simpson, lived here during the Second World War."

"Fascinating," Eva whispers, thumbing over the throbbing vein on the underside of my dick. "Tell me more."

"This is guerrilla warfare, you know."

"I recall a certain someone telling me that sometimes ethics can get murky . . . for instance, in love and war."

I tilt her face up and kiss her, cupping my hand around her jaw. Then I turn her head and put my mouth close to her ear. "You're not gonna win this round, so you can quit trying."

She stretches against me, her skin sliding over mine. "I'm not trying to win anything, sweetie. I just love touching you. I love how you feel. I love how strong you are. All these muscles . . . everything is so *hard*."

Her sigh is soft and happy, and holy shit is this woman steroids for my ego.

"What's that chuckle for?"

"I was just thinking you're good for my ego."

"Oh. I thought maybe you were thinking about this 'sort of' love-making that I was promised."

Just to be a brat, she lifts her chest from the water, giving me an eyeful of her wet, lush, bubble-coated breasts.

Without looking away from them, I say, "I can't understand how you can have such a serious medical problem and still be this horny."

She falls still and looks at me with widened eyes. "How serious? What did the doctor say?"

I quirk my lips. "Oh, *now* you wanna talk about the doctor."

She examines my expression, then obviously decides she's not in too much mortal danger because she smiles. "For starters, I know you'd have me in a hospital if things were really dire."

She waits for me to contradict her, but all she gets is a sour look. Of course, that makes her smile grow wider.

"So what's the prognosis? Besides rest, antibiotics, and no dick, I mean."

I blink, then start to laugh. "The prognosis, smarty-pants, is that you need to let your man take care of you until he's satisfied that you're out of the woods. Then you need to keep letting him take care of you, because that's the only thing he wants to do for the rest of his life, and if you *don't* let him do it, he'll get cranky. And I think we both know how ugly *that* can get."

Slowly, her smile dies. Then her eyes begin to fill with tears. She says in a shaky voice, "God must not have given up on me yet."

"What do you mean?"

"If he had, he wouldn't have sent me a miracle."

The feeling that goes through me is incredibly powerful, like a wave that lifts me high and sweeps me off my feet at the same time. It tightens my chest and restricts my throat, and leaves me unable to speak except with my eyes, which tell Eva exactly how much I cherish her. How god-damn good she makes me feel.

How loved.

She turns on top of me and throws her arms around my neck, bringing her sweet mouth to mine with so much passion it blinds me. Water sloshes over the side of the tub, but neither of us cares. We're too caught up in each other.

She says my name against my mouth, a soft cry that makes me desperate to be inside her. But her heart is so fragile right now, and she's been through so much—

"Eva," I groan, pulling away from her mouth.

She drops her head to my shoulder, clinging to me and panting. "Ugh!" She growls into my shoulder. "Let the record show that I *do not* like this horrific willpower of yours."

I can't help it: I start to laugh. Soft, broken laughter that shakes us both.

"And now he's laughing at me. Perfect." She sighs, twining her fingers through my hair, and relaxes against my body.

It's at this moment that we simultaneously realize her spread thighs are in such a position that if I flexed my hips, I'd slide inside her.

She lifts her head and looks at me with big eyes, biting her lip.

I warn, "No. The doctor said no activity that will elevate your heart rate."

All breathless and flushed, she says, "Okay. No it is. You're the boss."

I should've known what she'd do next. "You're the boss" is a dead giveaway a woman is about to do whatever the hell she wants.

She rolls her hips. I have to grab a handful of her ass to stop her from sliding the entire head of my cock inside her. I'm right at her entrance, rigid and hot. I feel her softness so ready to engulf me and have to exercise enormous strength of will not to obey the animal pulse of *deeper, more, now* pounding inside me.

We lie there, nose to nose, staring at each other and breathing roughly, until I say, "I don't know if this is the best moment of my life, or the worst."

"My heart is already pounding, Naz. Another few minutes can't do much more harm."

I lift my brows. "Another *few minutes*? Excuse me, but that's a terrible insult to my manhood."

"Well, how am I supposed to know that?" she says, pretending innocence. "The only time we've done it was when you were flat on your back in a hospital bed. I mean, granted, you'd just had surgery, but if memory serves, you've always had some excuse or another for not wanting to make love to me. Hmm. That's right. First it was your fake celibacy—"

"You're in dangerous territory, woman," I say gruffly, sinking my fingers into her hips.

"—then there was that weird cognitive dissonance excuse—"

"That's a real thing! I was being a gentleman!"

"—and in fact it was *my* idea we make love in the hospital, not yours." She looks at me accusingly. "And now, even when it's my heart that's sick, not my vagina, you're still saying no!"

I know what she's doing. It's obvious she's playing my ego like a violin. It also becomes immediately obvious that I'm her helpless puppet, because I stare straight into her eyes with a look of defiance as I thrust up inside her.

Her gasp of pleasure is the most beautiful sound I've ever heard.

I hold her there, my hands firm around her hips and my jaw gritted, as she shudders and closes her eyes. Flattening her hands over my chest, she lets out a slow, uneven breath, then says in a guttural voice, *"Yes."*

Her skin is rosy and gleaming from the hot water. Her head is tilted back. Her nipples are hard and pink, inches from my face, and far too powerful a temptation to resist.

I lean forward and suckle a pebbled nub in my mouth. Eva softly moans and clenches around me, but doesn't move, simply allowing me to lick and suck her nipples with my cock buried deep inside her tight heat.

As I move from one breast to the other, she whispers, "Tell me when I'm allowed to move."

"I don't know," I murmur, nuzzling her. "How's your heart rate?"

"So slow," she blurts breathlessly. "Oh, gosh, it's so slow I'm practically asleep."

Very gently, I bite down on her nipple. She gasps and sinks her fingers deeper into the muscles of my chest, her hips making an involuntary twitch.

I slightly increase the pressure of my hands on her hips so she knows I want her to remain still at the same time I start to suck harder on her nipple, drawing it deeper into my mouth. I lavish attention on it, then lightly bite into the succulent flesh just beneath. When that earns me a shudder of pleasure, I bite a slow, gentle circle all around one nipple, then move to the other breast.

She's trembling so hard the water ripples.

"Deep breaths, sweetheart," I murmur, sliding a hand between us so I can press my thumb against the sweet bud of her clit. She jerks, and the water sloshes.

"You're so . . . big . . ." She stops to catch her breath. "So hard. Can I please . . ."

"Slowly. Go as slow as you can."

When she realizes I'm not going to stop her, some of the tension leaves her body. She exhales, slides her hands up and around my neck, and licks her lips. Her eyes drift open, so we're watching each other when she finally starts to move.

Paradise isn't a garden. It isn't heaven, or some faraway, mythical place. Paradise is in the small, silent space between the faces of two lovers as they share their bodies and breath.

She moves, and my soul moves with her. She sighs, and my heart expands. She says my name in a small, wondering voice, and I know this is the only heaven a man like me will be granted, so much more than I could ever dream or deserve.

"I love you, Eva. I'll love you until my dying breath." My voice is broken but filled with reverence, echoing off the tile walls like a benediction.

"And I'll love you until mine," she promises, then leans down to kiss me.

The kiss is long, hot, and dizzying in its intimacy. The kiss of two people with no reservations, no secrets, no doubts. Everything is laid bare between us. My heart feels raw and exposed, so tender it's painful.

I squeeze her ass, digging my fingers into all that succulent flesh, loving the sensation of her hard nipples brushing my chest and the hot water sliding between our bodies. It's incredibly sensual, even more so because we're going excruciatingly slow. Her hips make the smallest of motions as she rocks against me, her thighs spread and trembling over mine. Under my thumb, her clit is a slippery, swollen bud.

"Oh God," she breathes, her eyes half-lidded. "Naz. Sweetie, you make me feel so good."

I flex my hips and slide deeper inside her, then withdraw half an inch and slowly do it again. Her groan is broken. Her fingers tighten in my hair.

I say gruffly, "Ride me, sweetheart. That cock is yours. Ride it and make yourself come."

I don't have to tell her twice.

She starts to fuck me, slowly at first, grinding her pelvis against mine in small circles. I rub my thumb back and forth over her clit as she moves, then capture a nipple in my mouth and draw on it, sucking and stroking it with my tongue.

She arches into my mouth and makes a small, inarticulate noise of pleasure. The sound is like a flaming arrow shot through my soul. I go back and forth between her breasts, suckling, hearing my own sounds of pleasure, grunts that rise from deep within my chest.

She starts a rhythm. A long, languid slide up and down the length of my dick, taking me deep, then rising back up until only the head is still buried inside her. Then she sits down again, exhaling raggedly, slowly sliding me back in. She does it over and over again while I stroke her clit and suck her nipples, until she's shaking and crying out and hot water is surging up and down the length of the tub as her hips move faster.

She stiffens and sucks in a breath. Her eyelids fly open so we're staring into each other's eyes when the first hard contraction squeezes my dick. That contraction is followed by another and another, so strong it feels like she's milking me.

"Fuck," I whisper. "Eva, that's so intense."

Her mouth is open but no sound is coming out. Her head falls back and she jerks, hard, her fingernails scratching my scalp and her breasts bouncing.

When she screams my name, primitive impulse takes over.

I drive up into her, hard, my hands on her hips to steady her as I thrust again and again, gritting my teeth as she rides me through her orgasm, quickly building toward my own. Water flies everywhere, splashing our bodies and slopping over onto the bathroom floor. Heat and pressure build at the base of my spine, coiling tighter and tighter until my balls are aching to explode.

Another thrust and I'm groaning, my body bowed and all my muscles straining, my cock buried so deep inside her I think I'll die of pleasure as I crack wide open and spill myself, twitching and hoarsely shouting her name.

It lasts forever. Time spins away and loses all meaning. I spend a lifetime in that endless moment, the image of her beauty as she climaxes on top of me burned into my retinas and the darkest, deepest reaches of my mind.

She's all there is.

This is all there is, this powerful thing that lives between us, this fierce and elemental force I'm no more able to control than I could control gravity.

I love her so much in this moment, everything I was before is incinerated. I came into this room one man, but I know I'll emerge from it another, a baptism of love so hot it's a fire that scorches me to the bone and leaves whatever I was before a smoking pile of ashes to be blown away by the wind.

Eva collapses on top of my chest, sobbing.

"I know," I say hoarsely, hearing my voice shake. "I know, baby. Kiss me."

I take her mouth, feeling how violently she trembles. How frantically my heart pounds. With my arms tight around her back, I hold her as close as she can get.

I'm in love.

I'm so fucking in love.

If I lose her, it will end me.

EIGHTEEN

Eva

We lie stunned and silent on the bed like two victims of a bombing, shell-shocked, ruined, left for dead.

His arm is under my neck. My leg is thrown over his. I'm tucked into the safe haven of his body, where he settled me after he dried me off with a fluffy white towel and led me here, quaking, every defense peeled away so I feel like one giant exposed nerve.

Finally, I say faintly, "That was . . ."

"Incredible. Unbelievable. Just . . . wow."

He sounds like someone who recently discovered an alien planet. Like he's setting foot for the first time on some amazing, distant new world.

I smile and press a kiss to his bare chest. "I was going to say wet. That was very wet."

His head lolls sideways. He gazes at me from under his lashes, his beautiful brown eyes warm and liquid, his lips curving up. "The wettest," he agrees in a soft voice. "Probably a good thing we had all that water, too."

I crinkle my brow.

"So you didn't crush me with your colossal weight, Elephant Girl."

"Riiight." I playfully nip his chest, and he grins.

"Oh no. I forgot. It's past feeding time. Better get you some peanuts before you start eating the furniture."

He makes a move to get up, but I tighten my arms around him in protest, forcing him back to the mattress. Chuckling, he kisses my cheek, my forehead, my hair, rolling to one side so he can gather me into his arms. I nestle against him, sighing in contentment.

"Oh, does the Elephant Girl *like* the zookeeper?"

I tilt my head up and look into his eyes, letting him see everything I'm feeling though I keep my voice nonchalant. "He's okay. Though I will say, his peanuts are pretty spectacular."

Naz dissolves into laughter, holding me tight against his chest so I feel the sound of his laughter rumble through my body, a weird ticklish sensation I enjoy very much.

"I'm glad you find me so amusing, sir."

He smooths my hair away from my face and kisses the tip of my nose. We're eye to eye, our heads resting on the same pillow, the bottoms of my feet resting on top of his, our combined afterglow so bright it's almost blinding.

"Only to look at," he says seriously, fighting a smile. "You've got a really peculiar face. What's the name for this hideous condition of yours?"

I think for a moment. "Awesome . . . intelligent . . . itis?"

"I see. Awesomeintelligentitis. Sounds frightening. Is there a cure?"

"No. But the symptoms are helped by certain things."

"Such as?"

I whisper, "Kisses."

He tries to look stern. "Yikes. It would take a brave man to subject himself to that. Very brave, indeed."

"So send out the bat call for Superior Man."

When he cocks an eyebrow, I say, "You know, that light in the night sky shaped like a bat that Gotham sends out when they're in trouble."

"I assume you're referring to the Bat-Signal?"

"That's the one."

He sniffs. "Ahem. Superior Man doesn't answer to Batman calls. That would be unprofessional. Not to mention demoralizing to Batman, who could never live up to the standards Superior Man would set if he did swoop in to save the day. Obviously."

"Obviously," I agree, keeping a straight face as if this is a sane conversation. "So what's Superior Man's call? For when the awesomeintelligentitis gets out of control and he needs to come save the poor citizens of Gotham from the terrible peril."

Naz thinks for a moment. "A giant pair of lips?"

"*What?*"

"You know, projected into the night sky."

"Uh, no. That's a weird and also lame superhero call signal. It has nothing to do with anything."

"It has to do with kisses! To save the citizens from the scourge of your awesomeintelligentitis!"

"No. I'm not sending up a giant pair of lips into the night sky when I need you. Think of something else."

"This is all about *you* now? I thought we were talking about the poor citizens of Gotham."

"Psh. Those people are tough. They can take care of themselves. Look what they've been through in all those stupid movies."

He laughs silently, his lips pressed together and his shoulders shaking.

"I have an idea."

"I can hardly wait."

"A microchip."

"How do you send up a microchip into the night sky? Cannon?"

"No, silly! A microchip like they put in dogs!"

Naz blinks several times in rapid succession. It's comical.

"Okay, follow along closely now, Superior Man. I know your brain is filled with a lot of very important superhero information, but make room for more." I pause to inspect his face. "Are you listening?"

He says drily, "My ears are literally inches away from your mouth."

"Okay." I take a breath, not sure I want to broach this subject at this particular time, but there won't ever be a really good time, so here goes. "Once when I was in the hospital having an MRI because Dimitri hit me so hard my vision stayed blurry for weeks, I overheard the nurses talking. One of them had just gotten a new puppy."

Naz stops breathing. All his laughter dies. He stares at me with a tight jaw, his pupils dilating.

"She said she was going to get the puppy microchipped, in case it ever got lost. My impression was that it was a simple procedure. Inexpensive and noninvasive, but great for reuniting the dog with its owner in case of an emergency. Whoever found the dog could just take it to any vet, and the information on the microchip could be read."

He hasn't moved, not an inch, not even to blink.

I clear my throat. "Except the microchip you put in me could be a GPS."

He closes his eyes and exhales a heavy breath. "Jesus."

"I'm sorry. I know my timing is bad."

"No, it's just . . ." He opens his eyes and gazes at me with a pained look. "I hate everything about that story, including the fact that a microchip isn't a bad idea."

It's my turn to exhale. My relief is overwhelming. "I'm so glad that didn't make you mad."

"Sweetheart, I could never be mad at you for thinking ahead." Naz tucks my head into the space between his neck and shoulder and starts to gently rub my back, his big hand warm and comforting.

My eyes closed, breathing in the smell of his skin, I whisper, "So you agree Dimitri will figure out eventually that I'm not with Killian?"

"Unfortunately, yes. It's only a matter of when. I don't know what Killian has planned, but when he doesn't produce you, Dimitri will know the jig is up. Christ, I hate that you have to worry about this. That you even have to think this way."

I won't have to after he's dead. "I knew when Killian said he'd told Dimitri that I was with him, not you, it would only buy me some time."

"Us," Naz corrects firmly. "Buy *us* time."

"But he isn't after you anymore—"

"Don't even go there," Naz interrupts, his body tensing. When I don't reply, he lifts my head with his fingers under my chin and examines my expression, his eyes dark and searching.

I reach up and touch his precious face. I say softly, "He'll always find me. One way or another, he'll find me. But you can be safe."

He rears up on one elbow and stares down at me, his anger palpable. "We're a team, goddammit. A *team*. Get this idea out of your head that *you're* somehow gonna fix this situation. *I'm* gonna fix it. That's *my* job."

"How are we a team if you do all the work?"

If a person could breathe fire, he'd have flaming orange plumes billowing from his nostrils right now.

"You promised me—literally *swore* to me—that nothing would ever separate us and you'd never put yourself in danger for me again. And now you're, what? What're you telling me? That you're gonna sneak away so when Dimitri finds you, I won't be anywhere near to help?"

"Well, if you want total honesty . . . the thought had crossed my mind."

He curses.

"But yes, I did promise you. I haven't forgotten."

"Did you *lie?*"

"You know I didn't. I'm merely saying . . ." I sigh and pull out of his arms, sitting up and swinging my legs over the edge of the bed. I complete my thought staring pensively at the floor. "If someone had

141

killed Hitler before he murdered millions of people, the world today would be a very different place."

Behind me, there's silence. It throbs with emotion. I don't even have to look at Naz to know what he feels.

"Stalin. Pol Pot. Mussolini. If someone in their inner circle had had the courage to take down one of those evil men before they committed the atrocities they did, before they caused so much suffering—"

"Dimitri isn't Stalin," says Naz, his voice clipped.

I turn and look at him over my shoulder. "Not yet."

He stares at me, his eyes flashing. "I'm trained in weapons. In search and rescue. In surveillance and self-defense. I've got years of experience in the military, on the police force, and as a bodyguard." He pauses. "What was it you're trained in again?"

"Ballet," I say calmly, holding his gaze. "And satisfying the deviant needs of a monster."

He shoves up to a sitting position, pulling his knees up and clasping his arms around them. It's a protective position, and it pains me to see it, because I know my words have hurt him. I know he's trying not to imagine all the terrible things I've suffered at Dimitri's hands, and not having much luck.

More gently, I say, "He'll see you coming. He's prepared for everything. Except me. I'm the only person he loses control with. I'm the addiction he can't shake. He's had and discarded hundreds of girls. Thousands maybe. But he kept me for seven years. Right by his side, at dinners and meetings and every Sunday at church. I'm his favorite. In his own sick way, he needs me. He needs what I give him. He needs my pain."

Naz thunders, "Well, I need you *safe!*"

"As long as Dimitri's alive, I'll never be safe."

He leaps from the bed and starts to pace beside it, naked and bristling, masculine and gorgeous, so gorgeous he's like a walking piece of art.

"You're not responsible for whatever it is Dimitri's got that Killian wants, or for worrying about anything other than getting well. The only thing you need to do right now is get better!"

I take a deep breath before I speak, because this is going to hurt.

The truth always does.

"I say this with love, Naz, because I know you have only good intentions. But what *you* need to do is stop telling me what I need to do. You told me once that my life is my own, and you were right. Respect what I'm saying, even if you don't like it. I won't be treated like anyone's property ever again."

He stops dead in his tracks, his face stricken. "I'm not . . . I could *never* . . ."

"I know, sweetie," I murmur, hating that I've caused that look. "But just consider the possibility that I'm a lot stronger than you think."

His voice is raw with emotion. "I know you're strong. I just love you too goddamn much to be cavalier about you wanting to put yourself in harm's way."

"I'm not asking you to be cavalier. I'm asking you to hear me out and admit that I might be right, even if you hate what I'm saying. If we're really a team . . . we have to take care of Dimitri together."

We stare at each other, the bed a thousand miles of space between us. I see how hard he fights himself to come to me, how wounded and helpless my words make him feel.

And I know I've pushed this conversation as far as I can.

For now.

I rise and go to him, silently folding myself into his arms. He hugs me so hard it hurts. His breathing is ragged. His cheek is hot and rough against mine.

Into his chest, I say, "You said no more sorries, but you deserve one more. I'm sorry I've upset you. I respect your feelings, and your need to protect me, and you. As a man, and as an expert in your field, and as a smart person in general. I'm so grateful I have you on my side."

I lift my head and gaze into his eyes. "Knowing you has made my wretched life worth living."

He kisses me, hard and desperate, then lifts me up in his arms. He strides around the bed, sets me back onto the mattress, and pulls the covers up around me. Leaning over to kiss me again, he says roughly, "I'm getting you food. You'll stay here and rest until I come back. I'm not trying to be a bossy asshole, but I'm gonna feed you and then we're gonna go to sleep and let this conversation rest until I don't feel like tearing my hair out and setting the building on fire. Yeah?"

I nod, squeezing his corded wrists and smiling.

He rises and looks down at me, his eyes shadowed. Then he shakes his head and sighs, stalking off to the bathroom to find his clothes where he discarded them, his limp more pronounced than usual. I watch as he drags on his trousers, drags his hands through his hair, and drags a heavy breath into his lungs.

Then he's gone, closing the bedroom door softly behind him.

NINETEEN

NAZ

This woman will be the death of me.

I know it, I've accepted it, and I don't care. She's worth it. Every risk and chase and heartache, she's worth it all.

I walk slowly into the kitchen, the muscles in my thigh throbbing, a pressure like a winch inside my chest. Now that the adrenaline has leached from my system, I'm feeling rough. Bone-tired and thick-headed, like my limbs are made of lead and my head's stuffed with cotton.

I take Eva's meds from the fridge and rub the bottle between my palms for a while to try to help it warm up, then set it on the counter and assemble a platter of fruit and cheeses. Connor was right about there being too much fruit, but there's also cold cuts stashed in a drawer that he was too impatient to find. I unwrap a few slices of turkey and roast beef and add them to the platter as well.

Then I scrub my hands over my face and lean against the granite counter as I consider the situation.

She's not gonna give in about wanting to be involved with taking down Dimitri, that much is clear. It's also pretty clear that she'll feel betrayed if I go ahead without her. She wants me to respect her wishes, which I do and always will—with one major caveat.

I'm the man. I'm the protector. I'm the one who's supposed to risk my life for her, not the other way around. It has nothing to do with my opinion of her intelligence, her capability, or anything else.

It's because *I'm the man*, goddammit.

It's my duty and my privilege to take care of her. It's in my DNA. Asking me to shrug and step aside while she goes out and fights her own battles goes against everything in my male nature. I have to protect her. I have to keep her safe. I *need* to, as much as I need to eat or breathe.

If that makes me old-fashioned or a chauvinist, so be it.

The only thing we seem to agree on is that Dimitri is a rabid dog who needs to be put down . . . but I'll be damned if I'll let her get anywhere near him. Just remembering his empty blue eyes when we had our weekly calls over the computer when Eva and I were still on Cozumel is enough to give me the willies. He's got more than one screw loose, and that's a fact.

And what he did to her—

"Fuck." Forcing the awful images of the hospital pictures of her injuries from my mind, I sigh heavily and scrub my hands over my face again.

It doesn't help.

The plastic bottle with Eva's antibiotics is still chilly, so I fill a pot half-full of water and set it to boil on the stove. Once it's simmering I remove it, set it on a cool burner, and submerge the bottle in the hot water for a minute. Then I take it out and test the temperature because I don't want it cold when it hits her veins.

Satisfied that it's warm enough, I find an IV infusion set in the medical kit in the pantry, shaking my head at how much it must cost Connor to have setups like this all over the world. But then again, the fees his clients pay are astronomical. Extracting your dearly beloved from the clutches of a kidnapper or nasty rival warlord in some godforsaken hellhole in the jungle isn't cheap.

I fill two glasses with water, set them on the platter with the food, then take it and the medicine back into the bedroom.

Lying in bed with the covers pulled up to her chin, Eva turns her head when I come in. Then she smiles, and the winch in my chest loosens slightly.

"You're so domestic," she says, watching me set the platter on the nightstand.

"Superior Man has all kinds of surprises up his superhero sleeves."

"Really? Do you do laundry, too?"

"Of course I do laundry. I was in the military."

"You say that like it's one of their required courses."

I sit on the edge of the mattress and tear open the plastic bag with the infuser set. "Master Sergeant McCall taught me basic tactical and survival skills along with how to shoot, rappel, and march, but he also required recruits to be meticulously neat in their personal appearance and maintain their bunk and equipment in pristine condition."

I have to grin, remembering how often I was screamed at for failing to pass muster. "I still make my bed with hospital corners so tight you can bounce a quarter off it."

Eva stares at me, impressed. "I thought that was only in the movies."

"Unfortunately, that's something Hollywood got right. If the quarter didn't bounce right back up into his hand, we had to drop and give him fifty push-ups, then make the bed again. Not even God could help you if it didn't pass the second time."

I make a little roll-up sandwich with a piece of turkey and a slice of cheese, then offer it to Eva. She takes it and starts to nibble. I watch until she's almost finished, then, satisfied, turn my attention back to the infuser set and get it assembled.

"He was a giant pain in my ass, ol' Sarge, and I hated his guts during basic, but it's him I have to thank for teaching me all the really important stuff I've learned."

147

Through a mouthful, Eva says, "I hate to break it to you, but hospital corners aren't that important in the grand scheme of things."

I smile. "I was talking more along the lines of loyalty. Duty. Respect. Selfless service, honor, integrity, and personal courage. All the things I've based my life on. The things that have made me the man I am. Here, I warmed up the antibiotics for you. Didn't want to inject ice into your veins."

I don't realize she's silent until I'm finished messing with the tubing and turn to look at her.

Her eyes are swimming with unshed tears.

"Eva?"

She sits up and gives me a sloppy kiss that tastes like turkey. "How are you so wonderful?" she asks in a strangled voice. "How are you so impossibly wonderful and good?"

I don't know what the hell I've done to get this reaction, but I'll take it. Chuckling, I brush a crumb of cheese off her trembling chin. "I keep telling you, sweetheart. I'm amazing."

She sniffles, nodding. "You do keep telling me that. And coming from anyone else, it would be completely obnoxious, but I have to tell you, Superior Man, you really pull it off."

I take her face in my hands and kiss her firmly, then smooth her choppy hair away from her cheeks. "I know. I'm so fantastic I can hardly stand myself."

She purses her lips. "It's a miracle you don't have two broken arms with how much you pat yourself on the back, honey."

"You're good for my ego, I told you that."

She flops back onto the mattress and beams at me, her eyes still watery but shining bright. "Apparently I've created a monster. May I please have another of your custom turkey rollie thingies?"

"As you wish."

When I hand it to her, she smiles. "I like that movie, too."

"Why am I not surprised you'd recognize a quote from *The Princess Bride*?"

"Maybe Superior Man has met his match . . ." She bats her eyelashes dramatically. "In Superior *Woman*."

I consider her for a beat, so happy all of a sudden that it's hard to catch a breath. Then I say seriously, "But you suffer from that terrible, terminal case of awesomeintelligentitis. I think that disqualifies you from the Superior title."

"Hmm." She chews thoughtfully on the cold cuts. "Maybe a minor title, then. Better Than Average Woman?"

I make a face. "Too long. Not catchy enough. Superheroes need a catchy name."

"That's true. I read that Stan Lee was originally going to call Spider-Man Stick-to-Wall-Man. Doesn't really have the same impact."

"Oh my God. You know who the creative leader of Marvel Comics was? You're every teenage boy's wet dream."

She wrinkles her nose. "There's a superhero name for me in there somewhere, but . . . ew."

I laugh, charmed by her as always. "Gimme your hand, sweetheart."

She extends her arm and rests it on my leg. When I open the small packet that contains an alcohol swab, she sighs wistfully, then swipes at her eyes.

Worried by her reaction, I ask, "Do needles scare you?"

"No, honey," she says softly. "Ignore me. I'm just crushing on you."

"Should I put on a shirt? I know all these bulging muscles of mine must be distracting."

"The only thing that's distracting is your ego. It's blocking the light."

"Are you sure that's my ego? It could be this." Grinning, I flex my biceps.

She looks at the ceiling and shakes her head, but I can tell she's trying not to smile.

"All right, then, unnamed superhero chick, here we go. Stay still so I don't stick you." I diligently scrub the back of her hand with the alcohol swab, making sure not to miss any spots. Then I get the catheter ready, make a quick check of her face to ensure she's okay, and slide the needle into her vein. Once it's set, I tape it down with a few strips of white medical tape, then swipe around those, too, just to be sure I haven't missed any stray bacteria.

She blinks at me dreamily, as if I've just done something really great.

I finish setting up the infuser and open the clamp so the medicine starts to flow. Then I start thinking about how Killian must've gone through these exact steps, and my smile turns to a frown.

"You're much better at it than he was."

Her murmured words startle me. "Oh. You can read minds now. How disturbing."

"Only yours."

I slant her a look. "Really? What else am I thinking?"

She examines my expression, then pronounces, "You're relieved I'm okay, furious at Killian, and upset with yourself for being hurt so you couldn't stop me from leaving, which you're wrongly blaming yourself for as some kind of failure to protect me. Also you're grappling with minor guilt about what happened in the bathtub and wondering how you're going to handle my insistence that whatever happens with Dimitri, I'm involved. And you're so tired you could drop, but you'd kill yourself making sure I'm taken care of before you'd let yourself get some rest. And your leg hurts."

My mouth stays open so long I'm lucky there aren't any insects circling the room.

She says softly, "It's not hard to know what someone's feeling when their happiness is more important to you than your own."

I have to squeeze my eyes shut and blow out a hard breath so I don't give in to the completely emasculating urge to cry.

She says, "Come here, sweetie."

I feel her soft touch on my arm pulling me toward her, and lean into a hug. I say, "Watch the tube—"

"It's fine. Stop talking."

I exhale into her hair, stroking her back and trying not to squeeze her too tightly, though it's all I can do not to crush my arms around her as hard as I can. She kisses my neck and shoulder, small, tender little kisses that are so sweet they could break my heart.

After a moment, she whispers, "How long do we have here together?"

"As long as you need to get better."

"And no one will disturb us?"

"No. The only person who knows where we are is Connor. Maybe Tabby. We're safe."

"And if we need food? Supplies?"

I lift my head and look at her. "I'll take care of everything. Why do you ask?"

She smiles shyly, ducking her head. "Because . . . we never . . . it would just be so nice to spend some time alone. I'd love to wake up with you. Watch television with you. You know, normal stuff. We'll pretend we're just two normal people."

I gather her into my arms again, overcome by that same powerful sweeping wave of emotion I felt in the bathtub when we made love. My voice comes out thick and rough. "That's exactly what we're gonna do, sweetheart. We're gonna have ourselves a little vacay and rest."

She snuggles against me, sighing in happiness, resting her ear over my pounding heart. "Good. We need it."

We do, though I don't respond. I'm too preoccupied wondering if we'll ever be normal people, or if this is the only chance we'll get.

Because I know Killian was right when he wrote that Dimitri would leave no stone unturned looking for Eva.

I just don't know how long it'll be until he turns over the right one.

TWENTY

Eva

Naz fusses over me and feeds me from his fingers, like I'm a wounded bird he found lying with a broken wing under a tree. He carefully watches to ensure the antibiotics flow smoothly into my veins, fluffs the pillows behind my head, brings the glass to my lips so I can drink water.

All the attention is wonderful. I suspect I could easily become spoiled and start demanding this treatment full-time.

I don't object, of course. If my superhero name ends up being Mega Diva, that's fine by me.

When I've eaten until I'm stuffed and all the medicine in the bottle has gone, Naz gently uncouples the IV tube from the catheter but leaves the end with the needle taped to my hand.

"I don't remember what happened to the last one."

"I took it out."

"You did? When?"

"When you were out of it on the ride over."

"Oh. Why'd you take it out?"

His face darkens. "Because I didn't want to take any chances that it was put in wrong."

My heart swells with love for him until it feels as if it will burst. I have to look away so he doesn't see the water pooling in my eyes, because I know he'd start to panic.

But oh, God. No one ever told me love would be like this. This . . . *much*. I feel like I'm constantly being swarmed by hurricanes and tsunamis of emotion, big tornadoes of feeling picking me up and spinning me sky high, only to drop me from so far up I'm in danger of shattering every bone in my body.

And this is the *good* stuff. I can't imagine what it must be like to have this and then lose it. I've survived a lot in my life, but I doubt I'd survive that.

There's only so much pain a heart can take before it breaks for good.

I watch with a feeling of supreme satisfaction as he turns off the bedroom light, shucks off his pants, and crawls under the covers next to me. He turns me gently to my side, then slides his arm under my neck and cuddles up against my back, drawing his legs up behind mine. Then he buries his face into my hair and sighs.

"You're a master spooner." I wriggle my butt into his crotch.

"And you're a master tease. Stop squirming."

"Why? Don't tell me you're already up for more bathtub action."

He's silent for a moment, just long enough for me to feel the new hardness pressing at my bottom. "Wow. I'm impressed. We need to rethink your superhero name."

He kisses the nape of my neck and winds his other arm around my waist, pulling me tightly against his solid warmth. "Don't name me something that sounds like a porn film."

"Super Penis? Biggus Dickus? Erection Man?"

"What did I just say? You're crap at following directions."

I hear the smile in his voice and smile myself. Then we lie there in comfortable silence while I idly consider if I should get up and turn off the bathroom light.

Naz murmurs, "Do you want that light out?"

Apparently I'm not the only one who can read minds. The thought makes me smile wider. "No, sweetie. Leave it. I'll be asleep in thirty seconds."

"Good, because so will I."

"Even with that situation happening between your legs?"

"I'll have nice dreams."

"Will I be in them?"

He cups my breast and gently squeezes, then whispers, "Always. Go to sleep."

And so I do, with his heat and strength wrapped around me and my breast still resting in his hand.

⟡

I awaken sprawled across his body like a blanket.

For a moment, I'm disoriented. The room is unfamiliar and so is my complete sense of well-being. Then I hear Naz's heartbeat thudding slow and steady under my ear, and I remember. I exhale, taking a moment to luxuriate in the altogether new sensation warming me down to my bones.

Joy.

I lift my head and look at Naz. His jaw is dark with scruff. His thick black hair is messy. He breathes deeply and evenly, his hands splayed over my back. He's holding me close, even in sleep.

I squeeze my eyes shut, rest my forehead on his chest, and say a silent prayer of thanks that I've been given this moment. I'm so happy I could poop glitter and rainbows. Then I prop a hand under my chin and indulge myself in gazing at my strong, handsome man, memorizing his features and enjoying this rare moment of calm.

He stirs, turning his head on the pillow, sliding a hand up to cup the back of my neck. He speaks without opening his eyes, his voice thick with sleep.

"Stop staring at me. I know I'm incredibly attractive, but you'll give me a complex."

I whisper, "I didn't mean to wake you."

"Mmm. I was dreaming."

"Of what?"

He cracks open an eye. "There was this woman. This beautiful, intoxicating woman."

"Oh?"

He nods seriously. "Tall and willowy, with legs like a dancer's and long blonde hair."

"Blonde!" I smack him on the chest.

He breaks into a gorgeous grin and drags me up his body so I'm aligned straighter on top of him, my chest and legs resting on his. "Are you jealous of a dream? How interesting."

"I'll give you interesting," I mutter.

His chest shaking with silent laughter, he tucks my head into his shoulder and rests his chin on top. "Good morning, sunshine."

I grumble.

When he wriggles his fingers into my sides, I shriek and roll off him. "No! No tickling! Gah!"

He doesn't let me get far. Laughing and pulling me back into his arms, he says, "Aha! I've found your kryptonite! Tickling makes you feel weak!"

"Tickling makes me feel stabby. Do it again and risk losing an eye."

He plants a big kiss on me, close-mouthed and firm. Then, grinning, he pulls back to examine my expression. "I take it you're not a morning person."

I fake glare at him. "Don't try to blame it on the time of day. It's your poke-y fingers and dream cheating that are the problem, my friend, not the morning."

"*Dream cheating?* That's not a thing."

"It's totally a thing. Do it again and you're toast."

He strokes his thumb over my cheekbone, smiling indulgently at me. "All right. Since you've threatened me with bodily harm, I promise I won't dream cheat on you again."

When I narrow my eyes, he adds quickly, "Or any other kind of cheating, either."

"That's right," I grouse, pretending I'm angry, because this is fun. "No more willowy blondes or it's lights out for you, Superior Man."

He dissolves into helpless laughter, squeezing me tight. Finally, when he's caught his breath, he says, "She wasn't really a blonde."

"Nope. Don't try to get out of trouble by changing your story now, pal. It's too late for retractions."

"Oh, so you don't wanna hear what the *real* dream woman was like?"

I tilt my head back and stare at him. "You're on such thin ice right now."

He ignores me completely. "Because no blonde in the *world* could ever compete."

"Mm-hmm. Keep talking, cowboy. I'll just be over here polishing my pistols."

His sigh is so dramatic he could win an award for it. "Okay. Fine. I can see you don't wanna hear about the real dream woman's grace, or her beauty, or her many other charms. I'll just keep how perfect she is to myself."

I pause, intrigued. "Perfect?"

He nods. "Not that you wanna hear about it, but yes."

"Perfect how?"

He struggles to keep a straight face as he looks at the ceiling and pretends to consider the question. "Well . . . she gets all my random movie quotes."

I scrunch up my face. "That's hardly a qualification for perfect status."

"You'd be surprised."

"That's it? That's all you've got?"

"If you'd stop shouting so I could get a word in edgewise . . ."

I do the fake glaring again.

"As I was saying before I was so rudely interrupted, the random movie quotes are only the start. There's also the wiener dog fetish—always a winner—the tendency to blurt out every little thing that crosses her mind, the absolute failure to tell a convincing lie, the weird sense of humor—"

"Weird! How is it *weird*? I'm funny!"

"—and the fondness for potato sack dresses. Oh, she's also kinda smart. And sweet. And she's got a rack to die for."

"A rack," I deadpan. "You're calling my breasts a *rack*. How gallant."

He glances down at them, smashed against his chest, and grins. "Sweetheart, those babies are literally the most gorgeous on the planet."

"Oh? You've seen all the breasts on the planet, have you?"

He blinks up at me, the picture of innocence. "Naturally. You try having X-ray vision and not seeing under everyone's clothes."

"Ah. Just another of Superior Man's amazing abilities, hmm?"

"Yep. It's a burden being this talented, let me tell you. Don't even get me started on my superhero strength. I can't tell you how many pickle jars I've shattered just trying to unscrew the lid."

We stare at each other for a moment, then break down laughing at the same time.

"And you say *my* sense of humor is weird. You're the one who's mental." As soon as the words leave my mouth, I stop laughing.

Killian had used that word to describe me: *mental*. It's not a word that was formerly in my vocabulary as an adjective, and it disturbs me that I'd repeat it. Especially here. Now.

In bed with Naz.

"Uh-oh." Naz inspects my face. "She's thinking. I can smell the smoke."

I swallow, my heartbeat picking up. "I . . . oh boy. You're not going to like this."

He falls still, the lines of his big body tensing. "I already don't. Spit it out."

"I was just thinking about . . . Killian."

After a moment, Naz says, "That's it?"

I tilt my head up and venture a peek at his face. "You're not angry?"

He arches an eyebrow, an invitation to continue.

"We're in bed and I thought of Killian. When I mentioned Dimitri before when we were in bed, you didn't like it."

"Of course I didn't like it," comes the instant response. "I don't want you thinking of anyone but me when we're in bed together. But it's not like you and Killian—"

He cuts off and stares at me, his face turning white.

I prop myself up on an elbow, flatten my hand over his chest, and look into his eyes. "We didn't. I told you, he didn't touch me in that way. But . . ."

He jerks upright so fast I'm startled. "But what?"

I sit upright, too, pulling the sheets up over my breasts. "He kissed me. Actually, that's not completely accurate. I kissed him."

"You kissed him," Naz repeats slowly, his lips so tight they're barely moving. "Voluntarily?"

"Yes."

"The man who kidnapped you, beat you, killed the crew of a ship, and cut off all your hair."

"I cut off my own hair," I say, but realize by the way Naz is looking at me that this isn't the most important topic at the moment. "Yes, I did kiss him, but it was under duress. He threatened to kill Raphael if I didn't."

He sits very still, simply looking at me. After a moment, he exhales. "Okay."

"Um. What do you mean, 'okay'?"

"I mean I hate the thought of his mouth on you, and I hate that you had to go through all that you did—including giving that fucker a kiss—but it wasn't like you wanted to. You did it because you thought it would help someone else. Thank you for telling me. I feel better that I know than if you'd kept it a secret. And I apologize that my feathers got ruffled and I startled you. I didn't mean to do that. I'll do better next time."

"Next time?"

His chuckle is low and dark. "I'm sure this won't be the last time I'll get jealous. There are probably gonna be a lot of men in our future who're gonna wanna kiss you. That's not your fault. But this *will* be the last time I'll question you. I trust you, and I need you to trust me. With everything. I know you can't if I act like some teenage dick."

He inhales, his nostrils flaring. "Also, I'm gonna tear that son of a bitch limb from limb and make a bonfire with all his body parts—"

I lean in and kiss him to stop the flow of words, because I can tell he's only getting started.

He winds his arms around me and pulls me closer, then takes us back down to the mattress and tucks me under his arm. We lie there for a while in silence as his heartbeat under my hand slows to a less murderous rate.

When he speaks again, his voice is oddly constricted. "In a way, I owe him."

That surprises me so much I can't speak for a moment. "How?"

"Because if it weren't for him, you'd be with Dimitri right now, suffering God only knows what."

"Oh, sweetie." I close my eyes and turn my face to his chest. He trails his fingers down my spine, tracing each bump, his touch achingly gentle.

He whispers, "Is there anything else you need to tell me?"

"Other than I love you?" I think for a moment. "I called Dimitri from the hospital."

"I know."

"Tabby?"

"Yeah."

"Did she mess with Raphael's money, too?"

"Yep."

I pause for a moment to reflect on the impressive intelligence and competence of my newfound friend Tabby, a woman unlike any other I've ever met. "Is there anything she can't do?"

"If there is, I haven't seen it."

I take a moment to gather my thoughts, then say, "I guess Raphael and Dimitri worked together. Killian mentioned girls. Dimitri's girls. He said Raphael caused more suffering than almost anyone he'd ever met. I took that to mean Raphael was some sort of courier."

"A trafficker. Of guns, drugs, and people."

When I make a small sound of disbelief, Naz says, "What?"

"It's just . . . he was so nice to me. He was sophisticated and elegant and just *nice*."

Naz says darkly, "Even the shiniest apple can be filled with worms."

I think of Dimitri's sweet, cherubic face, and shiver. *I know.* "Has Dimitri contacted you at all?"

"No. The last contact we had with him is when he called Metrix to cancel the service."

"When he was still pretending he had no idea about you and me and meanwhile had men lying in wait with car bombs to ambush us."

"Yeah."

"When I talked to him, he said you'd be left alone if I returned to him—"

"Not this again. Please. I'm not mentally prepared to discuss this yet."

"I'm just thinking out loud. Not going there."

He breathes a little easier, and I press a kiss to his chest. "Anyway, my point was that we made our deal, then Killian happened. We all agree Killian wants something from Dimitri, but do you have any idea who he is? Where he came from? I never saw him before, so he wasn't in Dimitri's regular circle."

"We think he's a spy."

"A *spy*? Like James Bond?"

Naz's voice turns dry. "God, I really hate that bastard's guts."

I know he isn't talking about James Bond, and that my tone of voice must've been a touch too impressed. "I didn't mean to make it sound like it was cool. I'm only surprised. He seems more like a street thug than anything else. I can't imagine him taking orders from anyone."

Naz exhales in a gust. "If he's what we think he is, he doesn't."

After a time, I say, "I'm almost afraid to ask."

Rolling to his side to face me, he kisses me, then gently tugs on a lock of my hair. "So. Tell me the deal about the hair."

"You're not going to tell me about Killian?"

"I think if I hear his name on your lips one more time, my head will explode."

"Gotcha. The hair. Well, Ki—um, He Who Shall Not Be Named grabbed it . . ." I trail off when Naz's eyes turn black. "You know what? I just felt like I needed a new 'do."

He starts to laugh, only it doesn't sound like he thinks anything is particularly funny. "We're so fucked up."

"So's everyone else. Big whoop."

His eyes start to look less like a serial killer's. "You don't mind?"

"Are you kidding? I think we're adorable. Mental illnesses, psychic scars, emotional wounds, massive dysfunctions, and all."

He pretends to look insulted. "Excuse me, but I don't have any mental illnesses."

"Really? Because I could name about five that you're suffering from right off the top of my head."

"Yeah, right," he scoffs. "You couldn't even name one."

I start to clinically tick them off my fingers. "Narcissistic Personality Disorder. Whatever the opposite of Body Dysmorphic Disorder is. Persistent Genital Arousal Disorder—"

"Like you're complaining."

"—and, worst of all, Cargo Shorts Attachment Disorder, which is unfortunately quite common in males of your age who've served in the military and were never properly taught how to dress in anything other than camouflage littered with unnecessary pockets."

He gazes at me as if I've got little floating cherubs playing harps and frolicking with unicorns on sunbeams around my head. In a voice filled with love, he murmurs, "That was only four, sweetheart."

"Give me a minute. I'm only getting started." I glance around the room, frowning. "Where'd I leave that mental health encyclopedia?"

He pulls me closer and kisses me, rolling on top of me and giving me his heavy, wonderful weight. "I think we can find something more interesting to do right now."

I'm not surprised to find him hard for me, but it does make me laugh. "I bet we can."

With no further interruptions, we do.

TWENTY-ONE

Naz

We spend the next six days in our own sweet bubble of privacy, the outside world forgotten. We don't watch the news, read a paper, or go online. An asteroid could be on its way to smash the earth to smithereens for all we know or care. The only thing that matters is each other.

I map every curve of her body with my hands. I learn the little noises she makes in her sleep. I discover exactly how long it takes to make her come with my mouth versus my cock, what makes her shiver or cry out, the infinite different ways she can say *I love you* with her eyes.

I unearth a part of me that's been buried for so long I thought it was gone forever. In so many ways, she brings me back to life. I'm Lazarus, resurrected from the dead by the power of love.

My gratitude is eclipsed only by my happiness. My sense of having been bestowed with undeserved good fortune is profound.

But with every passing moment, a darkness grows inside my gut. A black seed puts down roots and sends up an ugly flower.

Dimitri's presence looms, even when the man himself is out of sight.

It's in everything from the occasional sudden silence that descends over us out of nowhere to the way Eva steals glances at the clock, as if willing it to stop. We're both acutely aware this is a stolen respite from the storm we'll soon have to return to, and no matter how much we try to keep the thunderclouds at bay, they darken all our beautiful horizons.

Then, on the seventh day of our stolen paradise, I get a call from Connor that pops our sweet bubble for good.

"How you doin', brother?"

"Good," I answer, smiling at Eva, who's lying on the living room floor, engaged in some kind of elaborate stretching routine that looks like it should be painful. "Anything new since we spoke a few days ago?"

We've had a few quick check-ins, once when he returned to New York and wanted to let me know everything was copacetic at Metrix but the feds and the NYPD still wanted to interview me, and again two days ago for a general status update on Eva's health, which is steadily improving. The doctor came again yesterday and seemed pleased with her progress.

"Yeah, actually. There is something new."

The tone in his voice gives me pause. "That doesn't sound good."

Eva bolts upright and stares at me, her face paling.

"I honestly don't know what it is yet. Besides fuckin' weird."

I go sit on the sofa and Eva sits beside me, folding her legs beneath her, her gaze glued to my face. I say, "What's up?"

"We got a letter here for you."

I frown. "A letter? Like in the mail?"

"Yeah."

"From who?"

"Killian."

That knocks the breath right out of me like someone kicked me in the chest. Beside me, Eva stiffens.

"Honey? What is it?"

I hold up a finger. My mind is a blizzard of questions, not the least of which is how he knew where to send me mail. "Read it to me."

I hear the snap of paper, then Connor's rumble of a baritone. "I'm quoting here. 'Naz, we need to talk. Call me as soon as you get this.' Then he signed his first name."

I don't know what the hell this is about, but I'm gonna find out, A-S-A-fucking-P. "Gimme the number."

"There isn't one."

"How am I supposed to call him without a phone number?"

"Did he give it to Eva?"

I turn to her and ask, "Did Killian give you a contact number for him?"

She blinks, startled. "No."

"You're sure?"

Her startled expression sours. "Yes, I'm sure."

To Connor, I say, "Negative. What the actual fuck?"

"Dunno, brother. I told you. Weird."

"Lemme think." I do, furiously, my brain wrestling with and discarding dozens of different ideas in a flash. I decide the only logical explanation is that Killian left a way to contact him at the safe house in Angra do Heroísmo. But where? We didn't stay long enough to search the entire place.

Shit. Do I have to go back? Does he want *me to go back?*

Is this a setup?

Eva pokes me in the arm. "What's happening?"

I answer absently, still thinking. "Killian mailed a note to Metrix for me. He wants me to call him. I'm trying to figure out how the fuck that's supposed to happen since I don't have his number."

Without missing a beat, she says, "How would a spy leave another spy a message without a regular person knowing?"

I gaze at her with lifted brows.

She says, "Like with a cipher or at a dead drop, that sort of thing."

I mutter, "I don't even wanna know how you know about ciphers and dead drops." But then a light bulb goes on over my head.

165

Cipher.

When I jump from the sofa and run into the bedroom, Eva follows right behind me. Connor's saying something on the other end of the phone, but I'm not paying attention because I'm too busy riffling through the clothing I wore the day we found Eva at Killian's safe house.

My fingers close around a piece of paper in one of the pockets of my tactical vest. I pull out the note Killian wrote me on a piece of unlined white paper, and stare at it. Then I hold it up to the light.

"Sweetheart, get me a pencil."

Eva tears over to the nightstand, yanks open a drawer, and rummages around inside. When she doesn't find what she's looking for, she sprints into the living room. She's back faster than I could count to ten, holding out her hand.

"Connor, hold on a sec. Be right back."

"Copy that."

I take the pencil from Eva, hand her the phone, flatten the crumpled paper on the nightstand, and lightly shade around the borders with the flat side of the lead, looking for any impressions or indentations that might arise, a ghosted image of words written on another piece of paper that the pressure of a pen might've left.

There aren't any.

Okay, next.

With Eva following on my heels, I go into the kitchen and turn on one of the burners on the stove. Then I hold the letter above the flame at a distance far enough to heat the paper but not close enough to burn.

Peering around my right shoulder, Eva says, "God, I'm smart."

When I shake my head in disbelief, looking at the numbers that have appeared on the bottom edge of the paper, she says, "No, really. I'm *smart*, right? We're talking Einstein-level genius here. We're talking extraterrestrial intelligence."

"I see you've been taking a page from my humility playbook."

"Your galactic-sized ego playbook, you mean."

"Exactly. Please gimme the phone."

She hands it to me. I say to Connor, "You still there?"

"Yeah. What's the 411?"

"Killian left me his digits in invisible ink. I'm guessing citrus juice applied with a cotton swab."

After a pause, Connor says, "Kinda old school, but I gotta admit I like it."

I really, really hate that guy. "I'll call you right back." Before Connor can reply, I've ended the call and started dialing.

The line rings once before Killian picks up, his tone low and brusque. "Took you long enough."

"Fuck you, asshole. What d'you want?"

"How is she?"

Heat starts to creep up my neck. "None of your goddamn business is how. Why did you want me to call you? And how did you know how to contact me? And when can we meet so I can rearrange your face for the condition you left her in?"

I hear a hard exhalation, then quiet. Then: "Are the antibiotics working?"

I have to close my eyes and count to ten so I don't release the scream crawling its way up my throat. "Okay. I can tell we're not gonna get anywhere until you get a medical briefing. So here you go, then I'm never gonna talk to you about her again. Yeah, the antibiotics are working. Congratufuckinglations on doing one thing right."

"Any side effects? Is she eating? Has she asked about me?"

The heat spreads from my neck to my cheeks, then to my ears. Chewing on her fingernail as she stares at me with unblinking eyes, Eva hangs on my every word. The bruise on her left cheek is faint now, almost fully healed.

I growl, "No. Yes. No. Now *tell me what you want.*"

"I want you to put Eva on the phone."

My hard laugh sounds anything but funny. "The likelihood of that happening is somewhere south of zero."

"I need to apologize."

"I'll pass it along."

"The hell you will."

"Yeah, you got me. It's been nice chatting, asshole, but I gotta go now."

"She won't like it when she finds out I wanted to talk to her and you didn't let me."

"And you won't like it when I slice a foot-long gash in your belly and strangle you with your own bowels."

After a moment, he chuckles. "Ah, yes. Love. The emotion that turns you into a blathering moron with a flair for melodrama and no sense of self-preservation. I have to admit, the whole thing is fascinating to me. I'd never seen it up close before the two of you. Does it feel as ridiculous as it looks?"

I stare at Eva's beautiful face when I speak, my heart answering for me.

"It feels like Christmas morning and summer vacation and every wish you ever made over candles on your birthday cake as a little kid come true. It feels like finding something you didn't even know you'd lost and then wondering how you ever lived without it. It feels like lightning. Like fire. But also like the world's most comfortable bed. It feels like everything you could ever want but know you don't deserve and will never be worthy of. It feels, prick, like *magic*."

I hold the phone out to Eva. "If he says *anything* you don't like, I'm throwing this out the window."

She stares at me for a beat while I fold my arms over my chest and lean against the stove. Then she raises the phone to her ear.

She snaps, "Don't upset him like that again." She pauses, listening. "No, because it upsets *me*." Another pause, then a sigh. "Yes, he curses a lot. I'm aware."

I look around the room for something convenient to break, but Eva rests her hand on my arm and shakes her head, effectively staving off the imminent explosion.

She says to Killian, "How did you know Naz worked at Metrix?" Her expression turns guilty. "Oh. I don't recall that." She listens again, then says, "I don't recall that, either. Do you often interrogate people for information when they're half-dead?" She looks at the ceiling, as if requesting help from a higher power. "Killian. We've been over this. I *didn't* like it."

I motion impatiently for her to give me back the phone, but she holds up a finger like I did to her earlier, and I discover how irritating that is firsthand.

Then she begins to answer what must be a rapid-fire line of questions, because her answers come fast. "No. Yes. I'm not sure. Maybe. No—*no!* Oh please, get over yourself. You're not half as interesting as you think you are."

"That's it." I make grabby hands for the phone. "Hand it over."

She whispers to me, "One sec, honey," then gets back on the line with my archenemy as if I'm not having an aneurysm two feet away. "Did you want to talk just about the kiss, or was there something important you needed to say?"

She glances up at me, watching my face with a serene expression on her own. "Of course I told him. I don't keep secrets from him." Whatever he says in response to that makes her look at the ceiling again. "I regret telling you anything about that." She listens, batting away my hands as I try to snatch the phone, then says tartly, "You know, Killian, for someone who prides himself on being such a cold-blooded, independent killer who doesn't need anyone or anything, you sure are interested in relationships."

I say loudly, "I'll show him a relationship. The relationship between my bullets and his brain."

Eva rolls her eyes at whatever Killian says. "Yes, he threatened your life again, but how can you blame him? You're a profoundly irritating man." She holds the phone out to me with an exasperated look. "Here. I can't deal with him anymore."

She goes back to the living room floor and resumes stretching.

I spend a moment marveling at the flexibility of not only her muscles, but of her mind. Her mysterious, surprising, and sometimes unfathomable mind, which manages somehow to never snap under the awful weight of the memories it bears and the fears it must carry, but always to elegantly bend.

I put the phone to my ear. "You there?"

"I'm here."

I smile at the dejected tone of his voice. "You don't sound happy."

"Don't gloat. It doesn't suit you."

"While I've got you on the phone, what did you tell Dimitri about Eva?"

"I told him we fell in love and she was having my baby."

The next beat of my heart is oddly staggered, like a drunk stumbling over his own feet. "Did you now."

He sighs, and that sounds dejected, too. "No. I just wanted to make you angry."

"Sorry to disappoint you."

He says drily, "Aye, I can hear how sorry you are."

"Okay, I'm just gonna put this out there, but I'm having a really hard time figuring out the point of this conversation. You wanna fill me in?"

I hear him moving around and picture him pacing in an empty warehouse, a bloodied dead guy tied to a chair somewhere in the shadows behind him. "I've been thinking about something Eva said."

I'm instantly bristling, expecting some smart-assed remark about that kiss, but he surprises me by what he says next.

"She wants to kill Dimitri. I assume you know that."

Guarded, I say, "Go on."

"Well, so do I. I'm sure you do, too."

My brain capacity is strained by the sheer amount of disbelief it's dealing with. If he's saying what I think he's saying, the guy is fucking *nuts*. "You've gotta be kidding me."

"What?"

"You're suggesting we *team up*? Is that it? Some fucked-up version of the Three Musketeers off to fight the bad guy and save the day?"

"You know, you need to deal with that scathing hostility of yours. And your language. There's no need to use the word '*fuck*' like punctuation."

I say flatly, "This from the man who thinks it's fine and dandy to smack women around and murder the entire crew of a ship just for shits and giggles. Thanks for the manners lesson, dickhead, but your priorities are really outta whack."

He sounds insulted. "I left the girl alive."

"Excuse me. I'll submit your name to the Vatican for sainthood."

"Aren't you going to ask me why? There's a good reason."

Now I understand why Eva kept looking at the ceiling during their conversation, silently begging God for help. Another few minutes talking with this fucker and I'll stick my head in the oven. "I have a feeling you're gonna tell me whether I wanna know or not."

"She was new. It was her first voyage on the *Silver Shadow*."

That's all he says, but I know the underlying message. The female crew member he left alive had no part in the ugly business of Mr. and Mrs. Bergé. How he ascertained her innocence, I'll never know, but it's obvious he wants to impress upon me that he's got some sort of scruples, warped though they may be.

Except for one thing.

"So it had nothing at all to do with needing someone to give intel to the coast guard about where you might be headed."

He pauses briefly. "Don't take this the wrong way, but it seemed like you needed a helping hand."

"Great. Thanks for sharing. Good talk, Killian. Have a nice life."

"Don't hang up yet, there's more."

Through gritted teeth, I say, "Boy, I can hardly wait."

"Dimitri's going to meet me in Prague next week to do the exchange." When I don't respond, he says, "Oh, come on. I know the anticipation's killing you."

"Did your parents ever ask you to run away from home?"

"Of course not."

"Oh, that's right. You don't have parents. You were grown in a petri dish."

"Fine, if you don't want to know what we're exchanging, I won't tell you. It's not like I kidnapped your girlfriend for this or anything."

I mutter, "Jesus *Christ*, you're a dick."

"I'm actually pretty great, once you get to know me."

From the floor, Eva says, "Honey, there's a really scary vein standing out on your neck. You might want to talk to Killian later."

He says loudly, "I heard my name. What did she say? Does she want to talk to me again? Put her back on the phone."

I shake my head at his desperate tone. "You know, this little crush of yours on my woman is gonna be a big problem between us."

He fires back with a smug, "It shouldn't be, unless you're insecure about her feelings for you. Are you insecure, Naz?"

I spend a brief moment fantasizing about all the various ways I'd like to end his life before answering. "Tell me about the meeting in Prague."

"I'll take the evasion as a yes."

"It wasn't a yes. I'm trying to get this train wreck of a conversation back on track."

"Meet me in front of the Pötscher Madonna in Saint Stephen's Cathedral in Vienna at noon tomorrow and I'll tell you everything."

I say with disdain, "I'm not meeting you anywhere, especially somewhere *you* set up."

"I thought you wanted to rearrange my face?"

"You might be the single most annoying human being I've ever encountered."

"And bring Eva. She's part of this whether you like it or not."

"She's not going near you!"

"We'll see. And forget about calling me back because this cell's going into an incinerator now." The line goes dead.

When I stand there glaring at the phone in my hand for too long, Eva says softly, "So where are we meeting him, honey?"

It takes a moment for me to realize that Killian knew I'd refuse to meet him, that Eva was nearby and would hear me refuse, and exactly how she'd react to my refusal.

I'd really love to take a cheese grater to the bare skin of that bastard's back.

TWENTY-TWO

EVA

Naz doesn't talk for half an hour after his phone call with Killian. He simply stands in front of the living room window and glares at the view of the sea as if it's his mortal enemy, his hands clenched even tighter than his jaw.

When he's finally cooled off, he finds me reading a book in a wing chair in the bedroom. He kneels in front of me and buries his face in my lap. I thread my fingers through his hair and play with it while I wait for him to speak.

His voice muffled by my thighs, he says, "I don't want you to come."

It's obvious he's not talking about sex. "I know, honey."

"It won't be safe. I'd rather die than put you in danger."

"I know that as well."

"I'm sorry I wasn't talking for a while. I was trying not to break things."

"I could tell. It didn't bother me. He makes me want to break things, too."

He lifts his head and gazes at me with worried eyes. "It could be a setup. He could've decided he wants to kidnap you all over again, this time for himself. Or he worked out a new deal with Dimitri, a better deal, so he'll really hand you over to him now. Or one of a thousand other different scenarios, none of them good."

I brush a lock of dark hair off his forehead and smile. "Or it could be that he wants to tell you everything he knows so we can all make a plan about how to deal with Dimitri."

He rises and starts to pace, then abruptly sits on the end of the bed across from me and pins me with a look. "You can't possibly trust him."

I understand that he wants me to say I don't. I also understand that he'd rather I tell him the truth than a lie, so I try to say what I have to as gently as I can. "I don't trust him the way I trust you, no. But he did save my life. He didn't have to do that. I think we both know he's smart enough to successfully barter a dead body if he had to."

Naz closes his eyes and draws a breath. "That's another thing." He opens his eyes, and the look in them is somewhere between anger and anguish. "He obviously has feelings for you. The more time he spends near you, the stronger his feelings will get."

"No matter what he feels, he won't do anything I don't want. He'd never force himself on me."

That statement makes Naz draw in a slow breath through flared nostrils. "He forced you to kiss him."

"Technically he gave me a choice, but I hear what you're saying. But I also believe—though it might sound stupid, given his propensity to murder people—he has a certain code of honor that he lives by. There are some lines he'd never cross. Taking an unwilling woman being one of them."

"I have to admit, I hate how confident you sound about that. It makes it sound like you admire him."

"I don't admire him. I'm not saying I think he's a gentleman, only that he had plenty of opportunities to take advantage of me on the ship, but he didn't. He's simply intrigued. Most of that has to do with you, by the way, not me."

"Don't kid yourself," he says, his eyes flashing. "It *all* has to do with you. You're beautiful. He wants you. How could he not?"

I consider that for a moment. "I'm not so sure it's me that he wants, but what I have. What we have, together. I don't think he's ever experienced love."

Naz's expression darkens. "Oh, the poor thing."

I say quietly, "Have you ever known another couple who has this?"

A muscle works in his jaw. "One or two."

"That's one or two more than I've known. Imagine how it must look from the outside."

Naz's lips part. He stares at me for several beats of silence, then says gruffly, "Don't tell me you feel sorry for him!"

"Not even a little bit. My point is that as good as this feels, to someone who's never come across it before, it must look even better."

Naz closes his eyes and breathes slowly in and out, his fingers twitching on his thighs. When he opens his eyes again, they're burning.

"You have a good heart. You're a good person. It's one of the things I love most about you, that despite everything you've been through, somehow you're not bitter or hard. You haven't let life ruin you, though mostly it's put you through hell. And to a man like Killian, that's a trait that must be unbearably attractive.

"But whatever your opinion of him, I can tell you one thing for sure: He's capable of anything. *Anything*, including trying to smash something beautiful he knows he'll never have."

I sit with that, understanding that even having this conversation hurts Naz more than he'd ever admit. Then I rise, cross to him, and climb into his lap.

He winds his strong arms around me and squeezes me close. Into his neck, I say, "He can't break us, honey. Nothing can."

"He could try."

"Have I told you recently how much I adore you?"

A low sound rumbles through his chest.

"I do," I whisper, snuggling closer. "So much. And I love how much you worry about me, and how protective you are, and how safe you make me feel."

His big gust of an exhalation stirs my hair. "Now you're just buttering me up."

"I'm giving you genuine compliments. I haven't gotten to the part about how well-endowed you are yet, but if you'd shut up, I could proceed."

Something like a chuckle makes his Adam's apple bob. "You're shameless."

I kiss his neck. "Shamelessly in love."

He groans. "You need new material. That was just *awful*."

"It's working, though, right?"

"Unfortunately, yes. God, I'm pathetic."

"You're not pathetic. You're Superior Man, and I love you. Now let's talk about this meeting in Prague."

This time his exhalation sounds resigned. "Vienna. But don't get too excited. You'll be staying out of sight."

I don't say another word, knowing there will be plenty of time to argue about that later. I simply give him another kiss on his neck and smile.

⊷∾

In the end, I think the only reason he allows me to go with him is because he can't bear the thought of leaving me alone at the safe house in Cascais. He has a healthy, if grudging, respect for Killian's skill at manipulation, and decided the actual point of the call might not have been to arrange a meeting in Vienna, but to lure the lion away from his den so his competitor could slink in uncontested.

When he said that, I didn't bother pointing out that Killian isn't his competition because it would have fallen on deaf ears. When all the chest beating starts, men devolve to an earlier species and lose the power of logical thinking. If, at the meeting, the two of them drop their pants and a measuring tape makes an appearance, I won't be surprised.

There are phone calls with Connor and Tabby that last hours. They pore over schematics of Saint Stephen's Cathedral, mapping all the entrances and exits, arranging logistics, planning for contingencies, plotting war. I stay out of Naz's way through it all, sensing intuitively that the worries lurking on his mind are much darker than his normal protectiveness.

Things like superstition. Things like déjà vu.

We're both acutely aware that the last time we made plans to visit a church, those plans—literally—blew up.

First thing in the morning, Naz and I take a train to Lisbon. At the station, we meet an unsmiling young man in a black leather coat over a hoodie who has a smattering of acne on his chin and small, darting eyes. He pushes off the column on the platform where he's been idling, scanning the crowd, hands Naz an envelope in a casual pass that looks as if they simply brushed by one another, and lopes away without ever speaking a word.

"Friend of yours?" I ask, watching him melt into the crowd of morning commuters.

"Never saw him before."

"How did he know who to look for?"

He sends me a conspiratorial wink, taking my arm and leading me through the throng toward the escalators. "That's what we call tradecraft, sweetheart."

"Aha. In other words, Tabby set it up."

He smiles, but his eyes are busy scanning the crowd, too. When I ask him what's in the envelope, he simply replies, "Papers."

We take a taxi to the airport, where Naz supplies the passports of Mr. and Mrs. Kent to the portly sweating man waiting beside a small plane on the tarmac of the private jet terminal. He doesn't speak to us, either. He simply flicks a glance over our passports, then hands them back to Naz, nodding toward the pilot, who's peering down at us through the cockpit window.

"No security?" I whisper as the man walks off.

"Metrix is making good use of the money it diverted from Raphael's account" is the murmured reply, then Naz holds out a hand to help me up the few steps of the airstair.

The plane is small but luxurious, with wide leather seats facing each other, a table in between, and a bottle of champagne on ice that neither of us touch. After we've lifted off and the city is a speck far below us, I lean back in my chair and look at Naz.

"So, Mr. Kent."

"Yes, Mrs. Kent?"

"I didn't get a chance to look at your passport, but I was wondering if by chance your first name is Clark?"

"My darling wife," he drawls, tearing open a bag of nuts plucked from a basket beside the champagne. "Have you forgotten already? Of course it is."

Amused, I shake my head and watch him pop several peanuts into his mouth. "So I guess I'm Lois in this scenario?"

"Minerva."

"*Minerva?* You're joking."

"It's that face," he says, munching. "A woman suffering from such a horrible case of awesomeintelligentitis was either going to be Hortense or Minerva. Figured I'd be kind and go with the one that didn't sound like I was calling you a bad word."

"Well. At least it wasn't Eunice."

"What's wrong with Eunice?"

"Besides everything? It sounds like something you'd name your pet cow."

"Number one, nobody keeps cows as pets. Number two, I once knew a smoking-hot girl named Eunice."

I scoff. "Number one, I had a pet cow when I was little, and number two, you're full of baloney."

Naz lifts his brows and stares at me. "Talk to me about this cow situation."

"We lived on a farm."

He frowns. "A cattle farm?"

"No, more like a dirt farm. The cow was for milk. We had a goat, too. And a few chickens, but I didn't name them because I felt bad when they became dinner. Now tell me about this hot girl Eunice situation. Which I'm calling BS on, by the way, unless you're secretly immortal and lived back in the day when girls were all named Eunice and Bertha and the like."

Naz thinks for a moment, popping more nuts into his mouth and chewing. He swallows and says, "What was this pet cow's name?"

"I believe we've already moved on from that subject, Mr. Kent."

"I'm very much interested in keeping this subject alive, Mrs. Kent."

I look at the champagne, wondering if perhaps I should have a glass. Or four.

Naz relents. "Okay, fine. Eunice. It was a family name, her grandmother's and mother's both. And she was exceedingly hot. She was a dancer at a bar I worked at years and years ago."

Folding my arms over my chest, I gaze at him. "A dancer."

"Of the stripping variety. You know, where they twirl around on a slippery pole?"

I say, "I'm starting to get the idea this is a thing for you."

"A *thing*? What kind of thing?"

"You know, like dancers are your type. Did your friend Eunice twirl around on *your* slippery pole?"

Unexpectedly, he bursts out laughing. "Oh, I see. You thought I dated her."

"You said she was hot! *Exceedingly* hot! And why is that so funny?"

"Because you're cute when you're jealous."

I lift my nose in the air and sniff. "I'm not jealous."

"Oh, pardon my mistake." He lifts his hands in surrender, still laughing. "You're not jealous of a stripper, and you're not jealous of something that happened in my dream. Which we've already established I'm not guilty of, because I was only pulling your leg, and dream cheating really isn't even a thing anyway."

"It *is*. It's your subconscious giving a not-too-subtle hint that it wants you to stray. And just to clear up any misconception you might be operating under, I'm not saying I look down on strippers. People have to make a living. And I don't think they're slutty, either. Again, the living. If she sleeps with her clients, that's her business. Who am I to judge how a woman makes her money? At least she's not being forced to give it away for free."

"Whoa," says Naz, sobering. "That took a dark turn."

"Sorry."

"Don't be. You can always tell me whatever you're thinking."

We gaze at each other for a moment, until I say, "Okay. Here are some things I'm thinking. Don't look so freaked out."

"Not freaked out. Just listening. Go ahead."

"Are you sure? Because your listening face looks a lot like your freaked-out face."

"I'm sure."

After inspecting his expression for another moment or two, I continue. "I'm thinking it would be helpful if I knew what the plan was, for starters."

"We're headed to Vienna."

"And then?"

"We're gonna check into a hotel near Saint Stephen's Cathedral, where the meeting is taking place. There wasn't enough time to get Connor over here, but we've got half a dozen European assets diverted to work the op."

"What does 'work the op' mean?"

"In a nutshell, assist me with whatever I need."

I look out the plane window, gazing below us into a landscape of fluffy white clouds. They turn dark at the horizon, threatening rain. I try to shake off the little chill of premonition running down my spine and focus. "Why are we taking a plane to Vienna? Why not a helicopter like we did when we left Cozumel?"

"Because now Killian knows I'm associated with Metrix. Which means he probably knows everything else there is to know about the company, including that on short-range ops we almost always get where we're going in birds."

"So he might be tracking all the helicopter traffic into Vienna," I say slowly, thinking of all the other things a spy like him could be tracking, too.

"Correct," says Naz, nodding. "So this flight's off the books in terms of its passenger manifest and was paid for in cash."

"Why did we need the passports, then?"

"So the pilot knew who to expect, and also so anyone who might make it past the first two levels of disinformation would only see a Mr. and Mrs. Kent on their way to London."

I crinkle my brow. "But we're not going to London."

He smiles. "Exactly."

"Sheesh."

"What?"

"This spy business is exhausting."

He motions to the ice bucket. "Champagne?"

"Sure, why not. After all, it's not every day I get to be Mrs. Minerva Kent *not* on my way to London."

A jolt of turbulence makes me suck in a breath and grip the arms of my chair, but Naz ignores it, calmly unwrapping the foil from the cap of the bottle and untwisting the little wire cage thing I can never remember the name of. Then he pulls the cork and fills me a glass.

"You're not having any?" I ask as he hands it to me.

"When all this is done," he says, settling the bottle back into the ice, "we'll have a magnum."

"In France?"

He glances at me. "France?"

I sip my champagne, pleased by its cold, crisp effervescence, by the play of bubbles over my tongue. "I've never been. When this is all over, I'd like to have our magnum of champagne in France. On the Eiffel Tower at sunset, if that could be arranged. With candles and roses, too."

"Anything for you, Minerva. We'll see a plastic surgeon while we're there so he can tell us what can be done to help that hideous face."

His smile is playful, but his eyes are full of darkness. He's more worried than he's letting on.

I guzzle the champagne, then sit with the flute clutched in my hands as if it's a life preserver. Then I attempt to stifle a burp, without much success.

Naz sighs and settles back into his big leather seat. "Such a lady."

"I know. My mother would be so proud. Are you ready for more of my thoughts?" He appears to brace himself, and I produce a nervous laugh. "They're not too alarming. I think."

"Hit me."

"Okay. Um." I fiddle with the stem of the crystal flute, trying to decide how to say something. Then I lift my gaze back up to meet Naz's. "I may or may not have agreed to kiss Killian again."

The only reaction I get is silence, followed by Naz blinking.

Once.

Slowly.

I say, "It sounds worse than it is."

His voice as dry as bone, he replies, "I'm not sure that's possible."

"What I mean is that after he took me to his safe house, he threatened you—vaguely, not specifically or anything—and I said no, I wouldn't kiss him again, but then he made a strange speech about how he and I don't have rules and so we're dangerous animals—or something along those lines, I'm fuzzy about the details—and I can't remember if I agreed or didn't agree.

"I'm telling you now because I just remembered, and also because I wouldn't put it past him to bring it up in the worst, most insinuating way right when you're in the middle of talking about whatever it is you're going to talk about just so he could get the upper hand. The *perceived* upper hand, because he doesn't have any upper hand at all, he's just very good at throwing monkey wrenches into things in order to turn them to his advantage. So . . . that's it."

Naz looks at the ice bucket with champagne on the small table between us. He takes the other crystal flute from its small silver holder, pours himself a glass of champagne, drinks it, then sets the glass back on the table and calmly says, "I really, really, *really* hate that guy's guts."

"I thought it was important that you know."

"It is. Thank you for telling me."

"Are you mad?"

"Not at you, love."

His voice is gentle and his smile is soft, though his eyes are flinty. I have a feeling Killian is going to regret I told Naz about this.

I say, "So after we get to the hotel, what then?"

"Then we execute."

I raise my brows. "Who, Killian?"

"No, the op. Though if that rat bastard somehow ends up dead in a ditch on the side of the road, I won't lose any sleep over it."

"And what about me?"

"What about you?"

"What do I do during the meeting?"

"You'll be safe at the hotel under armed guard."

His eyes are flashing a Do Not Enter warning sign, but I'm going in anyway. "Honey—"

"No."

That was about as unequivocal as a *no* can get, but apparently he doesn't know me well enough yet. More firmly, I say, "Honey."

We stare at each other. He starts to drum his fingers on the table between us, a slow, steady beat that might as well be shouting DO! NOT! ENTER!

"Remember in an earlier conversation when I said you needed to respect my wishes?"

He nods. "Yes. Do you remember in an earlier conversation when I said I needed you to be safe?"

Okay, we're obviously at an impasse. Time to get creative. "What if Killian already knows which hotel we're staying at? What if you leave to attend the meeting . . . and then he shows up at our room?"

A muscle starts to twitch in Naz's jaw. "He doesn't know which hotel we're staying at."

He says it with cold finality, but I can tell he's already thought of the same thing. I'll leave that seed alone for now and let it sprout while I go in a different direction.

"Saint Stephen's Cathedral will be swarming with tourists at noon on a weekday, right?"

I get a wordless nod in response.

"It seems safer for me to be surrounded by other people than alone in a hotel room—"

"Not alone," he interrupts. "With armed guards."

"Uh-huh. As I recall, I was surrounded by armed guards on the way back from the church in Manhattan, too."

I can see how hard he tries not to react to that. His fingers still for a moment, his lips thin, but he recovers. "Ouch. And stop trying to convince me. I can't be convinced. It's bad enough that you're even going as far as you are."

I've met a brick wall of resistance, which is obvious by his tone and the rock hard expression on his face. Too bad for him I brought dynamite with me.

Softly, gazing directly into his eyes, I say, "If you leave me in that hotel room against my wishes, I won't consider it protection. I'll consider it patronizing. And disrespectful. And, worst of all, controlling. I lived for seven years under Dimitri's thumb, and I *deserve* to be there to hear what Killian has to say about him. I know you love me, but I'm not a child, or helpless, or a fool."

He says roughly, "I know you're not!"

"Then don't treat me like I am. Take me with you."

He closes his eyes and lets his head fall back against the seat, muttering, "You're killing me, woman. You're *killing* me here."

I lean forward over the table and grasp his hands. "I'll bet Killian won't talk to you if I don't show. And then all your and Connor's efforts to coordinate this thing will be for nothing."

With his eyes still closed, Naz makes a noise like a whimper low in his throat.

"Sweetie, please look at me."

He inhales, exhales heavily, then lifts his head and opens his eyes.

"You said we were a team," I say, squeezing his hands. "Teams work *together*."

He stares at me in silence, but I can already see him crumbling.

I press, *"Right?"*

He doesn't speak for a long time. He just gazes at our hands joined over the table with his brows drawn together and that muscle jumping in his jaw. Then, almost too low for me to hear, he says, "Right."

I'm so relieved I almost shout. Instead, I lean over and rest my cheek on our joined hands. I whisper, "Thank you."

"Don't thank me yet," he says darkly. "I have conditions."

I lift my head and beam at him, because I already knew he would.

TWENTY-THREE

Naz

Okay, maybe when I said I knew she'd be the death of me, I hadn't realized how *soon* she'd be the death of me. I think I've already had two strokes and a heart attack today, and it's not even lunch.

I mean, I know I'm stubborn. But Eva injects the word *stubborn* with steroids until it's about the size of the Incredible Hulk. I've known pit bulls less determined than her.

She keeps close to my side as we check into the hotel, so at least there's that. If I had to deal with her wanting to wander off on her own to tour the city, I might as well stab myself in the heart and get it over with.

"Nice view," she says from the window of the elegant suite.

"It's not about the view, it's about what's beneath it."

She looks down. "The canal?"

"Water's a good escape route if there's a fire, if streets are blocked with traffic, or if some other threat we can't anticipate occurs. We've got a boat ready if we need it in case anything goes wrong."

She turns and looks at me, her hair backlit in a halo of gold from the hazy light spilling through the gauzy curtains. "How depressing that you have to always be thinking of things like that."

I shrug, walking around our overnight bags where the valet left them on the marble floor in the foyer after I made sure all the rooms were cleared. He didn't even look at me strangely as I made my sweep, just waited patiently for his tip with his hands clasped behind his back while he stared at the ceiling. Maybe he thinks all Americans are some variation of Clint Eastwood or Bruce Willis.

"It's second nature now. Do you need anything to eat? Water? The little fridge in that console by the wet bar will be stocked."

She shakes her head, hugging her arms around her body and looking around the room as if expecting someone to jump out of a closet.

"Hey, Minerva."

She glances at me.

"I already swept the place. We're good."

"I know. It's just . . ."

"Just what?" I ask, my stomach tightening.

"Another strange room. Another strange city."

"C'mere."

I hold out my arms and she comes instantly, folding herself into me with a sigh. I squeeze her and kiss her on top of her head, drawing the sweet scent of her hair into my nose. *Jasmine. How does she always smell like flowers are blooming right under her skin?*

I say, "We'll have a place of our own soon. I promise."

When she wordlessly nods, I know she's homesick for something we've never had, never had a *chance* to have except for those short, stolen days in Cascais.

Fuck, how I wish I were rich. I'd build us an enormous castle on our own private island in the middle of the Caribbean where we could eat, sleep, and make love all day.

Into my chest, she says, "Could we get a dog?"

"Of course. You think I've forgotten about your fetish for wiener dogs? You can get as many as you want."

That earns me a small laugh. She says, "Careful what you promise, cowboy. I've got all twelve names picked out already."

I draw back and stare at her in horror. "*Twelve?* That's not having pets, that's hoarding. And probably illegal."

"Okay, how many can I have, then?"

"Four. One for each kid."

She blinks, her lips parting. "Oh no," she breathes, blinking faster. "You're not going to say one of those things that makes me cry, are you? One of those unbearably sweet, sentimental things you like to drop on me like bombs?"

I brush her hair from her cheeks, take her face in my hands, and murmur, "All girls, if we can manage it. I'd love to have a house full of your Mini-Me's running around laughing your beautiful laugh and smiling at me with your beautiful eyes and wrapping me around their beautiful little pinkie fingers, just like their mommy."

Eva's lower lip quivers. Her eyes fill with water. "You're *ruthless!*" She drops her head to my chest and starts to cry.

I laugh, hugging her, feeling my chest expand with happiness despite all that's yet to be done. "And you're a marshmallow. I've never met such an iron-willed negotiator and general all-around badass who was also such a softie. The contrast is like crack."

My laugh dies in my throat when I think that's probably Killian's exact opinion of her, too.

Eva lifts her red, tearstained face and examines my own. She sniffles, then says, "Don't let him get inside your head. You're Superior Man. Emphasis on *Superior*."

I sweep the water off her cheeks with my thumbs, shaking my head at the power of her intuition. "Can you read everyone's minds like that, or am I the only lucky one?"

Taking a breath and straightening her shoulders, she says, "I learned to read every muscle in a man's face and know with almost perfect accuracy what he's thinking. It doesn't work with women, though. Almost all of us wear careful masks. We pretend to be stupid and passive. It's like a leopard's protective coloring. We adapted to survive."

She stuns me when she does this. When she says these casual, cryptic things that speak to the horror of her life before I knew her and the depth of her intelligence, so painfully self-aware of most things yet blind to its own tragedy.

That she refuses to pity herself is astonishing.

I clasp her against my chest, one arm wrapped around her back and a hand cradling her head, and hold her until my heart slows its jagged beat.

She whispers, "Look who's the marshmallow now."

"Be quiet, Minerva. I was just thinking how much money I'm gonna have to come up with for the plastic surgeon. Might need to take out a loan."

Her shoulders shake with silent laughter.

Then I lift her head and kiss her passionately, putting all my feelings into it, giving her all the love inside me there is to give. She kisses me back, matching my passion.

For one short moment, my fear that we're about to walk hand in hand into hell is quiet.

Then my cell phone rings and the moment is gone.

⌘

The two men following Eva and me as we approach the north entrance to Saint Stephen's Cathedral are big, blond, and much too conspicuous for my taste, though Germans are a common sight in Vienna. It's not their size or gleaming platinum hair that stands out so much as their matching black raincoats, which bulge unnaturally in various places as they walk.

They might as well be wearing signs that scream "We're armed and dangerous and ready to make trouble! Whoopee!"

"Not exactly subtle, are they, our Teutonic Twins?" muses Eva. She's beside me, holding my hand, appearing much calmer than I currently feel.

"Christ. I can hear them clanging from here."

When Connor called to tell me everyone was in place and we'd have an escort over to the cathedral, I had no idea that by "escort" he meant "B movie extras overloaded with weapons who'll stick out like sore thumbs." I hope there aren't any police in the vicinity, or these two bozos will get stopped and searched for sure.

Damn Killian and his last-minute-in-a-different-country meeting demands.

Which of course he knew would be a logistical nightmare for me.

Eva says, "Who?"

"Who what?"

"You just muttered 'prick' under your breath."

"Nobody. Never mind." I squeeze her hand, looking toward the entrance and finding what I'm looking for: another two men in raincoats who look like they're armed and dangerous. They're smoking, lurking in a service doorway and glancing around furtively, shoulders hunched and pacing as they scan the crowd with narrowed eyes.

Because that's not at *all* conspicuous.

"Oh, good. It's amateur hour," I say, shaking my head. No doubt Killian has already made them all.

I weave through the swarms of tourists, holding Eva's hand tightly and keeping her close by my side. The day is bright and clear but cold, with a brisk wind that sends brown leaves skipping over the ancient square. Ahead of us, the huge carved wood doors of the north entrance stand open. There's no queue because fees aren't charged for general entry, so without delay, we head inside.

At the high altar far to our left, mass is being held. A choir sings hymns. The massive organ sends rich notes up to the high vaulted roof, which spreads them in waves over the stone canopy like ripples moving over the surface of water. It smells of incense and candle wax, worn stone and parchment, and a thousand bodies pressed too close.

I feel the presence of the four armed men behind us as I lead Eva farther into the nave, my eyesight quickly adjusting to the dimmer light. Tourists throng the main and side aisles, chattering in clusters near elaborately carved statues, taking picture after picture of priceless wood carvings, gold-leafed paintings, baroque altars, and gothic grates. Ignoring them all, I direct my gaze past the pulpit and a forest of columns and candles toward the opposite wall near the Roman towers, where the Byzantine icon of Saint Mary with the child Jesus is kept.

Called the Pötscher Madonna after the Hungarian shrine of Máriapócs where it was transferred from, it's our destination.

I take a step forward, but Eva's letting go of my hand.

I whip around, expecting danger, but she's merely sinking to one knee, facing the altar, and making the sign of the cross over her chest.

She murmurs something in Russian, crosses herself again, then rises and clasps my outstretched hand. "Sorry," she murmurs. "Habit."

I resist the urge to kiss her and go back to scanning the crowd instead. Slowly approaching from the north down the main aisle of the nave, I spot the shrine. Its elaborate medieval stone baldachin sticks out from the wall and is surrounded by a low wood barrier embellished with scrolled ironwork gates painted gold. The painting itself is elevated above an altar on which white taper candles burn in silver candlesticks. The frame is a network of gold sprays emanating outward, meant to symbolize mystical holy rays.

Over the past day, I've learned more than I ever need to know about this friggin' thing.

Several people sit on the low wood benches in front of the altar, but none of them are Killian. My heart thumping, I scan the crowd and the entire area, but don't catch a glimpse of him.

Until Eva says, "There he is," and points.

Leaning casually against a carved limestone column off to the right of the altar, Killian is almost unrecognizable. He's in a suit, of all fucking things, a ritzy-looking black suit, with a white dress shirt open at the collar and a pair of black leather shoes so polished they're reflecting random rays of light like mirrored glasses.

"He cut his hair," I note, regarding him with disdain.

"And shaved," says Eva. "He looks ready for a date."

I'm gonna put a bullet through both of his eyes.

I know there are two more men somewhere out of sight that Connor has installed, but I don't bother trying to spot them because I'm too busy glaring at Killian, who utterly ignores me as we approach. He's too busy looking at Eva.

His eyes drink her in the way a desert drinks rain.

We stop three feet in front of him. I snap, "Is that a gun in your pocket, or are you just happy to see me?"

"Bhrèagha," he murmurs, still staring hard at Eva. "You came."

It sounds like a sexual innuendo, which—as I'm sure he intended—sets every nerve I own on edge. "You don't speak to her," I say, loudly enough that it echoes off the walls and several tourists turn to look.

He flicks a cool glance in my direction and looks me up and down. Then, sounding disappointed, he says, "You're taller than I expected."

If I were a peacock and had plumage, my feathers would snap out and shimmy all over the place right now. "I'm exactly the same height as you are."

"I know. You sounded shorter on the phone."

We take the measure of each other while Eva softly sighs.

"Is this going to go on for long, boys? Don't we have some important stuff to discuss?"

Killian shifts his eyes in her direction, and I'm already sick of watching them melt like butter. He says, "Aye, *bhrèagha,* we do. But you know us men. Just have to swing from the branches a bit before we can get down to business."

193

I say between clenched teeth, "Whatever that pet name is that you're calling her, if you say it again, I'll rip your intestines out through your nostrils."

Eva squeezes my hand. "It just means 'witch,' honey. He's calling me a mouthy witch."

When Killian smiles at me, I bristle like a porcupine, a low growl crawling up my throat.

We both know it doesn't mean *witch*.

"Hey." Eva yanks on my hand, and I turn and look down at her. She's regarding me with an exasperated expression.

"I love you. Now cut it out."

Killian drawls, "Aye, Naz. Cut it out."

I slice my gaze at Killian, ready to rip out his tongue, but Eva snaps at him, "You too, idiot! Enough of this! If you bait him again, I'm leaving!"

I try so hard not to smile, I swear to God I do. But my lips curve up of their own will, and I stand there smirking at him in his new haircut and his dumb shiny shoes looking like a puppy that just got spanked on its butt with a rolled-up newspaper.

"Now *talk*," says Eva firmly, looking back and forth between us. "Like grown-ups, please. Killian, you go first. And let's get right to the important stuff: What's Dimitri got that you kidnapped me for?"

He pushes away from the column, straightens his cuff links, then looks me dead in the eye.

"A nuke," he says. "What else?"

My stomach drops down to my toes.

Dimitri has a nuclear weapon.

Because of course he would.

Fuck.

TWENTY-FOUR

Eva

"A nuke," Killian said, and just like that, everything comes together.

"I think I'm going to be sick." Breathless with shock, I drop Naz's hand and sink onto the end of the nearest wood bench, my hands shaking, my stomach in knots.

How did I not see this coming? How could I not have guessed?

"Breathe, sweetheart."

Naz is instantly by my side, kneeling down next to me and squeezing my leg. I'm too shaken to respond. He stands abruptly when Killian approaches, his big shiny loafers moving into my peripheral vision, then stopping short, as if forced to.

"Stay the fuck back," says Naz, his voice low and controlled but filled with fury.

"Get your hand off me, mate, or lose it."

Killian's voice is equally low and controlled, but he's obviously angry, too.

Staring blindly at the floor, I say, "Venezuela."

That shuts them both up, until Killian sighs. "Aye."

Naz says, "Somebody wanna tell me what this has to do with Venezuela?"

I look up at him, at his handsome face, his jaw so tight with stress and his expression a mixture of anger and confusion. "In the past two years, Dimitri had three visits with emissaries from the president of Venezuela. I don't speak Spanish, so I don't know precisely what was said, but they seemed very interested in what Dimitri had done for Syria with the dirty bombs. The Syrian president's name was mentioned more than once. So was the US president's."

Naz frowns. "The US threatened Venezuela with military action because of their human rights violations and economic mismanagement. There were sanctions, as I recall."

"And a good bit of saber rattling on both sides," cuts in Killian. "Which is also when the Venezuelan president got wind of the possibility that the US wanted to orchestrate a covert regime change." His tone drops, gaining an odd edge. "You know . . . as they do."

Naz and Killian stare at each other, but this time it's not quite as hostile. There's a quality to their frank gazes that speaks of some kind of mutual understanding, though I have no idea what it might be.

Naz says, "I see you've done your research on me."

Killian says, "You've led one hell of an interesting life."

Naz narrows his eyes, waiting for a cutting remark to follow, but there isn't one.

It seems to confuse him.

I say, "I hate to interrupt this nice moment of camaraderie, boys, but you've lost me."

Like quicksilver, calculation flashes back into Killian's eyes. "Don't tell me you haven't told Eva about your father, Nasir. Considering he's such a legend in the industry."

When Naz remains silent, a flush of red creeping up his neck, Killian smiles. "*Tch.* I thought you two didn't keep secrets?"

I jolt to my feet just as Naz takes a stiff step toward Killian and insert myself between the two chest-beating apes. I flatten my hand on Naz's chest, then turn and look up at Killian.

"We don't keep secrets."

Killian says with faux innocence, "Except for the part when he was lying to you about why he was on Cozumel, you mean."

If a body could turn to stone, Naz's does. He stiffens under my palm, his energy crackling with violence but his flesh as still and unyielding as rock.

"That's just shitty of you, Killian," I say calmly, "and, quite frankly, juvenile. Grow up. And don't you dare try that scowl on me because you already know I'm not scared of you. Now go stand over there next to the nice old lady in the red scarf and give us a minute."

When he doesn't move, I say more firmly, "Go. Don't make me ask you twice."

He snorts, knowing I'm throwing his own threat from when we were on the *Silver Shadow* back in his face. But he obeys me, shoving his hands into the pockets of his expensive suit trousers as if to keep them from curling around Naz's neck. Then he strolls away to a safer distance on the other side of the row of benches. Once there, he starts to chat up the elderly woman in the red scarf, who appears dazzled by the attention.

I turn back to Naz. "Honey. Hey, you up there. Got a second?"

His eyes tracking Killian's movements like lasers on the sights of a rifle, Naz says, "Yep."

"Could you focus down here? This will just take a minute."

His burning black gaze slashes down to mine. I say, "Hi, handsome."

He takes a slow, deep breath through his nose.

"Yes, just breathe. And while you're busy breathing, listen. Are you listening?"

He makes a sound like a bear disturbed from his winter hibernation.

"I told you this would happen. I also told you not to let him get under your skin. Everything he says and does is calculated to knock you off center. He's just playing chess with you, but you've already captured the queen. And hey—spoiler! *You're* the king. Don't let a pawn kick you off stride. Superior Man stays above the fray. Now get your game face on, honey, and let's do this."

For a long moment, he simply stares at me, his expression turning from rage to wonder. Then he cups my face in his hands.

"I must've done something truly incredible in a previous life to deserve you." He gently presses his lips to mine, his kiss so tender it's breathtaking.

Against his mouth, I say, "Oh . . . do you believe in reincarnation? That's fun. In my faith, we only have heaven, which seems really boring when you consider only the 'good' people are there. Who wants to spend eternity knitting doilies with nuns?"

There's a beat of silence as we stare at each other, then we smile and touch lips again.

Behind me, I hear a disgusted groan. Killian calls out, "Jesus, Mary, and Joseph, get a room!"

Naz chuckles. "I think I just figured out how to get under *his* skin."

He gives me another kiss, this one deeper. When we come up for air, a hard voice to our right says, "And you call *me* juvenile."

It's Killian, standing not three feet away, glaring at us from under lowered brows.

For the first time since this meeting began, Naz relaxes. He winds his arm around my shoulders, tucks me against his side, and smiles. "Oh, that's the least worst thing she's called you."

Killian shoots Naz a hostile glance, then looks back at me, his gaze searching. Then he spins on his heel and walks several feet away, running a hand over his hair. When he turns back a few moments later, his face is wiped clean of emotion.

All business, he approaches us again. "We discovered the president of Venezuela had made a deal with Dimitri to obtain a UR-100 warhead and have it delivered to him via cargo ship—"

"We?" interrupts Naz. "Who exactly do you work for?"

Killian waves a hand impatiently in the air. "You know I can't answer that. As I was saying—"

"The UR-100 was decommissioned by the Soviet Union in the late nineties," Naz says, interrupting Killian again.

Killian's jaws clamp together. He pauses a beat, as if to control himself, then says mildly, "Allegedly. May I continue?"

"Sure."

"Thank you."

"You're welcome."

Killian has to take another beat to compose himself, and now Naz is smiling wider.

Men.

"Dimitri has deep ties with the Russian Federal Security Service and the military. Money changed hands. He got hold of the warhead. He made arrangements for it to be shipped to Venezuela. Before it could be, however, a phone call was intercepted between Dimitri and our friend Raphael Bergé, who has long been a subject of surveillance by my people."

Naz says, "Whoever they are."

This time, Killian ignores him. "Raphael wasn't quite as scrupulous as Dimitri is in making sure his communications were secure. In the phone call, Dimitri instructed Raphael to make a detour from his current heading toward Halifax to pick up a passenger in New York." He glances at me. "I'm sure you can guess who."

"So that's when you entered the picture." I remember the night we met aboard the *Silver Shadow* and go cold all over.

"Correct." He pauses, gazing at me. When he speaks again, his voice has a new, husky tone, echoing with apology. "I thought you were his wife."

"Apparently, he tells everyone that," says Naz, sounding irritated.

Killian shakes his head. "No, Eva—I mean his wife and accomplice."

"I know what you mean." When I sigh, Killian swallows. His eyes start to burn.

Into the silence that follows, Naz calmly says, "If you reach out that hand and touch her, my friend, it will be the last thing you ever do."

The sounds of the cathedral suddenly seem very loud. Voices and music echo off the soaring limestone walls. Every footstep sounds like gunfire.

I say quietly, "We do what we think is right with whatever knowledge we have at the time. Honestly, Killian, if I were in your shoes and I had a chance to stop Dimitri from selling a nuclear weapon to a power-crazed tyrant, I probably would've—"

"Don't forgive him," cuts in Naz, his voice hard.

Killian murmurs, "Please do."

We stand in tense silence, Naz glaring at Killian, Killian gazing at me, and me in the middle, feeling all sorts of awkward.

Finally, I look at Killian and say, "I'll make you a deal."

"Name it" is his instant reply. It comes at the same time Naz growls, "No deals!"

"If you promise to behave yourself, I'll forgive you." I send a meaningful glance in Naz's direction. "And you know what I mean by 'behave.'"

Naz is appalled. "Don't forgive this bastard for *my* sake."

"Honey."

"I'm serious! *He hit you.*"

"Sweetie."

"You were covered in bruises! You could've died!"

I look at Killian, standing there saying nothing in his defense. "So? Do you promise?"

"Aye," he says, his voice thick. "I promise."

"Then I forgive you. But if you screw up, I'll revoke my forgiveness and you won't get another chance."

Naz groans, Killian smiles, and far up overhead in the tall Romanesque towers, bells begin to peal.

I look up and see a covey of doves flash through hazy beams of sunlight, their pale wings leaving whorls of dust motes in the air. "Oh, good. God approves of this plan. Now we can all get to work."

Killian says to Naz, "Does this mean you'll call off your goon squad? There are six of them, correct? Interesting fellows. A tad obvious, but they look competent. Germans always are."

Naz says sourly, "They're not the usual crew."

"I understand. I didn't give you much time to prepare for the meeting."

Naz squints at him suspiciously, but Killian is acting like a perfect gentleman.

For now. I better take advantage of it. "What have you told Dimitri? About me, I mean? Where does he think I am?"

"I've been stalling him. He thinks I'm holding you somewhere until you're well enough to be transferred."

"Did you tell him I was sick?"

Uncharacteristically hesitant, Killian shifts his weight from one foot to another. "I sent him . . . some footage of you."

I blink, taken aback. "Footage?"

Deadly soft, Naz repeats, *"Footage?"*

"When you passed out after I pulled you from the ocean—"

"What the hell?" Naz cuts in, his jaw tight.

I have to explain before a fight breaks out. "I jumped overboard. Killian saved me from drowning. Then I blacked out from exhaustion and the infection. What footage did you send him, Killian?"

Gazing warily at Naz, he says, "Video of you, uh, unconscious."

He displays a great deal of intelligence by not adding *and naked.*

Because yes, I remember waking from a fevered dream to find myself not only bruised but nude, with a balled-up washcloth near my feet that Killian may or may not have used to sponge sweat from my burning body.

My naked burning body.

This is so bad.

I try to keep my voice calm, though my cheeks have started to heat and my stomach is flipping. "I see. And his reaction?"

"I'd describe his reaction as ballistic. No pun intended."

Naz's arm around my shoulders has tightened to the point of becoming uncomfortable. I nudge him in the ribs. He exhales invisible plumes of fire, but immediately relaxes his grip.

"Sorry, sweetheart. Just trying not to have my third heart attack of the day."

"I hear you. This is all sorts of weird. Are you okay?"

He turns a warm gaze on me. "Don't worry about me. I'm good. Are *you* okay?"

"As long as you're okay, I'm okay."

Killian muses, "Keeping that promise is going to be much harder than I thought."

Looking into my eyes, Naz smiles.

I say, "Back to Dimitri."

"Dimitri," says Killian, "is expecting to meet me in Prague next week to exchange you for the warhead."

Naz asks, "Why Prague?"

"It's my favorite city."

When Naz and I stare at him, nonplussed, Killian says, "The architecture is truly magnificent. And, for my money, the churches are some of the most beautiful in the world." He smiles at me. "Have you been?"

"No."

He turns his attention to Naz. "You should take her to Saint Vitus Cathedral at Prague Castle. It's a Gothic masterpiece."

"Sure," says Naz drily. "We'll put that on the itinerary, right after divesting Dimitri of his nuke and lopping off his head."

"Saving the world shouldn't mean you have to skip the sights. I once had to do a black bag job in the pope's personal apartments at the Apostolic Palace, then took in a guided tour of the Vatican afterward."

That intrigues me. "So when you're not out spying on, kidnapping, or murdering people, you enjoy visiting churches. Odd for a man who doesn't believe in God."

He shrugs. "Architecture of the Gothic and Romanesque periods is one of my passions."

Naz makes a face. "Who *are* you?"

"No one of importance."

Naz rolls his eyes and mutters, "Oh, humility, too. That's just grand."

"I'm simply doing my job."

"Which is what, by the way?" I ask.

Naz deadpans, "If you say 'saving the world' again, I'll punch you right in the face."

After a moment's thought, Killian says, "Whatever's necessary. And what's necessary now is for us to come to an agreement about how we're going to handle Dimitri." He looks at Naz. "Eva's the key to the whole operation. Without her, Venezuela gets their nuke and wipes out Florida." He pauses. "No one much likes Florida, but that kind of thing would tend to get the US government a little riled up."

I look at Naz. "No doubt the response would be swift and deadly."

Killian adds, "If Venezuela targeted Miami, there would be nearly two million killed outright, not to mention how many millions more would soon die of radiation poisoning and other injuries."

Horrified afresh by those statistics, I insist, "We *cannot* allow that to happen!"

Naz looks back and forth between us, finally settling his narrowed gaze on Killian. "You said Eva's the key to the whole operation."

"I did."

"So what was your thinking when you dropped her off at the safe house on Angra do Heroísmo?"

"My thinking?"

"You must've had a backup plan, for fuck's sake! You kidnapped her, then decided that wasn't such a good idea after all, then left her at your safe house for me to pick up. How were you gonna convince Dimitri to trade the nuke without her?"

Killian stands still for a moment, simply looking at him.

Then Naz groans. "Fuck."

Confused, I ask, "What?"

"This asshole was never gonna continue the op without you."

"Why not?"

"Because he knew he wouldn't have to!"

"I'm lost here, guys. Would someone care to explain?"

Very gently, Killian does. "There's nothing you two won't do for each other, Eva. Love has made you strong, but also incredibly predictable."

It dawns over me slowly, like sunrise over a ridge. "You knew I'd convince him to let me be involved."

He spreads his hands apologetically. "Better a willing participant than an unwilling one." He looks at Naz. "Or two. Once I discovered who you were and worked for, I knew I couldn't risk having you show up unexpectedly down the line. There was too much riding on my success . . . and for me to be successful, I needed to deal with you."

I say, "But you'd already kidnapped me. You could've completed the trade without having to drop me off at the safe house, or take me to get medical attention, or anything. You didn't have to delay because I was sick!"

When Killian simply stares at me without responding, Naz grinds his teeth. "Yes, he did."

I throw my hands in the air. "Why?"

Naz mutters, "Because he's the *worst*, that's why." To Killian, he says, "And I want that video footage of Eva and any copies you made. *Today*."

With a perfectly straight face, Killian says, "I already destroyed everything."

We all know he's lying.

As the two men engage in a stare-off so charged with dislike it could make the cathedral explode into a fireball around us, I say, "Well, this should be fun."

TWENTY-FIVE

Naz

Oh, the irony. The man I'd like to kill with my bare hands for harming the woman I love is the same man who saved her life—twice, apparently—and promised to be nice to me on her request.

And is also obviously in love with her himself.

There's so much to hate this guy for I don't have enough fingers to count all the reasons.

"Let's get something clear before we go any further," I say to Killian, willing myself to remain calm. "I don't trust you. I don't like anything about you, and the fact that you got Eva necessary medical care is the only reason—and I mean *only*—that you're not lying in a pool of your own blood right now."

Killian is undisturbed by my scathing tone. "What about the fact that I didn't deliver her to Dimitri like I intended? That should earn me some bonus points, no?"

"Yes, and thank you," says Eva, squeezing my arm as she sends me a sideways look that says *Rein that horse in, cowboy.* "And now let's talk next steps."

His eyes warm as he gazes at her. "Always cutting straight to the chase and thinking ahead. You would've made a good military strategist."

She says darkly, "Living under the constant threat of violence has a way of paring things down to their bare bones."

Both Killian and I are stopped short for a moment by that statement, uttered with such unnerving pathos neither one of us knows how to respond.

A crowd of tourists chattering in Chinese pushes past us toward the Pötscher Madonna, oblivious to the far more interesting drama playing out right under their noses. The three of us are silent for a moment as they pass, then Eva says, "Speaking of thinking ahead, you can't be certain Dimitri doesn't already know what you're up to."

Killian lifts his brows. "Do I seem new at this to you?"

She stares at him with a strange look, one I've never seen before, a kind of world-weary hardness in her eyes. "Don't ever underestimate the devil."

Killian glances at me, frowning.

I say, "She's right. His connections are vast, but it's his cunning that's truly limitless. He enjoys playing games with his enemies. Spinning webs you don't see until you're helplessly entangled. Whatever measures you're taking to conceal your whereabouts and your plans, triple them."

"No one knows of my whereabouts or plans" is the confident response.

"Not even your people?"

"They know the desired outcome, nothing more."

"Still," says Eva, "take Naz's advice. Dimitri didn't get where he is by allowing surprises. If you think I've got the mind of a strategist, his is like a Stradivarius." She closes her eyes, draws a breath, and murmurs, "An instrument of evil, perfectly in tune."

It's fucking awful, standing there watching Killian fight himself not to reach out and touch Eva while at the same time fighting myself not to give him a hard shove and watch him stagger back. How we're gonna be able to work together, I don't know.

I say abruptly, "This isn't gonna work."

Eva opens her eyes and stares up at me. "What, honey?"

"This collaboration. I can't trust myself not to accidentally push this fucker into traffic."

Killian says mildly, "And here I thought we were finally getting along."

"If you'd stop looking at her like she's a juicy hot steak sizzling on a buttery plate and you've been wandering out in the wilderness with nothing to eat for years, we might not have this problem!"

He smiles. "What a vivid imagination. That's quite the picture you painted. My mouth is watering." He sends Eva a half-lidded look. "I can almost taste the juice on that steak."

She warns, "Killian."

He holds up his hands. "I know. I promised. This is me being good." He glances in my direction. "Apologies."

"Not accepted."

"Aw, now you've gone and hurt my feelings."

"Your feelings aren't the only thing about to get hurt."

"Careful, Nasir. I don't do well with threats."

"Do you do well with bullet holes? Because you're about to be riddled with them."

After another moment of Killian and me glaring at each other, Eva sighs. "You're right. This is a bad idea. I'll take care of Dimitri myself."

She's startled us both, because we turn to her with identical expressions of shock.

"Oh, don't look so surprised," she says, irritated. "There's a nuclear weapon somewhere out there and all you two are interested in is your pissing contest."

Killian was right about one thing: Eva sure knows how to cut to the chase.

Fuck. This crow I'm about to eat is really gonna taste like shit. "You've got a good point, sweetheart. All right, Killian. Apology accepted. Now I'm offering mine." I stick out my hand. "Truce."

He looks at my hand with faint distaste. After a moment's hesitation, he takes it, and we shake.

Then Eva says, "Good. Now can we please go somewhere quiet to finish this conversation? I need to sit down."

I look at her sharply. Two spots of color stain her cheeks, and her skin is damp around her hairline. "Are you all right? How do you feel?"

She looks up at me and smiles. "Strong as an ox." Then her eyes roll back in her head and her knees give out.

I catch her just before she crashes to the floor.

⌘

"I'm okay. Honestly, guys. Please stop hovering, you're making me nervous."

"*You're* nervous? How do you think we feel?"

I try not to be irritated that Killian included us both in that question, but decide it's not how I feel but how I react that's important. The last thing Eva needs right now is the two of us at each other's throats again, so I ignore him and focus on her.

"Do you need more water, sweetheart?"

Eva smiles at me. She's sitting on a wood bench with Killian on one side and me on the other, both of us leaning in.

"No. I'm not finished with this cup you brought me." She pauses, thinking. "You didn't scoop it out of the stone font over near that door, did you?"

"It's not holy water, I promise."

Killian asks, "Is this the first time you've fainted?"

Eva sounds annoyed. "I didn't *faint*. I simply felt a little dizzy."

"Are you having any other problems? With your balance, shortness of breath, anything like that?"

She looks at him in alarm. "No. Why?"

He flicks me a dark look. "Endocarditis can have some nasty side effects."

"Her blood work's good," I say. "White cell count is back to normal. No more signs of infection."

Eva says drily, "It's probably just all the free-floating testosterone interfering with my normal brain function. Let's go outside so I can get some fresh air."

"Or we could go back to your suite at the Hilton Riverfront," suggests Killian.

Eva sends me a pointed look. I glare at Killian in outrage and demand, "How did you know where we're staying?"

He pauses a beat. "I could tell you, but then I'd have to kill you."

Eva rolls her eyes and sighs. "Here we go."

Killian says, "Sorry. Bad joke. I installed a custom facial-recognition software program to crawl the security feeds of all the major hotels in the area."

Eva and I stare at him. I hate to admit it, but we're both impressed. I say, "Huh."

Killian says, "I know. I'm amazing."

Smiling, Eva says, "Oh, look, honey, he's starting to take after you."

The bastard looks at me and pulls his lips between his teeth, trying to suppress what's sure to be a shit-eating grin.

God, I really fucking hate this guy. "Just out of curiosity, why would you need to know where we're staying?"

"In case anything happens to you."

Eva looks confused by that cryptic statement, pulling her brows together into a frown, but I know exactly what he means. I hear the unspoken part of the sentence loud and clear, the slight emphasis on the word *you*, and understand with startling clarity that it's not a threat to me . . . it's an offer of support for her.

If anything happens to me, he'll step in and protect her.

I wait for the fury to crawl its way up my throat. Instead of fury, I feel a strange new emotion toward Killian, one that only moments ago I would've dismissed as impossible.

Gratitude.

Though I can't stand him, and I definitely don't trust his motives, he might be the only other man in the world she'd be safe with aside from me.

I still have to force the words from my mouth. Through gritted teeth, I say, "Thank you."

He examines my expression in silence, then simply nods.

Looking back and forth between us, Eva wrinkles her nose. "Lord, you two are strange."

Then a true miracle occurs: Killian and I smile at each other.

Maybe I can trust myself not to push him into traffic after all.

Maybe.

⁓

We don't go back to our hotel. We go to a quiet café on a side street a few blocks from the cathedral and sit at a table in a corner near a window, facing the street.

Killian orders espresso. I order Eva food. The three of us are silent until the waitress returns with Eva's vegetable soup and Killian's inky-black espresso, served in a tiny porcelain cup that somehow looks elegant, not ridiculous, in his huge hand.

I wish his parents had never met.

Killian and I watch Eva eat until she says between spoonfuls, "Anytime you two would like to stop staring at me and start talking, that would be great."

"How's the soup?" I say, instead of asking her for the hundredth time how she feels.

She glances up at me, her smile indulgent. "It's delicious, honey, and also I'm doing perfectly well. Stop worrying."

Killian says, "In case anyone's wondering, my espresso is delicious, too. Should we order a round for the goon squad?"

Following his gaze, I look out the window. Sure enough, there they are, hiding in plain sight, six glowering Germans in black raincoats lurking around corners like a bunch of rejects from a World War II documentary about the SS.

I say drily, "I'm afraid if we sent the waitress out, they'd open fire."

Killian observes, "They do look a bit jumpy."

Eva says, "Should I go out and tell them to go away?"

I frown. "No. Why would you?"

"Because I'm the only one at this table who speaks German."

I look sharply at Killian, wondering how she knows what languages he speaks, but he's suddenly very interested in examining his fingernails.

And now I want to kill him all over again.

To manage my impulse to drive a fork into his eye, I say, "Let's talk logistics. Tell me about the meet with Dimitri. What've you set up?"

"We're meeting at the Charles Bridge at midnight next Tuesday. It's a pedestrian-only bridge that crosses the Vltava River. I'll be at the east end, he'll be at the west. When he sees Eva alive and well, he'll send the coordinates for the location where the weapon is being kept."

I ask, "Send? How? To whom?"

"He'll give the information to the intermediary I'll bring with me to the meeting."

"And who's that?"

Killian stares at me with a level gaze, waiting for me to catch up.

After the light bulb goes on inside my thick skull, I say, "Just so you know, I've never been this predictable before."

He smiles, but it's not mocking or unfriendly, just understanding. "I believe you."

211

"Seriously, I'm not trying to brag or anything, but I'm extremely good at what I do."

"I know. It's not your fault. She has no idea how completely she can cross a man's wires."

Eva chimes in. "Wait, what are you talking about?"

At the same time, Killian and I say, "Nothing."

She looks back and forth between us, then mutters to her soup bowl, "Men."

"How will you verify the coordinates and get the weapon?"

Killian finishes his espresso, sets the tiny porcelain cup onto the table, then leans back into his chair. "You'll call a number I'll give you and provide the information from Dimitri to the person who answers. That person will, in turn, send assets to the location and retrieve the weapon."

It's obvious he won't answer questions relating to who that person might be, but that's not of great importance anyway. Something else is. "Dimitri will have snipers all over the area. The minute he sees Eva, he'll shoot us both. We'll be walking into a trap."

"I've already got my own snipers in place and surveillance set up. Whatever he does to prepare, I'll know about it, and it will be dealt with."

"A week out? You've got people in place a week out?"

Killian adopts a humble expression. "One can never be too careful."

"You said no one knew of your plans, only the desired outcome. If you've already got assets in place—"

"Freelancers," he interrupts, nodding. "None of whom know each other, who I work for, or who the target is, other than from a photo that will be provided to them moments before Dimitri arrives."

I drum my fingers on the table, thinking. "It could take hours, maybe days, to get your people to verify the whereabouts of the weapon. What if it's sitting in a cargo container on a dock in Tripoli?"

With total confidence, Killian answers. "My people can be any-where on earth within thirty minutes."

That makes me scoff. "Really? You've got assets in Antarctica? Who, penguins and fucking whales?"

His look sours. "I can't decide which is worse, your hostility, your language, or your sarcasm."

"Don't avoid the question."

"Aye," he says drily. "We've got trained penguins on the payroll. They're much smarter than you'd think."

With the air of an exhausted mother of toddlers, Eva says, "Boys. Play nice."

I lean back in my chair and fold my arms over my chest. Then I pronounce, "I don't like this plan."

Killian pinches the bridge of his nose between his fingers and sighs.

I insist, "Dimitri should provide you the location of the weapon *before* you produce Eva, not after. Even a delay of thirty minutes while we sit there exposed on the bridge is *way* too long a span of time. Too much can go wrong."

"And what happens once you get the weapon?" asks Eva. "He'll for sure have people watching to confirm you've located it. You won't be able to stall him."

"Oh, he'll be dead long before then."

Eva and I blink at Killian. I say, "Come again?"

"As soon as he gives you the coordinates, he gets a bullet through the brain."

I stare at him in disbelief. "You have to verify that he gives you the *right* coordinates. He could send you off on some wild-goose chase and, in the meantime, swarm the bridge with his men!"

Killian glances at Eva, then looks back at me. In a low voice, he says, "Would you risk it? Because I know I wouldn't."

He means would I risk providing incorrect intel when Eva's safety was on the line. I say through clenched jaws, "We're not Dimitri. We can't predict what he'll do."

"Maybe you two can't, but I can." Finished with her soup, Eva pats her lips with her napkin.

Killian says, "And?"

She looks at him, then at me. "Whatever you think he's going to do, you'll be wrong."

"I spoke to him," says Killian. "He couldn't hide what was in his voice. You're more important to him than that weapon."

Her smile is faint and holds a trace of gentle disdain. "There's something far more important to him than me, or that weapon, or anything else."

I prompt, "Such as?"

She turns her gaze to me. What I see in it gives me chills.

She says, "Control. It's what he's best at. It's his gift. He'll let you think you're winning, he'll even let you gain the upper hand . . . but only because it's ultimately advantageous to him. If you want to prevail in a game against Dimitri, you have to stop thinking you can outsmart him. He's already three steps ahead."

No one speaks for a long time after that, until I say, "So what do you suggest?"

"I suggest we prepare for what will actually happen at this meeting."

Killian and I lean in over the table. He says, "Which is?"

Her answer is chillingly simple.

"War."

TWENTY-SIX

Eva

I can tell by the expressions on their faces that they don't want to believe me, but they do.

It's a step in the right direction, but my stomach is turning and I'm feeling worse than I let on, so I ask if we can continue the discussion later.

I should've known that would make these two tigers pounce.

"Why?" says Naz, jerking upright. "What's wrong?"

"Are you ill?" asks Killian, going tense.

"I'm tired," I answer, avoiding both sets of searching eyes. "Don't overreact."

"Eva—"

"I just need to close my eyes for a while, honey," I say, resting my hand over Naz's. "I didn't sleep well last night, I didn't eat breakfast this morning, and Killian's news gave me a bit of a shock. You two can keep talking back at the hotel."

Naz says drily, "We're not going back to that hotel."

Killian spreads his hands open. "Come on. You still don't trust me? We shook hands!"

"Please don't make me stab you with this fork."

Killian looks at me. "I'm making an effort here, just so you know."

"I'll give you a gold star on your report card."

I rise from my chair. The two of them jolt to their feet, startling the waitress, who's just arrived with our check. "Someone please pay this poor woman," I say, waving my hand at her. "And dial down the machismo a few thousand notches while you're at it. People are looking at us like they think a duel is about to break out."

I don't bother waiting for an answer before I turn and head toward the door. There's some kind of commotion behind me, the sound of shuffling feet and chairs skidding over wood, but I keep right on walking until I've pushed through the front door and am out on the sidewalk, sucking in a bracing lungful of cold air.

Naz and Killian silently materialize beside me, one on either side, like hulking bookends.

Looking at one of the trench coat–wearing Germans loitering across the street, Naz says, "How do I get hold of you?"

Killian fishes inside his suit jacket, producing a crisp white business card. He holds it out to Naz between two fingers. Naz takes it and gives it a once-over with a cocked brow.

"A toll-free number?"

Killian nods. "It's international. Leave a voice mail and I'll be contacted immediately, wherever I am." He slants a look over my head at Naz. "Even in Antarctica."

Naz stares at the card as if he's about to stuff it into his mouth, chew it to a pulp, and spit it onto the sidewalk. I snatch it from his fingers and shove it into the back pocket of my jeans.

I say, "Thank you. We'll call you in a few hours and arrange for somewhere else to meet. Naz's choice this time, so we don't have to drag along Captain Obvious and the Standouts."

I nod toward the Germans, who have now clustered like a school of piranha beneath the awning of a dry cleaner down the block and are staring at us with narrowed eyes as pedestrians scurry by, giving them a wide berth. "In the meantime, I expect you two to think nice thoughts about each other."

Killian says innocently, "It might not seem like it, Eva, but I happen to have a very high opinion of your man."

Naz makes a retching noise. "Oh, for fuck's sake."

"You think I give just anyone my phone number?"

"Stop. You'll make me blush."

"There's no need to be sarcastic. I'm only speaking the truth."

"Sure. And I'm Dolly Parton."

"Hmm. You're less busty in person than I would've thought."

As they share a gaze of mutual dislike, I look back and forth between them and get the sense that underneath all the barbs and posturing, they're enjoying themselves.

Not that either of them would ever admit it.

"Goodbye, Killian."

He turns to me and smiles. "Goodbye, Eva. I'd kiss your hand, but I'm rather fond of my head. I don't want it to go rolling off down the street by itself."

Naz laughs. "Don't be ridiculous. Cutting off your head would be way too much work. I'd just shoot you ten or twelve times. Then reload."

I shake my head, trying not to laugh because I don't want to encourage them.

Killian glances at Naz. They do one of those chin-jerk things dudes do to each other, then Killian spins around and strides away down the street.

Watching him go, Naz pulls me closer to his side. "Let's find an internet café."

"Why?"

His eyes slightly narrow. "I wasn't kidding when I said we weren't going to stay at our hotel."

We take a taxi to pick up our bags from the Hilton, then go to a nearby internet café. Using a prepaid anonymous debit card over a secured Wi-Fi connection, Naz books us an apartment through Airbnb in the second district, only a short walk from the subway. It's modern, charming, and directly above another apartment that has a small yard with a huge angry dog that barks furiously at anyone who passes by on the street.

"Built-in security," Naz explains, staring down at the dog from the balcony. As we watch, it terrifies a mother pushing a stroller past the wrought-iron fence with a demonstration of vicious snarling while body-slamming itself over and over into the fence, apparently hoping to devour the woman's infant.

"What do they feed that poor creature?" I wonder aloud. "Kittens and razor blades?"

"The reviews said the apartment was great but the dog was a nightmare, so here we are."

He goes inside and removes his coat, pulling various weapons from pockets and holsters and depositing them onto the stand beside the television. I count three guns and half a dozen knives before he's finished.

"Wow. You're a walking arsenal."

He turns and smiles at me as I walk inside, closing the balcony doors behind me. "And I haven't even taken off my shoes yet."

Alarmed, I look down at his big black combat boots. "Is that where the machine guns go?"

Naz drawls, "Are you saying I have big feet, sweetheart? Because, you know, a man with big feet usually has a big . . ."

Into his dramatic pause, I say, "Ego. I've become very aware."

He comes to me and pulls me into his embrace. I wrap my arms around his big, solid body and exhale in relief. "I have to admit, the meeting with Killian went better than I expected it would."

"Even with all our bitching at each other?"

I smile, snuggling closer. "No one was injured. I'm counting it as a win."

"What d'you think of his plan?"

Surprised and pleased that he's asking my opinion on such a touchy subject, I pull back and look up into his face. "Honestly? I think it's as holey as Swiss cheese."

He smooths my hair off my face and presses a soft kiss to my lips. "Me too."

I chuckle. "Try not to sound too smug there, Mr. Kent."

"It's hard not to be. I knew I had a lot of faults. I'm just really disappointed to discover envy is one of them."

"Honey," I say softly, stunned by that unexpected admission, "you have nothing to be envious of. He's not in the same league as you. He's not even in the same solar system."

He pretends to be coy, lowering his lashes and pursing his lips. "Oh stop. Stop it some more."

I wind my arms around his neck, go up on my toes, and kiss him. "Are you fishing for compliments, Mr. Kent?"

"Yes, Minerva," he says gruffly, squeezing me tightly, his eyes liquid heat. "I need you to remind me what such a hideous crone as yourself wants with the likes of me."

I rub my chest against his. "Or I could just show you."

"I thought you were tired."

I whisper, "I'm never too tired for you," and kiss him again, this time deeper.

He fists a hand into my hair at the scruff of my neck and makes a noise of pleasure low in his throat, holding me hard against his body in that way he does that makes me feel so incredibly desired, but also protected. With his arms around me, I feel as if nothing bad could ever happen to me again.

His kiss is home. Heaven. The softest place I could ever fall.

He breaks away from my mouth with a husky chuckle and nuzzles the sensitive spot beneath my ear. "Lucky me," he whispers. "Because I'm never too tired for you, either."

He pushes my jacket down my arms and tosses it to the floor. Backing me up, he slides his warm hands under my shirt and pulls it over my head. It goes to the floor, too, discarded with an impatient jerk, then his hands are on my breasts and his mouth is on mine, and we're both groaning with the need flaring like a bonfire between us.

My legs hit the edge of the mattress. We break apart for a moment to tear off his jacket and shirt, then we fall onto the bed in a tangle of arms and legs, kissing frantically now, with a passion almost like panic. He's hot and heavy on top of me, pinning me beneath him as I draw my legs up on either side of his hips.

He's already hard for me. When I laugh breathlessly, he grins down at me, flexing his pelvis into mine.

He growls, "Erection Man strikes again."

"Good God, you're the best superhero *ever*. Hurry up and take off your pants."

It's his turn to laugh. It's breathless like mine, happy and a little wild, mirroring the look in his eyes. Then he's up in a flash, ripping open the buttons on my jeans and impatiently dragging them down my legs. He shucks off my shoes and socks, yanks the jeans the rest of the way off along with my panties, then whips off his belt and tears open the fly of his pants.

His erection pops out into his hand, proudly jutting, a rock-hard dare I simply can't resist.

I sit up, bat his hands out of the way, and suck it into my mouth.

His shocked groan is the sexiest sound I've ever heard. I wrap my hands around his rigid shaft and suckle the crown. "Fuck," he whispers. *"Oh sweet Jesus fuck please don't stop doing that."*

I circle my hands around the velvet heft of his balls, then open my throat and take his erection as far down as I can, until under my chin I feel the short curly hairs at the base of his cock, and I can't take it any farther.

Shaking hands sink into my hair. Naz's ragged breathing turns to another groan, this one lower and drawn out, as I reverse and suck my way back up to the head.

When I start a rhythm—one slow stroke down followed by a sucking tongue swirl at the top, both my hands wrapped around the base—his hands curl to fists. He gently thrusts his hips in time with my rhythm, until he's hoarsely grunting with each thrust, all the muscles in his abdomen showing, they're so tight.

He rasps, "Sweetheart."

Gazing up at him, I flick my tongue back and forth over the throbbing vein on the underside of his shaft. He shudders, his eyes glazed under drooping lids.

Then I'm suddenly on my back staring at the ceiling as his hot wonderful mouth finds the center of me and his tongue plunges deep inside.

My entire body arches. I cry out. I hear him make a sound, a muffled noise of masculine pride at my feral reaction, then his lips close around my clitoris and he begins to suck and I don't hear anything else because the pleasure is so intense I can't focus anywhere but on that burning white-hot spot between my thighs, the pulse like a heartbeat as he nurses me, sliding a thick finger inside as I writhe.

I come hard, screaming.

Before I'm even halfway through the orgasm, he's fucking me, thrusting into me with wild abandon, his desperation equal to my own. I've never felt this animal before, like some ancient cave-dwelling creature snapped its chains and has finally been set free to savage the countryside of my soul, tearing everything apart with insatiable, bestial hunger.

I claw my fingernails down his back. It only makes him wilder. He takes my face in his hands and kisses me as he fucks me, driving into me over and over, my breasts flattened against the hard expanse of his chest, my heart pounding like mad, the bedsprings squeaking frantically beneath us, the dog downstairs howling at the loud, hollow thudding of the headboard against the wall.

It's always passionate between us. It's always good. But it's never been like this before. So consuming it's close to scary. So wild it's close to crazy. So powerful it's close to dangerous, an uncontrolled force that threatens to crack us wide open and blow us apart.

Another orgasm hits me like a detonation. When I stiffen beneath him, gasping, Naz moans.

"Oh fuck yes give it to me, sweetheart, sweetheart, fuck—I'm coming, too—"

He cuts off with a strangled cry, jerking. Then I feel pulsing and a spreading warmth deep inside me as he empties himself, moaning my name.

A wave of emotion engulfs me. It's part love and part terror, both so strong I can barely breathe. I cling to Naz as he kisses me, his body slackening, his arms trembling, a sweet sheen of sweat on his chest.

I pull his head down and whisper vehemently into his ear, "I love you. Never forget that. Never forget that I'm yours."

He rolls over, taking me with him, careful to keep himself seated inside. On his back staring up at me, he's more gorgeous than ever, the look in his eyes one of total adoration, his smile as glorious as a sunrise.

In a gently teasing tone, still catching his breath, he says, "Figures I'd get stuck with the homeliest girl in the world."

When he flexes his hips, I inhale sharply and stare at him, wide-eyed. "You're not . . ."

His smile turns into the cockiest of grins. "Oh yes I am, Minerva. You bet your sweet ass I am."

He thrusts up into me to prove his point. Then, laughing, he pulls me down for a deep kiss and keeps on thrusting until neither one of us is capable of laughter anymore.

Later, sated, we drowse.

Running my fingers up his strong arm, I murmur, "You never took off your boots."

"Or my pants," he says, sounding proud of himself.

We're lying on our sides, facing each other, the late-afternoon sunlight shifting from pale gold to deep amber on the walls. It will be evening soon. Beyond the patio doors, the sounds of the city reach us: the distant wail of a siren and commuters rushing home from work before night falls, a couple laughing in the street.

Normal people doing normal things. Living normal lives out there in a cold, unsafe world that cares nothing for them and wants nothing more than to smash them into oblivion.

"Hey." His eyes searching, Naz cups my cheek. "What is it?"

"I wish . . ." I swallow, struggling to find the right words. "I wish I'd met you sooner. When I was young. Before I knew how vicious life could be. I wish I'd met you when my light outweighed my darkness. I could've given you so much more when I had hope to spare."

"Oh, baby."

He pulls me tight against him, pressing his lips to the top of my head. I feel his heart beating under my cheek and have to close my eyes because the sound is so unbearably sweet.

After a long time, in a quiet yet rough voice, he speaks.

"Without all our scars, we wouldn't be who we are. We wouldn't be able to understand each other the way we do. Falling in love when you're young and full of hope is nothing. It's easy. You don't have any idea what the final cost will be, what toll life will require before it's done with you."

He lifts my chin and meets my eyes. The endless love in his own is so beautiful it's heartbreaking.

"But we know. We know exactly how bad things can get, how ruthlessly life will take from you, and take and take until you're spent. We know how rare this thing between us is, and exactly how valuable . . .

and that's what makes it so precious. We said yes to love, even though our eyes are open to all the ways it can kill us. To all the demands and sacrifices it will force us to make.

"The strongest steel is forged by fire, and so are the strongest souls. Your light is so much more beautiful *because* of your darkness. Your heart is so much more open because it's been hollowed out by knives. And though I surely would've loved the younger, more innocent you, I adore you even more because all your broken pieces sing to mine."

I have to hide my face in his chest and take a long series of deep breaths so I don't dissolve into tears.

He wraps his arms around me and holds me tight, until my shaking stops and I'm breathing easier.

Then I say with as much nonchalance as I can muster, "Oh. Well. Since you put it that way."

"I know. I have a way with words. Shoulda been a poet."

We share a quiet laugh, then we're silent for a while, just breathing in each other's arms. When the shadows grow long and the room cools to blue, Naz stirs, kissing my temple.

"Wanna join me in the shower?"

"Mmm. Get the water hot for me. I'll be right in."

"Sure, Madam Diva," he teases, pinching my bare bottom. "I'll have the rose petals and candles waiting, too."

I grumble, "Damn straight you will," and give him a playful shove in the chest.

He kisses me again, then rolls away and stands. I'm treated to the sight of his muscular back as he stretches his arms overhead. The Arabic tattoos snaking down his spine look almost alive as they slide over his muscles. He told me once the ink on his back and on the insides of both arms was a message for what would meet him on the other side after he died, and thinking of it now sends a little shiver through me.

I'll ask him to tell me more later. I'll ask him about his father later, too, about what Killian meant by saying he was a "legend in the industry." I want to know everything there is to know about this man. I want to walk through all his secret places and learn all his darkest fears and worst regrets by name.

He blows me a kiss over his shoulder, then swaggers off toward the bathroom, whistling a tune I don't recognize. Smiling, I watch him go. When I hear the spray turn on in the shower, I roll over, swing my legs over the side of the mattress, and stand.

And immediately sit back down.

"Whoa." Grimacing, I press a hand over my churning stomach. I must've eaten something yesterday that didn't agree with me. I don't feel light-headed like I did at the cathedral, just off. Nauseated, but not feverish. Fatigued, which is undoubtedly a lingering effect of the infection. And that odd tenderness in my breasts is surely due to Naz lavishing them with attention . . .

From one heartbeat to the next, the room goes utterly still and silent. Everything in my brain shuts down, except for the part that's working at lightning speed to remember a date.

The date of the last time I had my birth control shot.

Like clockwork, Dimitri's personal physician arrived at the mansion every twelve weeks to administer the shot. Dimitri wanted nothing to do with children. A pregnancy would've interfered with his needs. It was the only thing I was grateful to him for, because the thought of bringing a child into the sickness that was my life was unthinkable.

But the shot isn't permanent. It loses effectiveness after several months. It has to be repeated to keep ovulation at bay.

Staring blindly at the wall, I whisper, "Cozumel was three months. The doctor came . . . six weeks? Two months before that?"

Naz and I were at the safe house in Cascais for a week. How long was I in New York? How long was I on the *Silver Shadow*? How long has it been since we made love in the hospital?

How soon do the symptoms of pregnancy appear?

"Oh God. I need a calendar."

I leap from the bed, ignoring how it makes my stomach lurch, and run naked into the kitchen. There's no calendar on the walls, so I frantically rummage through all the drawers. I don't find a calendar there, either.

I run back into the bedroom and begin to search the nightstand, when I hear a light knock on the front door.

I straighten, my heart pounding. Naz is singing off-key in the shower. The knock comes again, then a woman's cheerful voice, muffled by the door.

"Hello there! It's Mrs. Sanderson, your Airbnb host! I've got a little welcome present for you!"

I can't think, I'm so panicked about the calendar. All I know is that I have to get rid of this woman.

I find my clothes on the floor and dress as quickly as I can, my hands shaking. In bare feet, I walk into the living room, careful not to make any noise from old habit. Then I look through the peephole.

A smiling middle-aged woman in a plaid housedress stands on the stoop, holding a wine bottle with a gold bow stuck on the neck.

"Yoo-hoo! Anybody home?"

In the bathroom, Naz hits a high note, then starts laughing when his voice cracks. "Minerva! Water's hot! Get your butt in here!"

Through the door, I tell the woman, "Just leave it on the step, please. We're busy."

"Oh, I'm sorry, dear! I don't want to interrupt. I just like to greet all my guests, you see." Smiling madly, she waves the bottle of wine. "Hoping for a good review!"

I feel sorry for her. She looks harmless, a little desperate in fact, and probably does need some positive feedback on her rental to counter all the negative feedback about the dog. I scan the small stoop from side to side, but she stands there alone.

"Minerva!" hollers Naz. "Hurry up!"

I unlock the dead bolt and pull open the door.

And know instantly that something's wrong.

Through the peephole the woman's smile looked cheerful. Now I can see it's stretched so wide from terror, not cheer. Her eyes are big and full of panic, and the hand that holds the wine shakes like a leaf in the breeze.

Then it all happens in slow motion.

From the right side of the door, an arm appears. An outstretched arm clad in a black suit sleeve, terminating in a pale hand gripping a gun.

The gun is shoved into the woman's temple.

The owner of the arm steps up onto the stoop from his hidden spot on the stairs, materializing noiselessly in the doorway. His face is as pale as his hand. He's slim, blond, and immaculate, in a custom suit I know cost more than thirty-five thousand rubles and shoes made from the skin of an African crocodile. His eyes are the color of a midwinter Arctic sky.

Lifting a finger to his lips, Dimitri smiles.

ACKNOWLEDGMENTS

Big thanks to my team at Montlake Romance, including my wonderful editor, Maria Gomez, the copyediting and proofreading teams, the geniuses in marketing, and all the people behind the scenes who work so tirelessly to turn my words into something comprehensible.

As always, special thanks to my developmental editor, Melody Guy, who is a genius at spotting problems, big and little. You complete me!

To my husband, Jay, I own an incalculable debt. Without you, I would never have written a single word. Thank you for being my head cheerleader, butt kicker, best friend, and all-around amazing life partner. I'm well aware I won the husband lottery with you. (Despite how you can't help but shoo me out of the way when I'm loading the dishwasher all wrong. Friggin' Capricorns are so bossy.)

Thanks to my cover designer, the talented Letitia Hasser, who really outdid herself with this series.

To my readers, thank you a million times ten. Which I guess is ten million, but I can't do math. I'm so grateful for your support and enthusiasm for my work, and I love hearing from you. If you'd like to get insider information about works in progress and talk about my books with other fans, please join my Facebook reader group, Geissinger's Gang.

ABOUT THE AUTHOR

 J.T. Geissinger is the bestselling author of *Dangerous Beauty* and other emotionally charged romance novels and women's fiction. Ranging from funny, feisty rom-coms to intense, edgy suspense, her books have sold more than one million copies and have been translated into several languages. She is the recipient of the Prism Award for Best First Book and the Golden Quill Award for Best Urban Fantasy and is a three-time finalist for the RITA© Award from the Romance Writers of America. She has also been a finalist in the Booksellers' Best, National Readers' Choice, and Daphne du Maurier Awards. She lives in Los Angeles with her husband and their deaf rescue kitty, Ginger. For more information, visit www.jtgeissinger.com.

Made in United States
Orlando, FL
18 January 2025

57401145R00143